Frank 'n' Stan's Bucket List #6

Las Vegas

By

J C Williams

You can subscribe to J C Williams' mailing list and view all his other books at:

www.authorjcwilliams.com

Copyright © 2023 J C Williams

All rights reserved. No part of this book may be reproduced in any manner without written permission except in the case of brief quotations included in critical articles and reviews. For information, please contact the author.

All characters appearing in this work are fictitious. Any resemblance to real persons, living or dead, is purely coincidental.

Cover design by Paul Nugent

Interior formatting & design, proofreading and editing by Dave Scott

ISBN: 9798391106166

First printing April 2023

Books by JC Williams

The Flip of a Coin

The Lonely Heart Attack Club
The Lonely Heart Attack Club: Wrinkly Olympics
The Lonely Heart Attack Club: Project VIP

The Seaside Detective Agency
The Seaside Detective Agency: The Case of the Brazen Burglar

Frank 'n' Stan's Bucket List #1: TT Races
Frank 'n' Stan's Bucket List #2: TT Races
Frank 'n' Stan's Bucket List #3: Isle 'Le Mans' TT
Frank 'n' Stan's Bucket List #4: Bride of Frank 'n' Stan
Frank 'n' Stan's Bucket List #5: Isle of Man TT Aces
Frank 'n' Stan's Bucket List #6: Las Vegas

The Bookshop by the Beach

The Crafternoon Sewcial Club
The Crafternoon Sewcial Club: Sewing Bee
The Crafternoon Sewcial Club: Showdown

Life's a Pitch

Cabbage Von Dagel

Hamish McScabbard

Deputy Gabe Rashford: Showdown at Buzzards Creek

Luke 'n' Conor's Hundred-to-One Club

Chapter
ONE

A yappy pooch tethered to a lamppost lurched at passing shoppers, periodically gnarling with its teeth on menacing display. But the dog's threat level was minimal at best, owing to the fact it was no larger than a medium-sized squirrel and was likely transported about in its owner's handbag.

However, the little fella was game to be sure. Having marked its territory by soaking the base of the lamppost in urine, it was lord of the manor around these parts, the big kahuna if you will. Well, for a few minutes at least, while its owner was inside the butcher's shop. And despite its miniature stature, those passing gave it a wide berth for fear of receiving an unwanted chomp on their ankles.

But despite all its bravado and general annoyance, the dog's barking steadily decreased in both volume and frequency until it sounded decidedly spineless. Instead, it now gazed up Strand Street, the Isle of Man's main shopping avenue, fixated on something off in the distance, something currently unseen, but fast approaching. *"Grrrufff,"* it offered again, but it was a token effort at best as it tucked its tail between its legs, head bowed. It was as if it had a canine sixth sense or some form of heightened animal awareness, a feeling of impending doggy doom.

That looming fear may have been transmitted to some of the shoppers up ahead as well who, taking an unconscious cue from the spooked dog, could now be seen veering off to the side of the pavement, clearing a path. And now, rather than a shrill, migraine-inducing bark echoing through the street, a steady, repetitive thud filled the air of what sounded like heavy objects making uncomfortable, sudden contact with concrete.

Stella stomped with purpose, stout shoulders pressed back, her ample bosom jiggling each time the soles of her boots made contact with the hard pavement. As she came into view, she paid no attention to those around her heading for their work or perhaps making an early start on shopping. Without stopping, she glared briefly at the dog whose racket she'd heard from further away, offering it a scowl of such intensity that she received a timid, fearful whimper in response.

Rocking a thigh-hugging leather skirt and a white *The A-Team* t-shirt, Stella moved with the pace of a woman on a mission. As a relative newcomer to the Isle of Man, Stella was still gathering her bearings around this largely unknown locale. So the diagram she'd scrawled on the back of her hand was of some definite benefit as she trawled through the streets of the island's capital, Douglas.

After taking one more glance at her makeshift map, Stella soon emerged from an unassuming side street, her flared nostrils confirming that she was in the general vicinity of where she wanted to be.

According to her extensive and detailed research, Stella was aware of eleven cafés within a one-mile radius of her new flat. And for eleven mornings straight, she'd headed out early on her mission to sample their various comestible goods. It was funny, really, Frank had remarked previously, that she'd still not been to register with a dentist or find a new doctor in town, but she was already on first-name terms with many of the greasy-spoon proprietors in the area.

For the first time in as long as she could remember, Stella no longer had a regular eatery to satisfy her rampant appetite. As she had previously told anybody who cared to listen (and those that didn't) she wouldn't give Eric Fryer, of Fryer's Café back in

Liverpool, the time of day. But after moving to her new home, she'd give anything to be in his familiar (if distasteful) establishment right about now. She didn't know what it was, but the offerings in the Isle of Man, so far, just didn't quite live up to her exacting standards somehow. Perhaps it was their adherence to basic food hygiene protocols, or the absence of a grease-and-nicotine mixture dripping down the walls. But whatever it was that was missing, Stella was rapidly running out of available options.

So it was, on day eleven of her artery-clogging quest, Stella eventually found herself standing outside The Fried Piper. On first inspection, the clientele sitting beyond the condensation-covered windows met with her approval. She was never keen on the pretentious type of venues packed with suit-wearing office workers. Instead, Stella often found that the sort of establishments visited by high-viz-wearing manual labourers and the like often dished up the finest grub, as the kind of clientele frequenting these places had a more sophisticated palate, in her considered opinion. Sophisticated, that is, in the sense that it was in perfect agreement with her own.

Once inside, Stella inhaled deeply like a police sniffer dog at a music festival, her contented expression suggesting she liked what she was smelling. She extended a cordial nod of the head towards a table of four builders, taking a slight detour in their direction to inspect the contents of their plates. Again, she appeared to be pleased.

"Can I help, luv?" the lady behind the serving area asked, with her pen in hand and elbows resting on the countertop.

Stella proceeded forth, her eyes drawn to the menu scribbled in chalk on a large blackboard behind the assistant's head. Once at the counter she came to a halt, running her eyes down the list of menu items, and then back up it again. "Your sausages," Stella said, with her attention still fixed on the blackboard.

"Yeah? What about them?" the young assistant said, twirling her pen between her fingers.

"Fried or grilled?" Stella asked.

"Grilled," the girl replied without hesitation.

"Noice," Stella answered, nodding in approval. "Fried eggs…"

"Yeah?"

"How do you cook them?" Stella asked.

"In extra virgin olive oil," came the assured reply. "Gives the egg a satisfying crunch around the edges."

Stella seemed satisfied, almost impressed with the answers received. "Interesting," she said. She preferred her eggs cooked in lard or bacon fat, typically, but she was certainly willing to give this olive oil thing a go.

"Wait, hang on," the assistant said, suddenly removing her elbows from the counter and standing upright. She stared into Stella's eyes, gazing for several long seconds. "Oh… my… god!" she exclaimed. "Chester!" she called out, turning to the rear of the shop. "Chester, you need to come out here, now!"

"I'm busy back here!" Chester announced, poking his head out of the kitchen. "If you're wanting to go out for yet *another* fag break, Britney, you can think again," he said, aiming his spatula at her. "We've work to do, yeah?"

Britney shook her head, setting her bunches swinging from side to side. "I'm not after a break, Chester," she said. And then, whispering through the corner of her mouth, "I shink itch sher," she said, talking without moving her lips, like a ventriloquist (albeit a fairly rubbish ventriloquist, and one who sounded suspiciously like Sean Connery).

"Eh? What are you on about, girl? Honestly, if I hadn't done your dear mum a favour by hiring you, I'd—"

"Chester, just get your arse out here!" Britney shouted, all thoughts of discretion abandoned.

"Fine!" he said, emerging from where the magic happened. "What is it?" Chester asked, looking first to Britney and then the looming figure of Stella on the other side of the counter.

"I think it might be…" Britney offered, tipping her head several times in quick succession. "You know…?"

Chester presented himself before Stella, considering her like a lumberjack before a large tree. "What am I meant to be…" he began, confused as to what Britney wanted of him. He leaned forward, clapping eyes on the leather skirt, and then, heading all the way north, up to the mop of wire-wool curly hair, at which point his eyes gained a sudden look of recognition. "Wait, it's *you*, isn't it?" he asked, unable to contain his sense of euphoria. He paused for a brief moment, collecting himself. Then, after wiping his hand on his befouled apron, he extended it over the counter. "You're her, aren't you? You're the one they call Stella?"

Stella didn't usually shake hands, but this being a potentially important meeting, she begrudgingly consented. "I am, as that's my name," she said, before returning her attention to the menu with an indifferent shrug, not really interested in learning how these two knew who she was.

Chester followed the direction of Stella's eyeline. "Oh, don't bother with that," he insisted. "That's just for the tourists," he said. "Britney, show Stella to a table by the window and give her one of our exclusive, VIP, cloth-bound menus."

"We have exclusive, VIP, cloth-bound menus?" Britney asked, as this was news to her. "And where would I find these—"

"Yes, and fetch our guest an ashtray," Chester instructed, not allowing Britney to finish what she was saying.

"You can smoke indoors here?" Stella enquired, liking what she was hearing. "I thought it was illegal or summat?"

"*You* can smoke indoors," Chester advised. "And I won't tell anybody, if you don't."

"So does that mean I can as well?" Britney asked.

"No, you bloody can't, Britney. And hurry up with that menu."

With a fag in one hand, Stella soon considered the options on her VIP menu with an anxious Chester watching her every move from behind the counter.

"What's with the special treatment?" Britney moaned, back over with Chester now and rather annoyed that she would still have to step outside each time she needed to replenish her nicotine levels, unlike their new guest.

Chester extended his chewed-up pencil in Stella's direction. "Well, my intelligence sources tell me that—"

"*Intelligence sources?*" Britney scoffed, making no attempt to disguise her amusement.

"If you'd permit me to finish, Britney," Chester chided his colleague. "Stella," he started to explain, "is the stuff of legend in catering circles. You see, my second cousin's brother frequents the café in Liverpool which used to be her local. So, when he heard about her moving to the Isle of Man, he tipped me the wink just in case our paths crossed. And if what he says about her is true and she eats as much as they say, then I'll be putting a deposit on my new boat before you know it. I also have it on good authority that she's been doing the rounds of the island's cafés, sampling each of them. So the competition for her business will likely be fierce."

"I don't believe it," Britney said.

"I know. Exciting, right?"

Britney shook her head in the negative. "No, Chester. I mean that's just the most boring story ever, because you've told me all this before, remember? How do you think I recognised her when she came in? *You're* the one who bloody described her to me, if you recall. Anyway, and as to you buying a boat, how much do you reckon one person can actually eat? I mean, seriously?"

"Quite a lot. Bottomless pit, is what I was told," Chester said. "Right, she's looking up from the menu," he observed. "Get yourself over there and lay on the charm, yeah?"

Britney did as instructed. "What can I get you?" she asked, ready to scribble the order down on her pad.

Stella pinched the tip of her ciggy, placing the smouldering remains behind her ear to reignite after she'd eaten. "I'll take a sausage, bacon, egg, and mushroom bap," Stella said, snapping the menu shut. "I'll also order one to take away, and don't forget the large mug of tea for here. Oh, and for here, a large order of hash browns on the side as well."

"Right you are," Britney said with a smile, jotting down the order, and underlining it with a crude drawing of a yacht for Chester's benefit. "Coming right up."

A bit less than seven minutes later, Chester had worked wonders, producing a magnificent breakfast bap that wouldn't — in his considered opinion, at least — have looked out of place in the *MasterChef* finals. And he was soon encouraged to see Stella happily tucking into his creation, a trickle of egg yolk running casually down her chin.

"Do you think I ought to go and make some pleasant small talk with her?" Chester asked of Britney, seemingly oblivious to the outstanding order slips lined up on the pass like Christmas cards hanging from a length of string above the fireplace.

"I *think* you should get cooking, Chester," Britney suggested. "You know, what with you being the chef in a café half-full of ravenous and impatient builders?"

"Right. I'm going over to say hello," Chester said, ignoring the advice provided, wiping his hands on a tea towel, and setting off. "Everything okay?" he asked upon arrival, admiring the now-empty plate in front of Stella.

Stella looked Chester up and down. "I s'pose," she said, giving little away.

"When you're ready for your takeaway order, you just say the word, yeah?" Chester advised. "I'll make sure it's just as good as the first one," he promised. Then, glancing down at Stella's t-shirt, he hoped to gather material for his charm offensive. "Ah. I love it when a plan comes together," he said cryptically, flapping his eyebrows for effect, his gaze still fixed on the graphic of the iconic black van with red stripe from the classic 80's TV show, there on Stella's shirt.

"What are you doing looking at my tits?" Stella asked coldly, rearing up, and appearing to increase in mass. "Eyes up here!" she instructed, pointing in the direction of her thin, drawn-on eyebrows. "Honestly, I don't know what it is about men like you. Just because I'm wearing a figure-hugging outfit, you think you can come over here and leer at my knockers."

Chester rapidly moved his eyes in a northerly direction, away from Stella's chest. "I didn't– that is, I was just admiring your—"

"I know what you were *admiring*," Stella said, reaching behind her ear for her half-smoked fag. "You dirty old get."

"I'm a big fan, that's all," a flustered Chester explained, trying to dig himself out of a particularly deep hole. "Of the A-Team, I mean," he clarified, briefly pointing a finger at Stella's shirt. "I was doing my impression of Hannibal Smith from the show," he said, hoping to receive a positive reaction which didn't arrive. "You know. George Peppard...?"

"You've got a queue forming," Stella advised, blowing smoke in his general direction. "So I suggest you get your mind out of the gutter and you get busy with your frying pan, yeah?"

Chester nodded, reaching to collect her empty plate. "Right you are," he said, slowly backing up. "And I appreciate the suggestion."

"So?" Britney said with a broad grin once Chester returned, having witnessed his charm offensive collapse. "It went well?"

"Simply marvellous, Britney," Chester replied, heading back towards the kitchen. Then, looking over his shoulder, he added, "But I think me ordering a boat might be on hold for now."

With her mug of tea shortly drained and her purse in hand, Stella appeared at the till to settle her bill. "Don't forget I've ordered another bap to take with me," she told Britney. Then, looking up at the wall-mounted clock, "Here, is that time correct?" she asked with a frown.

"Give or take a minute," Britney answered, totting up Stella's bill. "Why, somewhere to be?" she asked by way of conversation.

Stella shook her head, setting her tight perm wobbling. "Nah, not really," she said. "I mean, yeah, I was supposed to be at work two hours ago. But I'm not bothered." She then flicked her eyes to the till's display, after which she handed over a freshly minted twenty-pound note. "Anyway, where did soppy bollocks get to?" she asked.

Britney needed no further clue as to who Stella was referring to. "He's hiding in the kitchen," she offered with a grin. "I think you must have frightened him off."

Stella let out a raucous cackle. "Tell him if he wants to be my regular chef, he needs to strap a pair on and know when to take a joke," she said.

"You mean you're coming back?" Chester asked, popping his head out from behind the kitchen door, having apparently been earwigging. "And here's your takeaway order, all ready," he said, fully emerging now and handing over a white catering bag with an impressive see-through smear of grease at the base. "I also popped in some more hashbrowns for you. Complimentary."

Stella accepted both her change and the bag of food. "Yeah, I'll be back," she said. "It's got a nice feel to it," she commented, taking a quick look around the place. She then cast a firm eye in Chester's direction. "Right, I know you're only a man. And I know these are difficult to resist," she said, glancing down at herself for a moment. "But I'm a married woman, so don't be getting any funny ideas, yeah? Otherwise, my hobnail boot will be getting up close and personal with your coccyx. Clear?"

Chester had the reprimanded demeanour of a schoolboy in the headmaster's office. "Understood, Stella. And I swear I'll try to resist any urges," he was happy to pledge. "So. We'll see you soon, then?"

But Stella didn't feel the need to respond one way or the other, simply stomping towards the front door of the café instead.

"Cheerio!" Britney said. And then, turning her attention to Chester once Stella had gone, "I think I'm going to really enjoy getting to know her," she said, before breaking into a laugh. "And you know what else?"

"No. What?"

"Soppy Bollocks is now officially your new nickname."

Chapter
TWO

Outside the kitchen door, a frayed extension cord dangled casually from a socket, wires exposed, an accident waiting to happen. Fortunately there was no power tool attached, at least, but half-completed jobs appeared to be the common theme running throughout the modest two-bedroom home, with plaster crumbling from the walls, some missing floor joists, and a partially constructed hallway bannister. It was as if the builders had disappeared to the pub on a Friday afternoon and not bothered coming back to finish what they'd started.

As a result, Dave Quirk was feeling decidedly underwhelmed as he progressed through the various damp-smelling rooms, taking care not to electrocute himself, or put his foot through a rotting floorboard that would offer little resistance to his generous frame.

"So," Giles, the hair-slicked-back estate agent, said once Dave had returned to the claustrophobically small living room. "What do we think of this hidden gem?" he asked. "The moment it came on the market you jumped straight into my mind," he said. "I thought, this has Dave Quirk written all over it."

Dave smiled politely, unsure if he should take offence that this hovel made Giles think of him. *"Hidden gem?"* Dave asked, repeating Giles's words back to him.

"Isn't it," Giles said, Dave's sarcastic tone washing over him. "We like to call this a blank canvas," he remarked, running a hand slowly through the air like he was helping Dave visualise the finished painting, so to speak.

"Yeah, it's certainly something, Giles," Dave replied. "Though what that something is, I'm not entirely sure."

"A doer-upper, as they say in the trade," Giles suggested, offering his surroundings a contented sigh, giving his client a moment to appreciate the obvious potential.

The property they were presently enjoying was, by Dave's reckoning, the thirteenth one he'd viewed in the last two weeks alone. And to say he was feeling dejected at present was the understatement of the century. It was in stark contrast to the joyous mood he'd enjoyed recently. Using the modest cash windfall provided by their new American friends, Brad and Chip, Dave was finally able to scrape together enough of a down payment to secure a mortgage. With visions of buying a dream home for the three of them (that being Dave, his significant other, Becks, and Becks's young son Tyler), Dave and Becks had scoured through the various estate agent websites with fervour. But what soon became abundantly obvious was that with the amount of money they were able to put down, and even stretching themselves financially as much as they could for the monthly payments, they would still likely need to moderate their aspirations and manage their expectations (or perhaps, as an alternative, sell a kidney or two). And it wasn't like they were being unrealistic by aiming for a five-bedroomed country pile with an indoor pool, either. No, all they wanted was a simple, comfortable place they could call home with a bit of outdoor space they could enjoy with Tyler.

However, with each completed viewing of properties within their limited budget, Dave was starting to realise that he would probably need to rob the same bank that had just offered him a mortgage. That or face the prospect of paying extortionate rent for the foreseeable. And faced with the choice of either of these unpalatable options, having to suffer through Giles trying desperately to polish a turd with his absurd estate agent rubbish sales patter was about as welcome as the cracked asbestos floor tiles in the kitchen.

Still, was it possible he was being a bit overly critical? Dave considered this for a moment. Perhaps he was being too much of a perfectionist here, setting expectations too high, and spotting issues where others might view them as an opportunity to put their own particular stamp on things. And in fact it was for this reason Dave had brought another pair of eyes along with him on this occasion, in this case, Monty's. And even if that separate set of eyes often operated independently of each other, Dave was still grateful for a valuable second opinion.

"Nah," said Monty, shaking his head, having concluded his inspection of the upstairs rooms and joining the others again. "Nah, no friend of mine is living in a dump like this," he declared. "You'd find a more inviting property in a bombed-out warzone."

With Dave's expression already gloomy before this critical assessment was delivered, old Giles may have felt his commission bonus was starting to slip through his greasy fingers. "Ah…" he said, frantically running through his 'handling client objections' playbook in his mind. But it would appear he was all out of ammunition, glancing at his watch in despair and appearing like he'd rather be anywhere else.

However, Dave wasn't daft, knowing that Giles likely had his finger on the island's property pulse. As such, having him onside and fighting in his corner was preferable to upsetting him too much, and so Dave extended a shovel-sized hand, placing it between Giles's shoulder blades. "I think I'll probably pass on this one," Dave said, giving Giles a gentle pat on the back and confirming what the fellow probably already knew. "But keep trying, buddy," Dave encouraged. "And, as a reminder, two to three bedrooms, some kerbside appeal, and a nice little garden would be bloody terrific, yeah?"

"How about one with a garage?" Monty added to the shopping list. "Something with plenty of room for our baby girl, right, Dave?" he said, referring of course to their magnificent sidecar.

Giles smiled politely, not answering, as it appeared the two were talking amongst themselves now.

"Believe it or not, he was actually speaking mostly to you," Dave clarified a moment later. "Whilst it may appear that he's looking at *me*, he's actually looking at *you*," he elaborated, for Giles's benefit. "You get used to it after a while."

"Oh, apologies," a flustered Giles replied, uncertain as to which one of Monty's eyes he should be directing his attention to. "Anyway, all duly noted," he said, scribbling onto his notepad. "And may I offer my sincerest congratulations on the arrival of your new daughter? I'll be sure to pull out all the stops to find the ideal home for the three of you."

Monty's face fell vacant. He felt sure there must be some kind of joke he wasn't getting. Only no one was laughing. "Eh?" he said eventually, along with a grimace.

"Your baby girl," Giles said, playing back Monty's words to him. "Do you know something? This is the part of the job I enjoy most, being tasked with finding the perfect home for a loving couple and their new child," he said, as much to himself now as to the others. "For that reason, I'll redouble my efforts, guys. You have my word," he told them. And then, "Oh, and the fact that you're a somewhat, erm, *unconventional* couple? Not a problem at all! In this day and age, we pride ourselves on being entirely inclusive," he added, smiling fondly at the pair.

Monty wondered if the musty aroma of the house, perhaps caused by toxic mould spores, was starting to have some sort of adverse effect on Giles and potentially explain the gibberish he was wittering on about. And then it started to slowly dawn on him. "Hang on a moment," Monty began. "If you think that me and—"

"Oh, it's fine," Dave quickly cut in, taking several steps to the side until he was standing directly next to his mate. "You don't need to be so shy about our love, Monty," Dave suggested, tenderly wrapping an arm around Monty's waist. Then, turning his attention back to Giles, he said, "Anything you could do to help us secure our dream home would be marvellous, Giles."

"And greatly appreciated, too," Monty chimed in, catching up and easing into character as he gazed lovingly at his partner and placed a wet, sloppy kiss on his cheek. "Here's looking forward to our new family home," he said, giving one of Dave's bum cheeks a firm squeeze just for good measure.

***

Dave was uncharacteristically quiet on their drive back to the TT Farm, unlike the exhaust on his trusty old Honda Civic. Indeed, from the throaty noise it emitted, curious children would often rubberneck from the side of the road, wondering what sort of expensive and exotic supercar was heading their way. Imagine, then, their underwhelmed surprise upon observing Dave's migraine-inducing lime-green paintwork, his car tootling along with a noise that'd shake your fillings loose. Granted, his Honda Civic Type R *was* a bit sporty. But it wasn't in any way a proper sports car, at least not the way you'd expect from the sound of it approaching.

"Sorry, was the kiss a little too much, maybe?" Monty asked, worried he'd crossed the line earlier, noticing Dave's silence.

"What? Oh, no. No, that's fine, Monty, don't worry about it," Dave answered, though still looking a bit glum.

"Ah. We can keep searching, buddy," Monty said, suspecting he knew the reason for his friend's oddly subdued manner. "The perfect house is out there just waiting for you."

Approaching the snaking stretch of road weaving its way through the village of Union Mills, Dave dropped down the gearbox, his overly loud exhaust scaring the hell out of an unsuspecting lady waiting at the bus stop, setting her beloved pooch off on a barking frenzy.

"I know, mate," Dave replied, in answer to Monty's comment. "It's just that I think I might have inflated the expectations of Becks and Tyler," he revealed with a weary sigh. "Ever since you mentioned that old Mavis near you was selling up, that's exactly the sort of property I'd imagined myself getting. You know, a lovely little pad like that, but sadly well out of my price range. And, stupidly, that's the future I've painted for them when they permanently move out of the TT Farm."

"Is that why you asked me to come along today rather than Becks?"

Dave nodded. "After viewing the photos of this house on the website, my hopes weren't exactly high. So I didn't want to put Becks through another dose of dire disappointment with Dave."

"It was a disastrous dump," Monty said, continuing with the D-themed alliteration. "Still, Giles might come up trumps and eventually find the perfect family home for you, me, and our lovely *baby girl*, yeah?"

Dave laughed at the prospect. "Well, in the unlikely event that I was going to set up home with a man in my life, Monty, I have to say, I'd want that man to be you, buddy."

"Cheers, mate. That means a lot," Monty answered, getting a little misty-eyed. "You want another kiss?" he asked, puckering his lips like a goldfish at feeding time.

"Bloody hell, Monty, not while I'm driving!" Dave said with a laugh.

It's a well-known fact that most folks aren't exactly jumping for joy as they head off to put in another turn at the office. But for Dave and Monty, it was something they didn't mind at all. And as the Little Lime-Green Love Machine (as Dave liked to occasionally call it) pulled into the TT Farm, both Dave and Monty smiled in unison, looking forward to another day in their own little rural paradise. For Dave, there was also the added bonus of working near his beloved Becks, which further contributed to his cheese-eating grin each morning.

As the recently appointed Administrative Manager at the TT Farm, Becks was tasked with ensuring the smooth running of pretty much everything, including the unenviable job of trying to keep both Dave and Monty in check — a duty she often joked was a bit like herding cats.

"Oh, here's the boss," Monty remarked as he climbed out of the car. "She's going to have the whip out for us being an hour late."

Dave blew a kiss, sending it across the farm courtyard in the general direction of Becks, who'd apparently come out to greet them. "Oi, Monty," he said from out of the corner of his mouth. "Remember to keep the viewing of that house to ourselves, yes?"

"Roger that. Mum's the word," Monty whispered in response as they approached the waiting Becks.

Becks was standing with her arms folded, offering the two of them a weary shake of the head. "Are you pair working on flexi-time?" she asked, but her radiant smile suggested she wasn't being overly serious in her disapproval.

"Quality, not quantity," Dave suggested, leaning in for a kiss.

"Have you both been for a fry-up without me?" Becks then asked, eyeing them both with suspicion. "Because we had a pact, remember?" she reminded them. "No sneaky breakfast skives without inviting each other."

"Never!" Dave said, protesting his innocence. "The fry-up is sacred, and we'd never indulge without inviting you."

"Never," Monty was quick to confirm.

"So what've you both been up to?" Becks enquired by way of conversation rather than interrogation.

"We've..." Dave started to reply, before trailing off. "We've..." he added a second or two later. "That is, we were going to..." he continued, caressing his chin as if this would provide him with some much-needed inspiration.

"Ah! We've been for a pedicure," Monty advised, giving his mate a knowing glance.

In response, Becks instinctively flicked her eyes down to both sets of hooves. "The two of you have been for a pedicure?" she asked.

"Yep," Monty replied, reaching a hand over his shoulder and kneading his back. "There were knots in these muscles I didn't even know I had!"

Becks stared into Monty's lone good eye. "Monty, you *do* know what a pedicure is…?" she asked.

"I do! And I'd heartily recommend it!" Monty insisted.

"Okay…?" Becks said, sounding unconvinced. "Anyway, I was just on my way to the barn to get it prepared for a children's pottery class when I heard your car coming, several miles off in the distance."

"So you thought you'd stop and offer us a warm welcome?" Dave asked.

"That, and I'd tell you about an email for you both that's come into the farm inbox," Becks countered, as the first of the pottery class was pulling into the car park. "And you can tell me why I'm acting as your social secretary perhaps another time," she gently admonished them before resuming her journey to the barn.

"Who's the email from?" Dave asked.

Becks spun around, walking backwards as she spoke. "It's from the other side of your bromance quartet," she said, making no attempt to disguise her smirk.

"Brad and Chip?" both Monty and Dave asked at the same time, gushing like schoolgirls on the front row of a Harry Styles concert. "What did they have to say?" asked Monty.

"Go into the office and find out," Becks replied with a laugh.

"She's lovely, isn't she?" Dave remarked, smiling like the cat that got the cream. Then, the moment Becks was out of earshot, his expression hardened. "A bloody pedicure?" he asked Monty, shooting his mate an incredulous look. "Honestly, that excuse was so lame she'll probably think I'm having an *affair*."

But poor Monty still wasn't quite sure what he'd done wrong, diligently following as Dave led the march towards the office.

It'd been seven weeks or so since the conclusion of the last set of TT races. And since Brad and Chip had returned home to the States, they'd exchanged several calls with Dave and Monty, with whom they'd formed something of a warm friendship. During those calls, Brad and Chip provided regular updates on their television documentary series, *Isle of Man TT Aces*, which was scheduled to air in the United States a few weeks hence. As such, excitement was building on the fair isle, with Dave and Monty knowing they'd soon be off on an all-expenses-paid jolly to help with the TV network's PR machine, as the pair were to be featured rather prominently in the upcoming programme. And, with four tickets on offer, it was also agreed that Frank and Stan would be accompanying them on the plane.

"Well?" Monty asked, after taking care of the all-important morning cuppas. "Have they sent over the flight tickets, then?" he asked, squeezing the life out of the second teabag with the back of his spoon. With no response received, he wandered over to the other side of the office with a cup in each hand. "Dave...?"

Dave reached out for his brew, eyes still fixed on the screen, reading through the entire contents of the email. "There's been a change of plan," he advised earnestly.

"Oh, for gawd's sake," Monty moaned. "I knew a free jolly to the other side of the world was too good to be true, Dave. Didn't I say it was too good to be true? And I've just paid a hundred quid to renew my passport, Dave."

Having finished reading, Dave eased back in his chair, blowing the steam from his cuppa. "It's nothing like that..." he teased, pausing to enjoy a quick slurp. "Don't worry, we'll still be going to the good ol' US of A," he revealed.

"We will?"

"Yessir. Only we won't be going to Boston anymore," Dave advised, the corners of his mouth rising into a sneaky grin.

"We won't?" Monty asked, uncertain if this was good news or bad. "So, where are we going?"

Dave placed his mug down on the desk, rubbing his hands together like he was starting a fire. "Apparently, reaction to the show has exceeded all expectations, producing quite a lot of excitement from both around the network's executive offices and from fans who've seen advance clips of it online."

"Well, we always reckoned it'd be wildly popular, Dave, as after all, *we're* the stars," Monty offered, modesty on full display. "But what else? Spit it out, man!"

Dave enjoyed watching Monty squirm, but he did have to divulge the news eventually. "Well, Clifford and co have decided to switch the premiere celebration event thingy from their HQ in Boston to somewhere associated with a bit more glitz and glamour," he related. "For that reason, we're off to the entertainment capital of the world."

"What? Benidorm?" Monty asked, confused, as he was sure Dave had said the event they were going to would be somewhere in the US, not in Spain.

"Benidorm?" Dave asked. "No, of course not Benidorm, Monty. No, we're off to Vegas!"

"As in Las Vegas?"

"Yes, Las Vegas," Dave said, leaping up and throwing his arms around his buddy. "And we're flying business class, too," Dave revealed, now jumping up and down, while taking Monty along for the ride with each excited, enthusiastic hop.

"I don't believe it," Monty said, scarcely believing it. "Team Frank 'n' Stan's Bucket List is going to Vegas, baby!"

Chapter
THREE

Life at Casa Frank 'n' Stan, a short walk from the iconic Isle of Man TT Grandstand, was a hive of activity of late. And they wouldn't have it any other way. When the boys had first viewed and subsequently purchased their abundantly sized home, there was a nagging doubt that the two of them might end up rattling around in empty rooms. However, now firmly established on the island, with new relationships and a considerable circle of friends, it very much felt like their house had a revolving door policy at times. Not that they were complaining, though.

Sitting at the breakfast bar in the kitchen, Jessie, Frank's wife (and, as it should happen, also Dave Quirk's dear mum), was leisurely enjoying her second cup of coffee of the day. "Good morning, sleepyhead!" she said, when Stan appeared in his dressing gown, looking uncharacteristically dishevelled. "Thanks for finally joining us!" she added brightly.

"Ugh, you're looking entirely too fresh and radiant, and I really don't know how that's possible," Stan, eyelids droopy, remarked with a tired smile as he made his way over to the large jar of coffee on the counter. "Holy Moses, I honestly can't remember the last time I slept beyond ten," he said, glancing at the clock as he made himself a cup of Joe.

"Well, I wisely decided on sticking to Diet Coke for most of the night, when you insisted we all go to the Saddle Pub for their *Saddleoke* karaoke evening," Jessie reminded him, cheerfully smug about it. "But may I say the microphone found you in fine voice, Stan."

"Well," Stan replied with a confident sniff, forgetting about his throbbing head for a moment. "It's often been said that I've got a voice like a young Tom Jones."

"Is that right?" Frank offered with a laugh, returning from the utility room with an armful of laundry. "So is that why they had to turn off the karaoke machine last night? Because your silky dulcet tones were simply too intimidating to the other patrons, knowing they could never measure up?"

"They turned it off?" Stan said, like this was news to him. "They didn't, did they...?" he asked, looking first at Frank and then Jessie. "Because I don't remember that at all."

"I'm afraid so," Jessie answered. "They had a queue of people waiting for their moment of fame," she told him. "But you were enjoying yourself so much that they were unable to wrestle the microphone away from your enthusiastic grip."

"So they ended up pulling the plug out of the wall, thinking that was the only sure way to make you stop," Frank entered in, along with a chuckle. "Only you didn't even seem to realise, and just carried on massacring that Elvis number you were working on for at least another two minutes."

Stan pressed the heel of his palm against his forehead, feeling embarrassed. But then, "You two are a bad influence on me. I'm placing the blame squarely on you," he suggested with a smirk, pointing an accusatory finger at the pair of them. "Anyway, I'm going to make Edgar a luscious bacon sarnie as soon as he brings himself downstairs, if you'd care to join us? The hangover cure of champions."

"Unlike some other people in the house, I'm not hungover," Jessie informed him, as a friendly reminder. "Plus, we've already eaten," she said. "But also, there might be a problem with your plan," Jessie advised. "You see, Stella and Lee appeared earlier, while you were still sleeping."

Stan placed his mug down on the worktop, making a dash towards the fridge. "Those gannets better not have eaten all the bacon!" he said, pulling open the door. "I bought the jumbo pack, specifically, so there was enough for us all."

"No, they didn't eat it all," Frank was happy enough to report. "But the same couldn't be said about Dave and Monty, who arrived a short time later. *They're* actually the ones who polished off the last of it."

Stan tilted his head back, beak in the air, now catching scent of his cooked bacon hanging tantalisingly in the air, bacon that he would no longer have the opportunity to enjoy. "But I was looking *forward* to that," he said, pouting as he closed the fridge door.

"I did tell them that you'd made a special trip to the butchers explicitly to secure that substantial bundle of lovely bacon for us," Frank said. "But knowing you'd gone to all that trouble only appeared to increase their appetites."

"He did *try* to tell them," Jessie confirmed, sticking up for her husband. "But, again, you know what my son is like when food is involved, and Monty as well."

Stan made his way to the cereal cupboard, inspecting the various offerings to be had there. "Well, I guess it's a *lovely* bowl of Kellogg's All-Bran instead," he said, extending a hand towards the box he'd chosen. "At least the fibre will help move my bowels along. Appropriate enough, I suppose, as this morning is already turning to sh—"

"There is one thing that may cheer you up," Jessie interjected, teasing Stan with some good news.

"They've also drunk all the milk, so I won't need to eat this?" Stan asked, appearing thoroughly uninspired by his healthy but, sadly, entirely grease-free breakfast option.

"No. But if you have a look in the living room, there's been a delivery that I'm sure you'll appreciate."

Stan didn't need all that much encouragement to delay his breakfast. "Is that right?" he said, eyebrows raised, as he set off towards the living room. A moment later, Stan reappeared with his nose pressed into an impressive, gorgeous collection of flowers. "These are for me?" he enquired, once he'd removed his face from them.

"Yessir," Frank answered. "Apparently, they were dropped off at Stella's flat but addressed to you. One of the reasons she'd popped around with Lee earlier."

"The other reason being to start demolishing my packet of bacon," Stan complained. But the bouquet of blooms appeared to make him largely forget about his hunger, at least for now. "Who is buying me flowers?" he wondered aloud, flicking his eyes between Frank and Jessie. "Ooh, maybe they're from Edgar?" Stan considered. "We were only admiring the display in the florist's window earlier in the week," he explained, rummaging about to see if there was a card attached, which there was. Stan placed the bouquet down on the kitchen worktop so he could open the miniature envelope to retrieve the insert. "What's this? I don't understand...?" Stan commented, once he'd read the note. Then, looking over to Frank, he said, "Sorry, if this is a joke, my noggin's too sore to get the punchline."

Frank shook his head. "Nothing to do with me, buddy. Why, what's it say?"

Stan cast his eye over the note once again. "It says, *Thank you for being such a valued and loyal customer. From all of your friends at The Meat Feast.*"

"Meat Feast?" Jessie asked, repeating what she thought she'd just heard.

Frank couldn't resist a juvenile snigger. "Here, Stan. Is Meat Feast not the title of those mucky DVDs you used to get delivered to the taxi office?"

Stan blushed in response, offering an apologetic smile for Jessie's benefit. "No, it wasn't, Frank. That was *Beefcake*, if I remember correctly. Beefcake something-or-other," he said. "And as I'd told you at the time, the postman must have confused our address with that of a neighbouring property," he explained weakly. Very weakly, in fact, if Frank's expression was anything to go by. And his wry smile also suggested to Stan that he may just know much more about the present flower situation than he was letting on.

"Frank Cryer," Stan snapped, "I'm hungry *and* hungover, so just tell me what's going on here."

And Stan knew his good friend only too well, as sure enough, "Okay, okay. Fine," Frank replied, confirming Stan's suspicions. "But only if you tighten that dressing gown first, yeah? Because, speaking of Meat Feast here, I think you're in danger of popping out," Frank added, before returning to the topic of the mystery delivery. "Anyway, I think Meat Feast might be a kebab shop," Frank finally revealed.

"Right. Okay?" Stan said, not having a clue what Frank was on about. "And?"

"A kebab shop only a stone's throw away from our new business office. Our new business office that just so happens to have Stella's flat located directly above it."

Stan ran a hand through his disarrayed bed hair. "So, a kebab shop has bought me a bunch of flowers and sent them to Stella and Lee's flat?"

"That's correct," Frank advised. "And they're nice flowers as well."

"Expensive, I should imagine," Jessie considered.

"I still have absolutely no idea what on—"

"Let me help you out," Frank gently cut in. "Now, don't get too angry..."

"Oi, that's never a good sign," Stan remarked. "Out with it, then, Cryer."

"Well, you know when we were trying to convince Stella to move over to the island?" Frank asked.

"Oh, you mean when we offered her a generous rise in pay, promoted her to the self-designated position of Commander-in-Chief of our new enterprise, provided her with complimentary accommodation, and..." he said, trailing off at the end.

Frank grinned, listening out for the cogs whirring inside his friend's head. "Yes?"

Stan sighed as the reason for his flower delivery presented itself. "We foolishly agreed to provide Stella with free takeaway food for the first year of her service on the Isle of Man, didn't we," he said, as more of a statement than a question.

Frank nodded, this information being something already in his possession. "We did, Stan, yes."

"When I provided Stella with that credit card," Stan said, his finger raised, "she was given firm instructions not to go crazy ordering food. I clearly told her, *Don't go crazy ordering food, Stella*. And I took her subsequent grunt as confirmation of her understanding and agreement."

"On the basis that a kebab shop is sending the owner of said credit card a rather fancy, expensive bundle of flowers," Jessie replied, "I don't think Stella has paid too much attention to that particular edict."

If Stan were a cartoon character, steam would most likely have been spewing from each ear. "As soon as I've drunk my coffee and taken two aspirin, I'm getting straight on the phone to Stella and– and..."

"And?" Frank pressed, wondering what the plan was. "Oh," he quickly added. "Now you mention it, Stella did actually want you to call *her*, as a matter of fact," Frank informed him.

"What for? Has she received a fruit basket for me from the local pizza shop?"

"Not that I know of, Stan. Apparently, Stella wanted you to phone her so you could thank her properly for the flowers, as generating that kind of response from the kebab shop had required quite a bit of effort on her part."

"*Frank!*" Jessie entered in, chiding her husband. "Frank, stop teasing poor Stan."

Frank started folding the laundry he'd collected earlier, still giggling away happily. "I'm sorry, Stan," he said, apologising unconvincingly. "But if it helps, Dave and Monty did bring news that should help cheer you up. Stan...? Stan, did you hear what I said? I said Dave and Monty brought news along with them that should help cheer you up."

Stan remained unconvinced, however, assuming this to be another ruse. Another bundle of flowers, pretty at first glance, but full of hidden thorns, so to speak. Choosing not to give Frank the satisfaction of responding, Stan instead rummaged through the kitchen-drawer-cum-medicine cabinet, searching for painkillers.

"Stan? Stanley, I said that I have good news," Frank repeated.

Stan glanced up for a brief moment, raising one eyebrow, just slightly, as his signal that he was listening but not amused.

"In regard to our little trip away to the USA," Frank offered, dangling a transatlantic carrot.

Stan removed an empty hand from the kitchen drawer, his mission to locate the aspirin apparently unsuccessful. "Yeah...?" Stan asked, his stern expression softening a bit.

"We're not going to Boston anymore," Frank related.

"Go on."

"The press junket or whatever they call it has shifted location to..." Frank teased, drumming his fingers on the worktop like he was, well, like he was playing the drums. "To Las Vegas!"

On the basis that Las Vegas was one of Stan's absolute dream destinations, what with all the bling and what have you, he took some degree of convincing that what Frank was trying to tell him wasn't a wind-up at his expense. Indeed, it required assurances from Jessie and finally a visual inspection of the emailed flight information before he eventually started to believe what he was being told.

"I've always imagined myself in Las Vegas," Stan admitted, drifting away. "There I am, right? On the front row of a Barbara Streisand concert," he continued, painting the scene in his mind. "I'm wearing my best Elvis jumpsuit, sparkly rhinestones and all, when she lowers her microphone, glancing down from the stage in my direction..."

"That conjures up a picture, I suppose," Frank offered. "So anyway, there was one—"

"I'm not done!" Stan cut in. "Barbara, as we're on first-name terms in my dream — in fact, *Babs*, as I call her affectionately — Babs steps forward, pointing an elegant, perfectly manicured finger down towards where I'm dancing. *You*, she says, *I need help*. So I point to myself and she nods, flashing me a smile. *I'm singing Woman In Love*, Barbara says, like I'm the only person in the auditorium. *And I want you to sing it with me*. Then, her security team appear, escorting me to the stage, the crowds of people trying desperately to touch my diamante-covered outfit as I'm being bustled along. And then there I am on stage, spotlight trained on me, belting out the classic song in front of thousands of spectators alongside Babs." Stan released a contented sigh, happy to have relived his imagined duet one more time. "And now, this has to be a sign," he suggested, flicking his eyes between Frank and Jessie.

"A sign?" Jessie enquired.

"It has to be. I was only singing karaoke last night, and now this," Stan said, pacing around the kitchen. "I'll need to get up in the loft and dig something out," he said, all concerns about his throbbing head now forgotten.

"You're not getting your suitcase down for the trip already?" Frank enquired.

"No, I'm going to get my jumpsuits out and make sure they still fit me," Stan said, tapping his midriff. "You see, I might be carrying a little more holiday weight than when I first purchased them."

"Wait, you mean you *actually* own an Elvis jumpsuit like you described? And you have more than *one* of them?" Jessie asked. "If so, I'm looking forward to the dress rehearsal."

"Me too," Stan said, rubbing his hands in giddy anticipation.

"Ah, before you go, Stanley," said Frank, delaying his friend's departure up the stairs. "What I was also going to tell you is that it's not just me, you, Dave, and Monty heading across the pond."

"It's not?"

"No, we're going to have some female company to keep us all in check."

Stan looked directly at Jessie, as he had to assume this was who Frank must have been referring to. "Ah, well you needn't worry about me," he assured her. "After all, I'll be much too busy rehearsing for my Las Vegas stage debut to get into any trouble. The same cannot be said for the other hooligans in our group, however."

"Oh, it's not me who'll be going," Jessie replied. "Sadly, I've got prior commitments I'm unable to switch."

Stan stared blankly for a moment or two. "Eh? Well if you're not coming, then..." he said, before trailing away as the answer presented itself to him in a moment of clarity. "Stella?" he said to Frank. "Stella is coming to Las Vegas with us?"

"Yes, indeed," Frank replied. "And you can blame Dave and Monty," he added. "They all met on the doorstep earlier, you see, and apparently, you're not the only one with a Las Vegas dream to fulfil," he explained. "You know the Bellagio?"

"Vaguely, I think," Stan answered. "Is it the hotel with all the fountains?"

"Yes, that's the one. Well it seems our Stella saw this display of aqua magic on the Discovery Channel."

"And she wants to go to Vegas to witness them in person?" Stan asked, putting two and two together.

"It's not just that, Stan. She wants to swim amongst them," Frank told him. And then, turning to Jessie. "Amongst them, or under them?" he asked. "What's the correct way to say it?"

"With them, maybe?" Jessie suggested.

"Well, whatever you call it, Stan, Stella wants to swim in the Bellagio fountains naked. That's her goal, according to her."

Stan tilted his head, trying to make sense of what he'd just been informed. "Naked...?"

"Starkers. Naked. *Au naturel*, as it were," Frank was able to confirm. "And who are we to stand in the way of a girl's dream?"

"Bloody hell, I think I can feel my headache returning," Stan said, deciding it best to leave the kitchen at this point and go try on his jumpsuits, as he'd planned. But a short moment later, just as Frank was attempting to conclude his laundry folding activities, Stan reappeared, leaning against the doorframe, as there was a question that had come to his mind. "Uhm, just one thing, Frank?"

"Yeah?"

"Stella was only whinging the other day about how skint she is," Stan recalled. "Brad and Chip are providing our flights, yes?" he asked. "Or Clifford Tanner, perhaps?"

"Correct," Frank was happy to advise.

"But not Stella's. Right?"

"Also correct," replied Frank.

"That's as I thought," Stan answered. "So, if Stella is as skint as she says she is, then how is she funding her unexpected trip to Vegas?"

Frank shrugged his shoulders. "Dunno," he answered. "After the pay rise we gave her, I doubt her bank balance is as dire as she claims. But considering she has an aversion to spending her own money, I'd say it's a fair guess that she—"

"Bloody Stella!" Stan exclaimed, having a fair guess at what Frank was suggesting. "Not content with having me bankroll every takeout restaurant in town, I'll bet my credit card is about to get busy on the British Airways website as well, yeah?"

"Oh? I think you've got a *suspicious mind*," Frank replied, flashing his wife a cheeky wink as he said this. "In fact, I think you're looking *all shook up*."

"I know what you're doing with the Elvis songs, Frank," Stan responded. "But you wouldn't be so relaxed if it was your credit card getting thrown around willy-nilly."

"Now, now, boys," Jessie entered in. *"Don't be cruel,"* she said, another Elvis title dropped in for good measure, much to Frank's obvious delight.

"I'll tell you one thing, it'll all be worth it, Stanley," Frank said with confidence. "After all, can you imagine all the fun we're going to have in the USA with Stella in tow?"

Stan considered that thought for a second or two. "Yeah," he replied, appearing to like the idea if the broad grin spreading across his face was anything to go by. "Can you imagine? Those Americans are not going to know what's hit them when the tornado that is Stella arrives in town!"

Chapter
FOUR

A familiar piano concerto, a classical music piece, played through the elevator speakers. Although try as he might, Brad couldn't quite recall the name of the composer despite the fierce concentration etched on his face.

"Everything okay?" his twin brother Chip asked, noting the troubled expression. "Just remember that we're invited guests this time, buddy. Unlike last time. We're not here like travelling salesmen trying to peddle encyclopaedias to bored housewives."

"I know. I wasn't worried," Brad said, pointing in the general direction of the speaker. "I was just trying to think of who it was that wrote this particular—"

"Bach," Chip offered helpfully.

"Huh?"

"Bach," said Chip, repeating himself. "You know, *Bach*."

Brad smiled politely as a man wearing far too much cologne vacated the lift on the fourteenth floor, leaving them with the overpowering aroma. Brad waited for the door to close, and once it was safely just the two of them in the lift, he cleared his throat in preparation for responding to his brother. *"Woof,"* he then offered up. *"Woof-woof!"* he added, even more enthusiastically this time.

Chip stared blankly. "What the hell was that? I said Bach, not *bark*. As in Johann Sebastian Bach?"

Brad chuckled to himself, his awkward faux pas not seeming to have bothered him in the slightest. "Ah, I thought it was one of those motivational *we-can-absolutely-do-this* moments. You know, like we did when we were in this elevator on our very first visit? I was just getting into the spirit of things."

Just then, the lift stuttered to a halt on the sixteenth floor. "It's a good thing we cleared that up when we did," Chip suggested. "Otherwise, I had this terrible feeling you were about to bend down to try and start licking your own—" he began to say, but the lift doors opening drew the conversation about canine personal hygiene to an abrupt conclusion.

The two brothers stepped out, feeling slightly more confident than the last time they'd arrived at the offices of NBC Boston some months earlier. As Chip mentioned a few floors below, the twins weren't there cap-in-hand this time, they were there on their own merit and at the behest of the big man himself — the Oscar-winning producer and NBC head honcho Clifford Tanner.

But to suggest there weren't any nerves present as they approached the reception desk would be something of a stretch, For this meeting with the great and the good at NBC could be the springboard for their future careers, as they both knew. Of course, Brad and Chip had been in regular contact with the marketing team at the network. Today, however, was the day when the boys found out what the most important people in the industry thought of their now-completed documentary series, *Isle of Man TT Aces.* And that wasn't the NBC executives; rather, that was the great American viewing public, or at least a small, select portion of it so far.

Success for any new television series depended largely on the reactions of a focus group, a collection of viewers invited by the network to advise what they like, what they'd change, and crucially, what they hated. And it was this all-important feedback that had content makers, like Brad and Chip, on tenterhooks. However, on the basis that the network had already announced the show's official launch campaign in Las Vegas, it was unlikely (they hoped) that the feedback would be too critical. As such, the boys remained quietly confident of receiving a glowing endorsement of their work. And, if this were the case, they knew this would result in a major tick on their collective resumes and, potentially, a second series of their Isle of Man TT documentary commissioned.

Approaching the reception desk, Brad nudged his brother. "At least it's not the same douchebag as last time, remember?" Brad remarked from out of the corner of his mouth, in reference to the less-than-personable welcome they'd received on their first visit there.

"Good morning, gentlemen. And how can I help you today?" the receptionist, Isabella, greeted them warmly.

Chip flashed her a toothy smile. "Good morning to you, too," he said. "Brad and Chip Freestone to see Mr Clifford Tanner," he announced, answering for the two of them. Then, slightly leaning in just a bit, but not enough to encroach on Isabella's personal space, Chip whispered conspiratorially. "And can I just say that you're a lot friendlier and more pleasant than the Grumpy Gus we met the last time we were here," he added, looking to his brother to back him up on this.

"You got that right," Brad agreed. "Someone sure got out of the wrong side of bed that day," he added, though slightly distracted by the TV on the opposite wall replaying the NFL highlights from the previous evening's action.

Isabella offered an uneasy laugh, pointing a discreet finger in the general direction of the floor directly behind her.

In response, Chip stood on his tippy toes, craning his neck to get a clearer view of what she was indicating. Spotting a man crouched down with his back to them, rummaging around at the base of a filing cabinet, the blood instantly drained from Chip's face. "Is... is that him?" Chip asked, mouthing the words.

Isabella nodded, looking to her phone like she was hoping it'd ring before her colleague returned to normal height, at which point things might get even more awkward than they were now.

"Yeah," an oblivious Brad continued, breaking his attention away from the big game that he'd already watched in its entirety the night before. "That guy sure had a stick up his—" he said, before receiving a sharp kick in the ankle from Chip. "Ow! That really hurt, what was that for?" Brad complained, lifting his leg to shake off the pain. But before Brad could find out what he could possibly have done to warrant such an assault...

"Brad? Chip?" a firm but friendly voice called out, its owner marching out of the door they knew to be the boardroom from their previous visit. That visit being when they'd successfully pitched the idea of the *Isle of Man TT Aces* and, even though they were best left in the dust bin of the past, several other not-so-great concepts.

"Clara!" Chip said, delighted to see Mr Tanner's executive assistant. Then, placing a palm on his brother's back, he guided the both of them away from the reception desk. "Great to see you again, Clara," he said extending his other hand.

"Yes, thank you for coming in," Clara said, meeting them halfway and greeting them both. "Shall we...?" she asked, leading the way towards the boardroom.

However, Brad appeared reluctant to do so, standing rooted to the spot for a moment. "Um... Clara?" he said, squirming like he was trying to pluck up the courage to ask her out on a date. "Clara, I just wondered..."

Clara came to a halt, turning around. "Yes? What is it, Chip?"

"I'm actually Brad," Brad advised, waving the confusion away like it was only a minor issue.

"Oh, darn. Sorry, Brad."

"It's fine, it happens all the time," Brad assured her, building up the courage to ask her what he wanted to ask her. "Just before we step into the lion's den, uh, I don't suppose you can give me — or should I say *us* — an idea of what we can expect? It's just that we haven't been given any indication of... well, we don't know if they actually like our work, you know?"

Clara had been nodding along as Brad spoke, indicating she'd been listening intently and was sympathetic. "I understand. But, no," she replied, smiling graciously, just before resuming course towards the boardroom.

Brad and Chip followed a few steps behind, like two misbehaving students being escorted to the school principal's office.

"Ready?" Clara asked, reaching for the door handle. But sensing the pair's unease, she delayed entry for the moment. "What's wrong?" she asked, darting her eyes between the two of them. "Look," she said. "Each of you are talented creators, right? Better than most people that go through this door. So just take a deep breath, relax, and remember that you absolutely deserve to be here. Okay? Are we ready?"

"Ready," Brad replied, after taking the suggested deep breath.

"Well let's do this," Clara said, opening the boardroom door and encouraging the men to follow her in. And then, "Gentlemen? Brad and Chip Freestone," she announced, for the benefit of those waiting.

Brad swallowed hard as he emerged into view of those inside, offering a timid wave and an uneasy smile. Similar to their previous visit, a sea of faces was positioned around an expansive hardwood table that appeared as if it'd been polished to within an inch of its life.

"Come on in, boys!" the energetic voice of Clifford Tanner called over. "Get yourselves comfortable over here," he said, inviting them to fill the two vacant seats to his left-hand side.

Brad and Chip did as instructed, swapping cordial nods along the way with the various executives staring back at them. "It's good to see you all," Chip said as they settled themselves in.

Clifford ran a careful hand across his slicked-back, greying hair, his deep-set green eyes considering the new arrivals. "Lock that door, Clara!" he said after a moment, his gaze unwavering. "Because I'm going to tear these two a new one!" he growled.

Chip looked to his brother, and then to Clifford, offering an uneasy laugh at this sudden change of tone.

"You boys have gotten me into a whole heap of trouble with Mrs Tanner," Clifford gravely advised, pointing an accusatory finger in their direction.

"We... we're very sorry, Mr Tanner," Brad said apologetically, knowing he hadn't done anything untoward with Mrs Tanner, and hoping to Christ his brother hadn't either.

Chip, for his part, glanced over to check if Clara was locking the door as instructed.

"Relax, gentlemen," Clifford said, slapping a hand down onto the table and letting out a big, booming laugh. "I'm just busting your chops," he told them.

"Well, I've never been so relieved to have my chops busted, Mr Tanner," Chip suggested, on the verge of hyperventilating. "So you're *not* in a whole heap of trouble with the wife, then?" he asked, by way of conversation.

Clifford shook his head. "No, I *am* in a whole heap of trouble," he said. "And It's all your fault, gentlemen. Do you know why?"

"Um, no we don't, sir," Brad answered, looking to his brother for any clues.

The suits around the table leaned forward, like Romans baying for blood in the Colosseum, watching the twins squirm.

"I'll tell you why," Clifford said, his hands now steepled before him. "Mrs Tanner was expecting a vacation in Paris next year, but because of you two, that's not happening."

"It's not?" Brad asked. "I'm so sorry to hear that, sir," he said, although still having no idea as to the why of what Mr Tanner was saying.

"No. And I'll tell you why it's not happening, boys. It's not happening because I'm taking Mrs Tanner to the TT races next year instead of Paris. And not only that, but after watching that bunch of crazy bastards in your show, I'm figuring on buying my own motorcycle, much to Mrs Tanner's disapproval."

Brad didn't want to be too overconfident at this juncture, but he was starting to get the impression that Clifford was a fan. "So you like what you've seen?" Brad ventured.

"Liked it?" Clifford replied. "Gentlemen, it was about the finest thing I've watched in years. It has all the right ingredients for some awesome programming. Tension, intrigue, suspense, passion, pulse-pounding action. It's got it all. Hell, by the time I finished, my fingernails were worn down to nubs from all the nibbling I'd been doing." Then, shifting his attention to the opposite end of the table, "Clara, can we now share the focus group feedback with the boys and the rest of the team?" he asked.

"Sure thing, Clifford," Clara replied, fidgeting with a remote control, which sparked a wall-mounted monitor to life. Then, pushing her chair back, she walked across the room, taking up a position standing within pointing distance of the screen. "Okay, let's dig down into the data," she said.

Both Brad and Chip listened intently, offering regular head bobs to demonstrate the contents of the slides were registering in their brains. But a lot of the information Clara relayed was complex data analysis which was, in truth, a challenge to keep up to speed with. What the boys did appreciate, however, was the enthusiastic atmosphere in the room, and also that a significant portion of the detailed graphs was coloured in a healthy shade of green — something they assumed to be good, as green was usually a sign of something positive (as opposed to red, which was generally a sign of something rather more negative). And that certainly appeared to be the case when, at the conclusion of the presentation, the majority of the seated executives erupted into rapturous applause, with several hearty whoops of delight thrown in as well.

Among those expressing their delight was Clifford Tanner. "Whaddaya think of those numbers?" he asked of the twins.

"Pretty good...?" Brad put forth, perceptive individual that he was.

"*Pretty good?*" Clifford scoffed, although not in an unkind way. "You hear this guy?" he asked of his colleagues around the table. "They just landed the sweetest set of focus group numbers I've seen in nearly thirty years, and this is how they're playing it."

"Maybe it's the start of their negotiation tactics for an increase in pay?" one of the suited men proposed. "Better get them signed up for a second series right now, while the door is locked!" he followed up with a laugh.

Chip instinctively glanced over at the door for a moment, allowing what he'd just heard to register. "There's going to be a series two?" he asked, looking over to Clifford now with a hopeful expression.

Clifford placed his palms on the table, head bowed, appearing temporarily lost in thought. And for a gut-wrenching moment, Chip panicked, worried that he'd perhaps overstepped the mark. Seconds passed in what felt to the boys like hours, with the others in the room sitting in hushed silence.

Eventually, Clifford looked up like an angry librarian after hearing some boisterous chatter, despite nobody in the room having said a word. "A second series?" he said, brow furrowed. "Well of *course* there's going to be a second series, you dunderheads!" he erupted with a laugh, putting Brad and Chip at ease. "But there'll need to be some changes, though," he added.

Brad reached for the notepad he quickly realised he didn't bring along with him. "Um, such as...?" he asked, deciding to just take mental notes instead.

"The public loved what they saw, boys. They just want to see more of the little guy," Clifford instructed.

"No problem, Mr Tanner," Brad immediately replied, agreeable to just about anything if it meant more episodes for him and his brother to create. But in processing the request, he wasn't sure if Clifford Tanner meant *little guy* in a figurative sense, or if he meant it in the actual literal sense. "Which little guy, exactly, do we need to show more of, Mr Tanner?" he asked.

Chip was equally as perplexed. As far as he knew, nobody had ever referred to 'Big Dave' as little, and Monty was light-years away from being categorised as being diminutive as well. "The little guy, Mr Tanner? Do you mean Frank or Stan, maybe?"

Clifford wasn't good with names. "Clara, was it Frank or Stan the focus group raved about?"

Clara flicked through her handwritten notes. "Neither," she said, a short moment later. "It was Rodney. Rodney Franks."

"That's the one!" Clifford said. "The short, nasally guy in the cravat, right? I mean, who even wears a cravat anymore? It's brilliant!"

"Oh, so when you said little, you really did mean little, as opposed to an underdog...?" said Brad, though still confused.

"Wait, the focus group *liked* Rodney Franks?" Chip asked, echoing his brother's bewilderment. "But he only had minimal screen time in the show's final cut. And when he did appear, he was, to put it as nicely as possible, kind of abrasive?" he pointed out. Of course, reducing Rodney's role to practically nothing had been a deliberate move on their part, payback for Rodney's role in stealing their filming equipment amongst other shenanigans and, in their own words, *for being a complete douchebag.*

Clifford shrugged. "What can I say? People love themselves a cartoon villain," he advised. "And that tension between the race teams? Pure TV gold! And also, it might be a good idea to invite Rodney Franks and his racing team over here for the premiere celebration. The people there will definitely lap it up, and plus it'll make for some good publicity."

"It's more than just the usual kind of tension or typical rivalry you'd see between teams, Mr Tanner," Brad offered. "You see, Dave, Monty, Frank, Stan, and pretty much everybody involved with the Isle of Man TT races would love to punch Rodney in the face. They hate his guts, sir. He's not a well-liked man at all. Like, not at *all*."

Clifford clapped his hands together in delight. "Excellent!" he said. "That'll just add to the drama!"

"Truth be told," Brad cautioned, "I don't know how receptive the guys will be to seeing Rodney join them over here. They really don't like the guy, sir. I mean they really, *really* don't like the guy. Big Dave, in particular, has threatened to throttle him on more than one occasion. And when I say 'throttle', I don't mean a motorcycle throttle, either. I mean—"

"Ha! I'll bet! You couldn't write a better script if you tried, boys!" Clifford interjected, appearing unconcerned by any of the information he'd just been presented. "But if anybody can get all parties to play nicely together, I know you two are up to it!" he cheerfully added, giving both of the brothers more credit than they perhaps deserved in any imagined referee or peace-keeping duties or abilities.

"Yes, of course, Mr Tanner," Chip agreed, rolling his eyes on the inside. "We'll certainly see what we can do."

"Just one more thing," Clifford said, pushing his chair back in indication that the meeting was nearly reaching its conclusion. "The show already has a large and ever-growing fanbase from the snippets we've released on social media, right? Well, I've got an idea for something they're really going to go nuts about! But I need your help to make it happen...."

Ten minutes or so later, a physically drained but generally satisfied Brad and Chip were waiting for the lift. "Dude, they loved our work," Brad commented, appearing exhausted from their meeting but pleased by the outcome. "We did it."

Chip offered a laboured fist pump, appearing to be equally sapped of energy. "Bro, I know, right? But how in the hell are we going to get Dave and the others to work with Rodney Franks?"

"I dunno, guy. But it's possible that might be the least of our worries," Brad remarked, as the two of them entered the lift. "Because what about Clifford Tanner and this batshit crazy plan of his?" he asked, reaching for the ground floor button. "There's no way Monty and Dave are gonna sign themselves up for any of it, I don't think. Not a freaking chance."

Chapter
FIVE

After many months of steady work and an eye-watering amount of funds deployed, the refurbishment works at the island's TT Farm were now entering the final stages. The last of the outbuildings was now completely renovated and ready to be utilised as a community space. Further, the guest accommodation block was nearing completion, meaning the charity, Frank 'n' Stan's Food Stamps (the fundraising initiative that was originally conceived by Frank and Stan back over in Liverpool to help the homeless), were able to extend their welcome to even more folks at a time when it was needed the most.

The ongoing success of the charity was something that both Frank and Stan were immensely proud of. From humble beginnings, it had grown from strength to strength. Among its many social endeavours, it now operated homeless shelters across the UK, providing vital support to thousands of people each week. And it wasn't lost on anyone in Team Frank & Stan's camp that the charity's ongoing success was due, in very large part, to the tireless efforts of Stella's husband, Lee. Indeed, witnessing Lee flourish, from a desperate existence living on the streets to a successful charitable pioneer, was one of Frank and Stan's most cherished legacies. And being part of his journey and watching him prosper offered them the reminder, if one were ever needed, that there was good in most folk if offered the chance to showcase it with a bit of hard work.

And someone else putting in a solid shift, as it should happen (in this case, with some of the TT Farm's newest animal residents), was none other than Dave Quirk, happy as a pig in shit. A striking coincidence, in fact, as he was currently surrounded by pigs covered in shit...

"Honestly, what have you lot been eating?" Dave asked with a weary shake of his head, using the sturdy pitchfork in hand to attend to the mounds of soiled hay. "And whichever one of you is responsible for this output..." he said, casting an accusing eye at the possible suspects, "needs to see a vet as soon as possible." But Dave couldn't be annoyed for too long, grinning as he listened to the three dozing Welsh pigs snoring like drunks after a heavy drinking session. Indeed, Dave wondered if they might've also stopped for a particularly spicy curry after their hypothetical night out if the state of the hay was anything to go by.

The pigs, a welcome addition to their ever-expanding petting zoo, were, for the time being, left nameless. Young Tyler was eager to assist in that regard, but after christening the two farm donkeys *Dave* and *Monty,* it was decided that the naming rights for the pigs would be subject to a well-publicised competition on social media instead. For now, until such time as their official naming ceremony should occur, Dave had provisionally dubbed them *Hamlet, Sir Oinksalot,* and *Trash Can.*

"Dave!" the familiar voice of Monty called out abruptly, just outside, from somewhere near. "Dave...? Where are you, Dave?"

"Appears when all the hard work's done," Dave muttered to the sleeping pigs. And then, "Yes, darling!" Dave replied, poking his head out of the pig stable with a rogue strand of sticky hay fixed to the side of his cheek. "It's so nice of you to show up," he remarked, resting his elbows on the chest-high stable gate as Monty approached.

"I did tell you I had some admin to do first," Monty advised. "Here," he said, handing over one of the two mugs of tea he'd brought along with him. "Hang on, have you got Becks in there with you?" Monty then enquired, eyeing Dave with suspicion.

"Eh?" Dave replied, before blowing the steam from his cuppa.

"Well, you've got a bit of hay stuck to your cheek, sweat running down your face, and your hair looks like it's been styled by a blind, one-armed barber," Monty observed. "Rather like you've been *exerting* yourself in the stable, if you take my meaning."

Dave straightened himself up, standing at full height now. "Oi, are you calling my girlfriend a swine?" he asked, stepping to one side, revealing the only other stable occupants as being the three sleeping porkers. "I'll be sure to tell Becks what you've been saying," he continued, removing the strand of hay from his cheek with his unoccupied hand and giving whatever adhesive had secured the thing there a tentative sniff. "And that, after she's always spoken so highly of you, Monty! For shame."

But Monty wasn't really biting. "So that admin I was talking about," he answered, clearly moving on.

"Yeah?"

"Well, the thing is..." Monty began, taking a step or two back to increase the distance between them. Almost as if he knew Dave wasn't going to like what he was about to say.

"Out with it, Monty."

Monty set his mug down on something nearby and reached into his pocket, retrieving a carefully folded sheet of paper. "We've received an email, which I've taken the liberty of printing off for you," Monty explained. He prepared himself to hand the page over, stretching his arm all the way out in order to maintain maximum distance between them. "Here," he said, cautiously handing over the paper like he was offering a tissue to someone with a particularly phlegmy cold.

"This better not be yet *another* photocopy of your bare bum cheeks, Monty," Dave warned him. "Because you know Stan wasn't happy after you left smears on the glass of his machine the last time you unfastened your belt in the name of comedy."

"I told Stan that I'd already wiped the glass clean," Monty replied. "So that smear was ab-so-lute-ly nothing to do with me," he insisted, holding up a hand to protest his innocence.

Dave unfolded the page he was given, offering a furtive glance in Monty's direction before allowing his eyes to wander down to the printed note.

"Holy—! Was that you?" Monty asked abruptly, in response to the sudden noise, like a clap of thunder, emanating from just inside the stable door.

"Eh... no, Monty," Dave said, shifting his weight from one foot to the other. "Probably one of the pigs," he suggested, before returning his attention to the note.

"Because that sounded wet to me, Dave. So if it was you, I think you should go and check your—"

"Is this a joke?" Dave asked, cutting his friend off.

"What? No, it really did sound like you..." Monty began, before realising Dave was referring to the email he was currently reading. "Ah. No. They're deadly serious, I'm afraid," Monty replied. "Apparently they tried to phone at first, but when they couldn't get hold of anybody that way, they then sent the email through."

Dave crumpled up the paper into a tight ball, holding onto it in the palm of his hand as he took up his mug of tea. "Why would they even think this was a good idea?" he asked, after pausing to swallow a mouthful of his brew. "I mean, as if we were a couple of D-listers, is that it? Like a pair of washed-up, has-been celebrities? That's what they say, isn't it? That those are the kind of people who do this sort of thing?"

"Wait, *who* says that?" Monty asked, wanting to make sure he fully understood Dave's train of thought.

"The people who say that," Dave clarified.

"Ah," said Monty, entirely satisfied with Dave's answer.

"I mean, in what possible world would it strike them as an idea we'd be completely onboard with, let alone even consider?" Dave continued. "Honestly, I hope you replied and told them to stick it right up their—"

"Of course!" Monty promised. "But they phoned me straight away, as soon as I did," he advised. "And while speaking to them, however, they did just happen to up their offer," he related, rubbing the tips of his thumb and forefinger as if he was playing the world's smallest violin, or, in this particular case, counting out a wad of imaginary cash.

"Oh?"

"Yeah, five hundred quid."

Dave considered Monty's words for a moment. "Five hundred quid, you say…?" he asked a moment later, the consternation on his face now beginning to recede like the tide.

"Each," Monty revealed.

"*Each*?" Dave asked. "Right. Tell them we'll do it, Monty."

"We will? So you're not offended by the idea?"

"Monty, for five hundred spondulicks each, I'd lick the stable floor clean with my tongue," Dave advised, glancing down to the lovely filth behind him. "This is a no-brainer, I should think. We just turn up, smile for the camera, and Bob's yer uncle, we're that much richer. Bish-bash-bosh, done and done, yeah?" As he said this, Dave released his grip on the scrunched-up piece of paper he'd been holding onto, casually tossing it towards the rim of Monty's mug.

"So I'll go and phone them back, then? Tell them we'll do it?" Monty asked, deftly moving his mug out of the way, saving its remaining contents from disaster.

"Yeah, why not, buddy. Money for old rope, right? And who'd have thought it, Monty? Me and you being paid to promote the opening of a bloody supermarket."

"It's crazy, innit?" Monty said, shaking his head slowly. "Although it's not a supermarket, really," he pointed out, not wanting to dampen the enthusiasm, but wishing to keep the record clear. "It's more of a convenience store, yeah? But, still."

Dave appeared unperturbed. "Maybe we should get ourselves an agent?" Dave asked, sounding only half serious. "Once this TV show finally airs and we're world-famous celebs, they'll be queuing to sign Dave and Monty up to—"

"A *full-sized* supermarket?" said Monty, daring to dream.

"Well, that's not what I was about to say, Monty," Dave answered with a laugh. "But who knows, mate? Who knows. Anyway, once we're done with our brews, are you going to help me finish mucking out the three little pigs here?"

"Uhm, no," Monty said, thinking on the spot, "I'll, erm, need to get right back on the horn to the convenience store before they book a replacement for us," he explained, pointing in the general direction of the office.

"Good idea, Monty. Oh, and when we see Stan, we should ask him about an agent, as he's always going on about his illustrious acting career."

"Acting career? It was an advert for eggs, wasn't it?"

"It was," Dave confirmed. *"Seen by over four thousand people,"* he added, doing his finest impression of Stan.

Monty drained the contents of his mug. "Right, I'm going to make the call," he advised, heading back in the direction from which he'd arrived. "Oh," he added as an afterthought, speaking over his shoulder as he continued along, "Dave, if that wasn't one of the pigs letting rip earlier, then I do think it'd be wise to have a quick inspection. It's nothing to be embarrassed about. Happens to the best of us. But it's always best to check, as my old mum used to say."

"Words to live by, Monty. Thanks."

"That's what friends are for, Dave. Always looking out for one another."

***

Over on the other side of the Atlantic, a perspiring Brad was just completing his morning run, a good several minutes behind his brother this time, which was unusual for him. He appeared preoccupied, like there was something on his mind.

"I was just getting ready to send out a search party to go and look for you. I thought you got lost or something," Chip said with a grin, offering a bit of applause as his brother finally finished with their regular circuit through the bustling metropolis that was downtown Boston. "Did you stop to talk to that pretty brunette I noticed standing outside Dunkin Donuts?"

"Which one?" asked Brad.

"Which brunette?"

"No, I meant which Dunkin Donuts," Brad clarified. "There's like a jillion of them in Boston alone," he said. "And it's not called Dunkin Donuts anymore, either. It's just *Dunkin* now."

"Yeah, I know, but that's stupid," Chip answered. "It'll always be *Dunkin Donuts* to me."

"I know what you mean," Brad offered, checking the Fitbit device on his wrist for his vital statistics. "Anyway, I'd like to use the attractive brunette as an excuse for coming in late, but—"

"But your brother is a lean, mean running machine?" Chip suggested, striking a pose and flexing each of his quadriceps in turn.

"Naw, it's this whole thing with Dave and Monty. It had me distracted," Brad revealed, right before launching into a round of stretching. "There's just no way they're ever gonna agree to work with Rodney Franks, are they? I mean, they despise the guy on a cellular level. And as far as that crazy, chowderheaded promotional idea that Clifford Tanner has come up with—"

"Chowdah!" Chip interjected.

"Uhm… you okay?" Brad asked, concerned his brother might have developed a sudden case of Tourette's.

"What? I just like chowder," Chip answered with a shrug, as if this should have been obvious. "Anyway, yeah, Frank and Stan aren't exactly big fans of Rodney either," Chip added, back onto the subject. "So have you thought of a plan while you were out on your run?" he asked, running his eyes over his brother's face. "You have, haven't you. I can tell by the way your left eye is narrowed."

"Huh? You can? And it is?"

"Sure, and I do the same thing when I'm coming up with a good idea. Or at least I think I do. Only for me, it's my right eye. Don't forget we're twins, Brad. So, anyway. Your plan…?"

Brad raised both hands, building up to his big reveal, the formulation of which had seriously impacted the time required to complete his morning jog. "Okay, so all our guys over on the Isle of Man hate Rodney Franks's guts, right?"

"Sure. Stan once called him an *odious little skidmark*, which I thought was funny," Chip recalled, in fond remembrance. "And when he said skidmark, he didn't mean the kind you leave with your tyres on the road," he added. "He meant—"

"Yeah, yeah. I get it," Brad interjected. "Anyway..."

"Anyway, if we tell them they'll need to work with Rodney, they're probably going to refuse," Chip said, mirroring his twin's line of thought.

"Yeah. And if that happens, then there's no chance of making Clifford Tanner's promotional idea a reality, and we can probably kiss the promise of a second series to our show goodbye," Brad said, starting up the steps to their shared apartment.

"And I don't think NBC Boston will be busting down our door with too many offers for future work, either," Chip offered. "So with that in consideration, I'm all ears for this great master plan of yours, my good man. Which is...?"

Brad stopped, turning to face his brother, who was still on the sidewalk below. "Master plan?" he said. "Well it's simple, really."

"It is?" Chip replied, ready to hear more.

"Sure. We just don't tell them," said Brad.

Chip waited, mouth agape, desperately hoping there was perhaps a bit more meat on the bones of his brother's proposal. Several further seconds of waiting, however, and that didn't appear to be the case. "That's it? That's your plan?" he asked. "I mean, granted, I didn't have any ideas of my own, but... well, what you just said is the same thing as doing nothing. Basically, it *is* doing nothing. And also, it's kinda dickish, too, don't you think?"

Brad descended half of the steps he'd just climbed. "Don't get me wrong, I love the guys," he insisted. "But if we tell them Rodney is involved, then it's game over, right? So we *don't* tell them, and we hope that once they've already travelled the whole five thousand some-odd miles to get to Las Vegas, they might be a bit more receptive to the idea. Because what choice do they really have at that point, right? Especially when we hold the promise of more episodes in front of them, and all the money that's going to bring."

Chip shrugged. "It's a big barrel full of *what-ifs*, bro. And you seriously expect Rodney Franks to keep his trap shut about the whole deal? I mean, we've gotta tell him he's going to be featured much more prominently in the second series, right? Otherwise, why would he fly all the way to Vegas? Especially after the way we screwed him over by seriously diluting his screen time in the first series."

However, this appeared to be something Brad had already considered, if the expression on his face was anything to go by. "And why was Rodney so angry at us for pretty much completely cutting him out of the show?" Brad asked, half rhetorically.

"Um..." Chip said, thinking over the question for a moment. "Well, because Rodney Franks is the most narcissistic, self-serving little douche canoe we've ever had the mispleasure of bumping shoulders with?" he offered.

"And...?" Brad answered. "That means?"

"That means Rodney will do whatever we need him to do if it results in him being the star of the new episodes," Chip deduced. "Keeping his trap shut included."

"Bingo!"

Chip bounded up the few steps between them, offering his brother a cheerful slap on the back. "Dude, what you lack in running prowess, you more than make up for in cunning," he said. "All we need to do now is think about how to stay on good terms with Dave and Monty throughout this whole sordid process."

Chapter
SIX

In her light and airy office at the premises of Frank 'n' Stan's Hire Cars, Stella used her thumbnail to try and remove a bit of dried blood from her trusty miniature cricket bat. She smiled fondly, recalling each and every time when she had unleashed the bat in anger. But try as she might, Stella struggled to recall which occasion resulted in the reddish-brown tinge on her prized enforcer that was currently attracting her attention.

As she'd come to realise, life in the Isle of Man was a rather more sedate experience than what she was accustomed to in her previous home in Liverpool. And while the present location was not without its charms, Stella couldn't help but reflect on her former career in the taxi business. Sure, it had been long hours with constantly ringing phones contributing to the onset of tinnitus. But it was a time she reflected on with affection. There, she'd been the queen of her castle, relishing the opportunity to berate tardy taxi drivers or, as on many a happy occasion, throw out an obnoxious and often excessively inebriated punter, using that person's head to open the taxi office's front door.

However, since her arrival on the island to commence her new position as Commander-in-Chief at Frank and Stan's newest enterprise, her beloved cricket bat hadn't yet been put to its proper use. Not once. Which was a sad, sorry state of affairs, in Stella's opinion. Her hopes of some kind of violent altercation were briefly raised the previous week when the lusty postman enjoyed a preview of her low-cut top and the goodies contained therein, with him glancing a little longer than she'd usually permit. But she was out of practice, struggling to free the cricket bat from its Velcro moorings before Postman Perv (as she now referred to him) saw the error of his ways and scarpered, quick-smart, before he ended up with a cracked skull. Still, if nothing else, that little encounter had reminded her that there was no room for complacency, and to always be at the ready to deploy her weapon at a moment's notice.

And there was another aspect in which there was absolutely no room for complacency, too, and that was in regard to the efficient operations at Frank 'n' Stan's Hire Cars. Say what you like about Stella, as the two happy proprietors of the business noted, but she certainly ran a tight ship. Indeed, both Frank and Stan couldn't be more thrilled with the financial performance of their new endeavour (Stella's excessive takeaway food ordering notwithstanding). So much so that they had already expanded their impressive fleet of vehicles, as well as Stella being authorised to expand the numbers of her front-of-house staff. And with Stella agreeable to a more back-office type of role, leaving direct client contact with the reception staff, the customer complaints and subsequent assaults were the lowest in any business they'd been involved with so far. So all in all, life at the Isle of Man's newest hire car business was looking pretty rosy for all concerned.

"Knock-knock," Lizzie (one of the customer-facing team members) offered, tapping her knuckles on Stella's half-opened office door. "Sorry, I'm not interrupting, am I?" Lizzie asked, after noticing her boss appeared consumed with whatever it was that she was working on.

Stella lifted her head, taking a pause in her efforts. "Just some stubborn old blood stains on my bat," she offered, now giving Lizzie her attention.

Lizzie smiled as politely as she could, still a bit uncertain about Stella's unique quirks at this early stage in their professional working relationship, although warming to Stella just the same.

"The postman's just been," Lizzie advised, holding out a brown package.

"Dirty get," Stella remarked with a scowl, instinctively tightening her grip on the bat.

Again, Lizzie smiled, seemingly unaware of any apparent sexual tension between Stella and the postie. "It's marked private and confidential, otherwise we'd have taken care of it for you," Lizzie suggested.

Lizzie stood for several long seconds, arms extended like she was playing pass-the-parcel at school, or, perhaps, like she was holding a bomb she wanted rid of (although she had no way of knowing the precise contents of the package she was carrying). "I could..." Lizzie started to say, when Stella made no move to take hold of the item. "Erm... I could open it for you if you like? I mean it's not a problem or anything," she offered, running her eyes over the printed label attached. "Ah. It says it's from *T-Shirt Heaven*," she helpfully noted.

This titbit of information appeared to finally gain Stella's attention, as she had up until this point remained distinctly uninterested. "Oh?" she said, one of her hand-drawn pencil-thin eyebrows rising up. "Right. I've been waiting for this," she revealed, rubbing her calloused hands together. "Take a seat," Stella said, inviting Lizzie closer to her desk. "There are fresh doughnuts in the box, if you like. You can help yourself, but *don't* take one of the jam ones."

Lizzie parked herself down on a chair, laying the parcel carefully on Stella's desk before turning her eyes towards the opened box of doughnuts which, she had to admit, smelt absolutely delicious. Several or more deep-fried delights were teasing her olfactory senses, only she didn't know which ones were stuffed with jam as they all looked pretty much alike. A cursory glance at the lid didn't help, only revealing the contents as being 'assorted' rather than offering any clue as to what filling each of them might contain.

"Uhm..." Lizzie said, raising a finger like she wanted to ask the teacher a question, but Stella was now ripping open her parcel like a little girl early on Christmas morning. "Erm, how do I know which ones are jam?" Lizzie asked, not wanting to upset her host by nicking her favourite variety, as she'd been warned.

Now with a neat pile of t-shirts lying next to strewn bits of packaging covering her desk, Stella leaned over, reaching inside the box and removing a particular doughnut for consideration. "Like *this*," she said, revealing a bit of worldly, accumulated wisdom to her inquisitive student, as in one rapid movement, she ripped the doughnut in half, releasing a dollop of strawberry jam that started to flow ever so slightly, majestically, towards its comrades sitting in the box below it.

"Nope, not this one! This one goes back in!" Stella declared, quickly pressing the two halves of the doughnut back together to stem the tide of delicious ooze, before returning the selection to the box. Stella repeated this process a few more times, before finally exposing a gooey yellowish substance. "Ah! Custard!" she was happy to advise. "You like custard?"

Lizzie nodded in response. "Sure. Custard is good," she said.

Stella handed over the defiled doughnut. "Don't go spilling any on my desk," she told her.

Just then, before tucking into her doughnut, Lizzie spotted a red smear on Stella's fingers. Now, this could quite easily have been a remnant of the strawberry jam, of course. However, as there'd been talk of a blood-splattered cricket bat just earlier, young Lizzie didn't really feel quite so hungry all of a sudden. "Thanks, I think I'll save this for my afternoon cuppa," Lizzie advised. "So anyway," she quickly added, steering the convo away from anything involving the potential harbouring of hepatitis C. "Anyway, what's with all the t-shirts, then? It's not a new uniform for us all, is it?"

Stella picked one of the folded garments up, shaking it open until the printed design was visible. "Nope," she said, breaking into a boisterous cackle, the sound of it coarse like sandpaper from Stella having smoked far too many ciggies over the course of years. "No, these are for our trip to Vegas," she revealed. "I've bought one for me, and one each for the rest of the plonkers who are going."

"Ah, that's nice of you," Lizzie remarked. "It's only a couple of weeks before you go there?" she asked by way of small talk, receiving a nod in response. Once she got a proper look at what Stella was holding up for her, though, Lizzie's lower jaw slowly fell open. "You... you *bought* those shirts?" she asked. "I mean, you're going to get Frank and Stan and the others to *wear* them? Seriously?"

Stella's brusque laughter intensified. "Yeah, can you imagine that soppy sod Stan wearing this?" she asked, as a tear of happiness wound its way through the laughter lines on her face. "Oh, I cannot bloody wait!"

Chapter
SEVEN

A stiff breeze threatened to steal the hat from an elderly chap wandering out of the butchers, purchases in hand. Fortunately, his swift reaction prevented his bonce from being exposed to the elements for too long, although his sudden movements brought him directly into the path of two young lads tearing up the side of the street at a fair old rate of knots.

Both lads initiated evasive action as best they could, but it still didn't prevent them from tumbling into the unfortunate gentleman. "Sorry, mister!" one of the lads immediately apologised, reaching down to pick up the man's shopping, which had fallen to the ground. "Here you go," the boy said, looking the old fella over for signs of injury. "Are you okay?" the other lad asked.

"I think so," the man replied, taking custody of his goods, and then checking to make sure his hat was still correctly positioned on his head. His initial reaction had been to give the careening lads a piece of his mind, but once he realised there was no harm done there seemed little point. "Where are you two young ones rushing off to?" he asked them. "Have you got tickets to the circus or something?"

"Circus?" came the hopeful reply, from one of the two lads. "There's a circus…?"

The old man laughed, shaking his head. "Next time, mind how you go," he cautioned, gently chiding them. "Not all of us OAPs are quite as flexible as I am," he said. And then, "That means old-age pensioner," he felt the need to clarify, after receiving a pair of blank looks.

"We're going to the toy shop," the other of the two boys said, in answer to the earlier question. Then, hooking a thumb in his mate's direction, "Because it's his birthday," he revealed.

"My gran's just given me twenty quid to buy some Lego," the birthday boy announced, along with a huge grin. "But you're sure there's no circus? Because maybe I could—"

"There's no circus, lad. It was just a figure of speech," the man said with a chuckle. "Now you two get yourselves to the toy shop. See what you can find with that twenty quid, yeah?"

And with that, the two Lego hunters went one way and the older gent the other way, his hat firmly in place.

A moment or two later, a cravat-wearing man emerged from the door of the neighbouring solicitors' office after concluding his first meeting of the day, barking orders into his mobile phone as he exited the building. "And how is it *my* fault if she's just lost her job?" he asked, rolling his eyes in frustration. Then, nearing the butchers, he slowed and came to an eventual halt, distracted as he was by his call. "So *what* if she's a single parent," he replied to the person on the other side of the call. "Do I need to remind you that Rodney Franks is not a charity?" he asked, referring to himself in the third person. "I want you to issue eviction proceedings without delay. Just do it," Rodney demanded through gritted teeth, before terminating the call.

Rodney pocketed his phone. And then, as he also presently found himself under assault from the firm breeze, he set about in fastening his olive-green blazer. "They think I'm a soft touch? *Nossir*," he muttered to himself, evidently annoyed with his recent phone conversation. Now ready to resume his journey, he looked straight down to glance briefly at his watch. But as he did so, he gave a bit of a start.

Rodney looked over one of his shoulders, and then the other. And then he shuffled forward, ever so slightly, until he came to rest a half a pace or so from his starting point. There, he stood quietly, looking for all the world like he was lost in thought, or perhaps waiting for the next bus. After a minute or two of this, Rodney slowly crouched down, casually falling to one knee and then fiddling with one of his shoelaces, giving the impression — should anybody be looking on — that it was requiring his attention. Discreetly, he turned his foot a few degrees clockwise, revealing the face of the Queen now staring regally back up at him.

"Marvellous," Rodney said, offering the pretence of tying off his shoelace as he snatched the crisp twenty-pound note from where he'd just been concealing it beneath the sole of his shoe. With a satisfied grin, he rose to full height (which, to be frank, really wasn't that far), appearing perfectly contented with himself and continuing on his merry way back to his office HQ.

However, Rodney's progress was soon delayed by a pair of panicked youths causing something of a kerfuffle up ahead.

"We think he dropped it somewhere over there," one of the lads was heard to say, motioning with his hand in a very general, non-specific way, as neither of them seemed to really have any idea as to where they might have dropped it, exactly.

"It's—it's—it's—" the other lad stammered, struggling to get his words out, owing to the tears currently running down his face. "It's my birthday money for Lego!" he was eventually able to explain, speaking to a passerby who'd been kind enough to stop and listen. "My gran gave it to me!" the boy revealed, just before the blubbers reappeared, rendering him effectively mute again.

The woman attending to the lads turned full circle, looking for the sobbing boy's missing money. "Excuse me," she said, now addressing Rodney as he approached their location. "You've not seen any cash lying about, have you?" she asked. "Only the boys have misplaced it, and reckon it's somewhere in this area."

"Cash?" Rodney asked with a shrug, tightening his grip on the curled-up note presently secured in his grubby mitt. "No, I can't say that I have," he lied, taking a quick step to his left. "Now, if you'll excuse me," he said, with no apparent interest in the young lads' desperate plight, "some of us have work to get to."

FRANK & STAN'S BUCKET LIST #6: LAS VEGAS

***

Marlene, Rodney Franks' long-serving, long-suffering assistant — plus receptionist, plus valet, plus dry-cleaning administrator, occasional alibi in criminal investigations, et cetera — sat behind her desk, applying her emery board to a slightly uneven fingernail. It wasn't as if she didn't actually have anything to do, however, as life was never what anyone could call dull working for such a self-proclaimed captain of industry as Rodney Franks.

Access to the reception area at Rodney's HQ came via an ageing lift that creaked like a rusty ship being tossed around with the tide each time it was called into service. For many, it would be an awful distraction but, for Marlene, it was strangely comforting after so many years and also had the added advantage of pre-warning her that a visitor was on their way.

Marlene lowered her emery board, closing over her half-read *Cosmopolitan* magazine, wondering if Rodney's ten o'clock appointment had perhaps arrived a bit earlier than expected. In response to the impending arrival, Marlene readied her warmest smile, perfected over the years. As the lift spluttered to a halt, the doors stretched open, revealing the slight, Lilliputian figure of her boss.

"Ah, good morning, Rodney. Coffee?" she offered.

Rodney unbuttoned his blazer, flashing her an unexpected smile. "Ah, you've had your hair done," he noticed, whistling a happy tune. "And a coffee would be lovely."

"I see *someone's* in an uncharacteristically good mood this fine morning," Marlene answered. "You've not been on the sauce already, have you?" she said, sniffing the air for any tell-tale scent.

Rodney removed his jacket, and then carefully straightened up his cravat. "I'm sober as a judge, Marlene," he insisted. "But sometimes good fortune lands unexpectedly on the breeze," he related with a chuckle, tapping his trouser pocket. "And, as a result, you just know you're going to have a terrific day," he added, walking towards his office with his jacket draped over his narrow shoulder and a certain spring in his step.

Once seated at his desk, Rodney turned his attention to the day's post, and to any documents requiring his attention and/or signature, all carefully laid out for him.

"One mug of fresh coffee, Rodney," Marlene said, soon placing it down in front of him. "Oh, and I took a *very* interesting call from Brad Freestone while you were meeting with your solicitors," she advised, with a teasingly arched eyebrow.

"Brad Freestone?" Rodney asked, between dainty little sips of his coffee. "As in Brad the double-crossing American shyster? *That* Brad Freestone? Honestly, Marlene, there I was, having a perfectly enjoyable morning, and you have to go and ruin it all with talk of—"

"Rodney," Marlene cut in, her considerable experience telling her that his complaints would otherwise continue for the foreseeable if she didn't. "Rodney, it's positive news."

"Oh?" he said. "Ah. Well go on, then," he requested, setting his coffee down, and then leaning back in his chair, using his hands to support the back of his head.

"Well, that show you were supposed to be in but then weren't, really?" Marlene started to explain.

"Thank you so much for the reminder, Marlene," Rodney said, his voice dripping with sarcasm.

"Rodney, let me finish!" Marlene shot back, giving him a brief scowl. "Apparently the portions of the TV show you *did* appear in, limited as they were, were very well received by the American focus group," she disclosed. "In fact, they were a huge hit."

Rodney's ego was starting to receive a welcome boost. "Focus group, you say?"

Marlene nodded her head. "Yes," she said. "Before a new programme goes out on the air, television studios will often invite a select demographic to gauge whether they like what they see."

"I see. And they liked themselves a bit of Rodney Franks, did they?" Rodney asked, assuming this to be the crux of the present conversation. "The old Yankee doodles can't get enough of yours truly?" he added, jabbing his thumbs into his chest.

"It would seem so. I'm told the show has generated quite a lot of excitement, with talk of a second series already in the works."

Rodney leaned forward, resting his elbows on the surface of his desk. "A second series, you say...?"

"Yes, and there's more," Marlene replied. "Something I think you'll like," she suggested.

"Oh, this day just keeps on delivering, Marlene. Do continue," Rodney said, gesturing with a twirl of his wrist, eager to hear more, as the conversation centred on him, his favourite subject.

"Okay," Marlene answered, happy enough to pass the info along. "Brad hoped you'd be available to appear at the show's premiere launch party thingamajig," she advised, recalling the general details of her conversation. "And if you'd find yourself agreeable to that, he suggested that you could talk about a much more prominent role in series two."

Rodney slapped a hand on his desk, startling poor Marlene in the process. "Yes!" he yelled. "I always knew Rodney Franks was the *real* star of that show, and not those wretched losers!"

"Gracious as always, Rodney," Marlene commented with a smirk. "Anyway, the premiere celebration is scheduled to take place at the end of the month in Las Vegas," she said, revealing this bit of pertinent information.

"Las Vegas?" Rodney asked. "As in Las Vegas, Nevada?"

"That's right. And they want the riders in your sidecar team to join you as well. All expenses paid. So should I let Brad know that you're agreeable?"

Rodney looked like a child who'd just been offered a trolley dash around the local sweet shop. "Marlene, fetch me the phone number for Dave Quirk when you have a moment, would you?" he asked, not paying attention to Marlene's last question, as he was currently too giddy. "Or that imbecile who races with him, Montesquieu, or whatever his name is. Or, for that matter, those two dim-witted sponsors of theirs, Francis and Simon, or whatever they're called." Rodney knew everyone's correct names, of course. He simply had no interest in using them just now.

"No!" Marlene responded, firmly, lest there be any doubt. "If you're thinking of gloating, Rodney, then you absolutely *cannot*," she cautioned.

Marlene then went on to outline the details of her conversation with Brad, those details including how it was absolutely vital, and a condition for Rodney to appear at either the premiere event, or subsequently, any part in the second series, that he absolutely *must* keep things to himself, at least for the time being. And if any part of this proverbial cat should escape from this proverbial bag, then any and all offers and invitations would be rescinded immediately, without hesitation, and there would be no second chances.

"So you're clear on that?" Marlene asked, once she'd finished laying out the terms. "Yes, Rodney? No gloating!"

Rodney held out his hands. "Okay, okay, I hear you, Marlene," he said.

"So you won't say anything to them? Dave Quirk and the others, I mean?"

Rodney shook his head. "Nossir. Rodney Franks is going to be bloody famous," he said dreamily. "And I wouldn't do *anything* to jeopardise giving the public what they wanted all along. *Me!*"

"So I should tell them you're in agreement?" she asked. "Is that what you're saying? Just to be clear."

"Yes, yes! Get on the phone, Marlene," he answered, shooing her along. "Tell them that, yes, mum's the word, I promise," he said, pressing a slender finger to his lips.

"No need," Marlene said with a grin. "I've already confirmed that you'd be amenable to everything."

"Ah! And that's why I employ you, Marlene. Because you're one in a million," he said, rubbing his hands together in delight. "Oh, and Marlene?"

"Yes?" she replied, halfway out of his office.

"I'll need your help in finding my passport," Rodney said, relaying what he was thinking. "Oh, and suntan lotion, Marlene. I'll need that, too."

"What about swimming togs, Rodney?" she asked, in her best sarcastic tone. "Do you want me to go Speedo shopping for you during my lunch hour?"

"Oh, would you?" Rodney asked. "That would be splendid," he said, with it being unclear if he was serious or not. "Nothing too revealing, though, Marlene. I need to keep a little bit back from my adoring fans. Tease them, if you will."

Rodney was now in his element, like the family dog resting comfortably in front of a warm, cosy log fire on a cold winter's eve. "This is it, Rodney Franks," he said, going for the third-person approach once more. "This time next year you're going to be a global superstar!"

Chapter
EIGHT

"You've changed, Monty," Dave declared, along with a fierce shake of his head. "The old Monty would never do something like what you've just done," he offered, before hurrying across the road in advance of an approaching bus.

Monty, for his part, waited patiently, allowing the bus to come and go before safely navigating his way to the other side. Then, once across the street, he picked up his pace a bit, sort of half-running, half-walking, moving like he was desperate for the loo but didn't wish to advertise that fact to the world.

"I've not changed, Dave," Monty protested, once he'd caught up with his mate. "It's just that I like the coconut smell, is all," he explained with a shrug. "And also, I like the way she runs her fingers through my hair," he added, a look of serenity washing over his face.

Now on Duke Street, a section of the island's main shopping district, Dave came to an abrupt halt, with Monty following suit. Dave, expression stern, turned to his chum, taking a short step towards him. Then, he moved in close, leaning in, planting his snout amongst the follicles on Monty's bonce and taking a long, lingering snuffle. To any passing shoppers, it may have appeared like two lovers, after a brief spat, were now enjoying a somewhat tender moment.

"Coconut, you say?" Dave asked, filling his senses, continuing on with his snuffling. "And do I also detect a hint of mango?"

Monty clapped his hands in delight. "Bravo, my friend. You've got the nose of a bloodhound!" he declared. Monty then ran a satisfied hand over his freshly styled hair. "Plus, along with the lovely scent, it also leaves you with a silky glow," he pointed out.

Dave considered this for a moment. "Hmm," he offered. "Now you mention it, your hair does have a certain sheen, Monty. It reminds me of spilt oil on a wet road."

"Thanks, mate, that's kind of you to say," Monty replied. "And she only charges an extra three quid for that shampoo service," he advised. "So next time we go for a trim I'd definitely recommend you treat yourself, yeah? I expect your tresses would come up lovely after Faith has worked her magic on them."

"I have tresses now?" Dave asked, surprised yet intrigued, as this was the first time his unruly, slightly thinning mop of dishevelled hair had ever been described in such a way.

"You will by the time Faith has worked her magic on them," Monty insisted.

It was now only a few short days until their much-anticipated flight to Las Vegas, and the boys reckoned they had needed to smarten themselves up with a long-overdue visit to the local barbershop. After all, they both wanted to look sharp for any media who might be in attendance at the official premiere celebration of their new TV show, *Isle of Man TT Aces*, of which they were of course the stars.

Indeed, going one stage further, knowing their hotel had a whopping great pool, Monty had taken his personal grooming mission to the next level earlier in the day. By his own admission, attending to one's bikini line with a pair of kitchen shears hadn't been the easiest or most straightforward of tasks. Dangerous, at times, even. But Monty hadn't wanted the flourishing overgrowth of his intimate area to possibly curtail his swimming pool activities, hence the pre-holiday resculpture. And despite Monty's assurances of discretion and a gentle hand, Dave had seen fit to reject Monty's generous offer of also smartening up his own gentleman's area.

"You won't tell Stan I've used his scissors, will you?" Monty asked, the topic evidently still on his mind. "I tried my own, but I don't think they were sharp enough," he added, extending two fingers to replicate the scissor action. "You see, the curly hairs kept getting caught between the blades rather than making a clean cut. As a result, they started to pull and hurt after a while," he explained, going into unnecessary detail.

"Tell Stan about the scissors? Not on your nelly," Dave scoffed. "Well, at least not just yet, I won't," he clarified, along with a devious grin. "You see, I've personally witnessed Stan using those very shears for many things in the kitchen, including trimming the fat from a leg of lamb. So mum's the word, I promise. At least until the next time he tucks into a Sunday roast."

Monty slowed as they came upon the travel agents, checking the sign hanging over the automatic doors. "This is the one," he advised, looking through the vast front window, hoping to gauge the size of the queue for the bureau de change. "I won't be long, if you want me to catch you up?"

Dave shook his head. "Nah, I'll wait outside for you, Monty," he said. "I think I'll enjoy anonymity as I stand here and watch the world go by. At least a short while longer, yeah?"

"What, is the world about to stop soon?" asked Monty, wondering if he should be worried.

"No, I meant the anonymity part," said Dave. "We won't be able to do this in a couple of weeks, you see."

"Eh? What are you on about?" Monty asked.

"Fame, Monty. I'm talking about fame. After the show comes out, you don't think we'll be able to walk down the street like mere mortals anymore, do you?"

"You don't think so?" Monty asked, giving this some thought.

"No. We'll be household names, mate," Dave advised. Then, pointing a less-than-discreet finger towards the passing shoppers, he said, "They'll all want a piece of you, old son. You won't be able to walk five feet down the road without autograph hunters chasing you or women throwing themselves at you."

"Women? Do you think so?" Monty asked, with panic etched across his face. "But I already enjoy the love of a good woman, Dave, and the missus would kill me."

"That's the price of fame, good buddy. You'll be tripping over all the pairs of knickers thrown at your feet soon."

Monty ran that scenario through his mind's eye, shifting his weight from one foot to the other as he did so. It was only when he spotted the glimpse of a smirk on Dave's chops that he began to relax. "You're kidding, Dave. You're kidding, right?"

Dave unleashed a hearty slap on Monty's upper arm. "Yeah, of course I am," he replied with a laugh. "It's the Isle of Man, after all. They're a relaxed bunch over here. I reckon David Beckham could walk through Strand Street, carrying a football with him, and he wouldn't get more than a quick glance."

Monty appeared relieved. "I s'pose you're right," he said with a chuckle. "If David Beckham wouldn't get a second glance, then what hope have two fellow prime specimens like us got?"

Dave patted his rotund belly in response. "Prime specimens indeed, Monty," he said in agreement. "Anyway, once you're all finished here, we'll head over to the greasy spoon for a fry-up, yeah? Does that sound like a plan?"

"I'll go and buy my dollars, then. Quick-smart," Monty said, smacking his lips at the thought of impending food.

"You do know you can get dollars there, right? Over in the US of A?" Dave added. "Just asking. Because they have cash points over there, same as here, or ATMs as they call them."

Monty raised a hand in defiance. "No, no, Dave. If I bring cash *with* me, then I can only spend what I have," he explained. "Otherwise, I'd have a beer or six, and the next thing you know I'll be flashing my credit card around, thinking I'm J R Ewing."

"Nice. All you'd need is a cowboy hat," Dave said, instantly recognising Monty's reference to the old TV show in question. "So I guess you did learn a few valuable lessons after that stag weekend in Amsterdam?"

"Some things you can never forget," Monty answered, stepping towards the shop doorway. "But the less said about that sorry affair the better," he suggested, talking over his shoulder as the glass doors parted for him.

Once inside, Monty walked through the travel agents section towards the bureau de change office situated at the rear. Fortunately, there were only a couple of people in the queue ahead, so it wouldn't be too long before he was tucking into a delicious fry-up, he reckoned. In the meantime, he waited patiently, admiring the various posters on the wall of his present location depicting various exotic holiday destinations. He'd never really been one for foreign travel, necessarily, quite happy where he was most of the time. But the thought of going to Las Vegas, with his mates, was something he was certainly looking forward to.

A few moments later, a gentleman at the front of the queue moved aside, placing the plastic travel wallet he'd received, now stuffed with currency, inside his jacket pocket. On his way out, he offered a cordial smile to those still waiting, with Monty now shuffling forward, one step closer to being served.

Once again, Monty returned his attention to the posters, imagining himself stretched out on a lounger, cocktail in hand, soaking up the sun's glorious rays. He also reflected on his earlier conversation with Dave, wondering how or if his life would indeed change once the television series aired. But it didn't matter. Not really. As far as he was concerned, he already had his dream job working with people who were friends rather than colleagues, and he had no intentions of giving that up regardless of any fame or fortune that might fall into his lap.

"Can I help?" asked the chap behind the security screen, a dapper-looking fellow with a splendid red bowtie. "Yes, hello, sir...?" he added, when Monty didn't move or acknowledge him.

"I think it's your turn, dear," said the woman ahead who'd just been served, tapping Monty on the arm as she passed by, waking him from his daydream.

"Ah, thanks for that," Monty answered. "And I hope you enjoy wherever it is you're going on holiday," he offered, assuming that was the purpose of the helpful lady's visit today.

The waiting cashier was seated in a secure booth, surrounded by protective glass which presumably protected him from the unwanted advances of armed raiders, brigands, and thieves.

"Can I help?" asked the cashier, with a finger poised over his well-used calculator.

Monty looked around the counter area, unsure if he needed to talk into a speaker — like he did when visiting the bank — or if he was meant to just shout his order through the glass. With no obvious speaker device present, Monty opted for the latter.

"I should like to order one thousand dollars, please!" Monty announced, directing his head towards the serving hatch like a horse drinking from a trough.

"American?" came the response.

With his order given, Monty had returned to full height, smiling in anticipation. "Say again?" he asked.

"American?" the cashier repeated.

"Me? Nossir, I'm local," Monty insisted, along with a shake of his head. "Although people do say I have an unusual accent. Or speech impediment, rather. But I think they mean accent."

The cashier held his gaze for a moment, unsure if his latest client was being difficult or not. "Not you personally, sir," he eventually clarified. "What I mean is, do you require American *dollars*, as opposed to, say, Australian or Bahamian?"

Monty took a moment to register what he was being told, as he wasn't aware of any other countries using the dollar, and neither did he consider himself a bohemian, really. "I'm going to Las Vegas," he replied, after a moment. "Las Vegas in America."

"Not a problem, sir," the cashier said, getting busy with his calculator. "I'll just need to see some identification, please."

Fortunately, Stan had warned him that a photo ID would be required for any currency exchange, so Monty retrieved the passport he was carrying, placing it through the serving hatch.

"There you go, my good man," Monty said, one step closer to the sun lounger he'd imagined earlier.

The cashier opened up Monty's passport to the photograph page, inspecting it, then looking up to Monty, and then looking back to the passport. "Erm," he said, moving the passport closer for an improved view. "This is your passport?" the man asked, in a tone suggesting that he didn't believe it was.

Monty panicked, wondering if he'd perhaps taken the wrong one from the sideboard. "If you could just...?" he asked, indicating that he wanted to double-check. "Yes, that's me," Monty was quick to confirm, when the passport was pressed up to the other side of the glass. "Why? Is there a problem?"

The cashier stuck the passport under his nose once more. "It just doesn't look very much like you, sir. And as that's one of the principal duties of a passport, it presents us with some trouble in concluding this transaction." Then, tilting his head, he added, "I mean, it *sort* of looks like you, if you view it a certain way, but then again... no. It doesn't belong to a cousin, does it, or perhaps some kind of distant relative?"

"Ah, I believe I see what's going on," Monty replied, nodding like he was certain he understood what the problem was. "I've just been for a haircut," he said, pointing to his head. "When that photo was taken, my hair was a lot longer than it is now," he explained, pushing his chin forward, striking a pose while the cashier ran his eye over him once more. "It's also been subjected to a deep shampoo. Coconut and mango," Monty added in, providing more detail than was actually necessary again. "So it's probably also shinier than it was in the photo, you see."

However, the cashier simply wasn't buying it. "I'm sorry, sir," he said, closing over the passport. "I'm afraid you'll need to bring in an alternative ID," he instructed, passing the document back through the serving hatch.

"What? But I'm going away in just a few *days*," Monty complained. "I need those!" he insisted. "I need those American dollars!"

Having been frustrated by both the continuing delay and a rumbling tum, Dave suddenly appeared inside the building, his expression somewhat vexed.

"What's going on? Has he flown all the way over to America to pick up your dollars?" Dave asked, walking over to his chum. "I'm wasting away to bloody nothing out there," he added, pointing back outside, to indicate where *'out there'* was.

"He won't serve me, Dave," Monty moaned, tipping his head towards the glass screen. "He claims my passport photo looks nothing like me."

"Here. Let me see that," Dave responded, picking up Monty's passport and opening and examining the photograph page, just as the cashier had done. "What do you mean that's not you?" he asked, looking at the document, and then at Monty. "It's you, all right. I mean, who *else* looks like that?"

"Nobody!" Monty insisted, although, truth be told, he wasn't sure if this was a good thing or bad.

Eventually, Dave laughed, sliding the passport back through the serving hatch to the cashier. "Can I borrow a pen for a moment?" he asked through the glass partition.

The cashier provided the implement, as requested, uncertain how it was going to remedy the situation but likely hopeful it would help bring their interaction to a quicker conclusion.

"Open up the passport," Dave politely advised the cashier. "Right," he said, now addressing Monty, holding the pen at arm's length, in such a way that both the cashier and Monty could easily view it. "Look at the pen, Monty," he instructed, slowly moving the pen closer. "Are you watching?" Dave asked the cashier, with his attention still focused on Monty and the task he was performing for both the cashier's and Monty's benefit. "Keep watching the pen," he advised Monty, as the writing device approached ever closer to Monty's nose. And then, once the pen had reached an inch or so away from Monty's face...

"Ah, that's him!" the cashier suddenly called out.

"You see it now?" Dave asked.

"Yes! It didn't look like him a minute ago, but now it does," the cashier replied, impressed by Dave's magic trick and now satisfied that he wasn't dealing with some sort of fraudster.

"It's the wonky eyes," Dave was happy to explain. "When the passport photo was taken, he probably had both of his eyes fixed on a stationary object, amazingly enough, which in this case was the camera. And on the rare occasion when this happens, the stars align, so to speak, and they're uniform for a brief moment. To be honest, it can actually be quite unnerving when you're not used to seeing him that way."

And Dave's explanation was further demonstrated as correct because, as soon as he pulled the pen away and returned it to the cashier, Monty's eyes quickly parted ways with each other, both travelling in a different direction once more, as if they'd just met with an argument and had a severe falling out with each other. "And there we are," Dave declared, successfully demonstrating his case and putting that mystery to bed.

After another cursory glance at the passport for one final, quick confirmation, the cashier appeared pleased. "Ah, splendid, Mister Montgomery. And will twenties and tens be okay, sir?"

Chapter
NINE

Frank took a deep breath, deciding he'd nursed his cup of tea longer than was entirely appropriate. "Right," he said, giving himself a gee-up ahead of the short walk from the kitchen in their house on Glencrutchery Road towards the office he shared with Stan in the same home.

It wasn't that Frank minded attending to the outstanding paperwork piled up on his desk, appreciating it as a necessary evil after many years in business. What he did mind, however, was the fact that his partner in crime, Stan, had buggered off at first light and not been seen since.

With their collective jolly/adventure/business trip to Las Vegas due to commence first thing the following morning, it was confirmed with Stan — over a glass of chardonnay the previous evening — that they would address all outstanding paperwork together before leaving the island. And although they were only to be away for several days, it was agreed that it'd be nice not to be faced with a pile of invoices and whatnot upon their return.

Sitting at his desk, Frank removed the thick elastic band that bound together a pile of unopened envelopes, fanning the envelopes apart like a deck of cards. "Hmm, you know what," he considered, "I reckon I'll come back to you in a bit," he said, now opting instead to review the weekly summary report from the car hire business which, of late, had proved to be pleasurable reading indeed.

And this, as it should happen, proved to be the case once more as the spreadsheet loaded up on his trusty laptop. Frank leaned back in his chair, offering a contented smile at the figures presented before him. In merely a few short months, Stella and the team at the hire car company had not only met their targets but had completely obliterated them. And from what both he and Stan could tell, their employees appeared perfectly comfortable with their new boss despite any initial concerns they may have harboured. Indeed, with things going so swimmingly, if the company's performance continued at this rate, there was now even talk of opening another branch in the south of the island to cater to the obvious demand.

Buoyed by this positive news, Frank felt more motivated to get busy with his chequebook now and pay some invoices.

Feeling the need for some background music, Frank looked towards the magical cylindrical apparatus on the sideboard that still amazed him each and every time he spoke to it. "Alexa?" he said seductively, like he was about to chat her up. "Alexa, play..." he continued, before briefly considering his options. "Alexa, yes, please play songs by Dolly Parton," he decided, pleased with his selection.

"Playing *Dolly Parton's Greatest Hits*," Alexa obligingly replied, efficient creature that she was.

Frank reached for his letter opener — a miniature version of the fabled sword Excalibur, which Stan had given him one year for Christmas — thrusting the implement forward, cleaving the air, as if he were fighting a mighty dragon. Frank appeared easily distracted, continuing with his imaginary assault for several additional seconds, flourishing his sword, parrying and poking, before applying what must have been the final, fatal blow, as Dolly belted out the chorus to her iconic hit "Jolene."

The conquering hero reached for the envelope at the top of the pile and, sword arm now warmed up, sliced it open in one impressive movement. Satisfied with his efforts, he hummed along to Dolly's singing, quickly dispatching the first of many bills.

And it wasn't too long before Frank eased into his stride, now making serious inroads into the shrinking stack, giving the occasional glance to the wall-mounted clock, along with a shake of the head, in response to Stan's continued absence. Dipping into the next envelope, Frank groaned the moment he spotted the Mastercard symbol printed on the letterhead. He'd completely forgotten about how, in a moment of red wine-induced weakness, he had ordered a steam mop from one of the TV shopping channels. Of course, Stan had advised against the purchase, suggesting it would likely only get used once before being consigned to the utility room to see out the rest of its days. And Stan was correct, as it turned out, with the mop now being used as an additional coat stand rather than as the designers had intended.

Frank unfolded the bill — consisting of several pages — taking a mental note to hide his credit card the next time he watched TV shopping channels while over the drink-drive limit. "What the bloody hell?" he said with a gasp, the moment his eyes fell on the 'Amount Due' at the foot of the statement, his pulse rate greatly increasing as a result. "How can a mop possibly cost *that*?" he asked, wondering just how much wine he'd actually consumed on that fateful evening. Frank quickly moved his attention further up the statement, looking for the transaction details. To his horror, he could see line after line, running down each page and spilling over and onto the next. Indeed, there was so much text that it read more like a novel than a credit card statement.

"I've been scammed!" Frank exclaimed, with no other explanation presenting itself to him as he scanned the statement for any reference to a steam mop, without any success. Instead, all he could see were dozens of transactions to the Taj Mahal restaurant, The Spice of India, Neo's Pizza, and so on. All fine establishments, of course. But definitely none of which sold mops.

However, it was only when Frank ran his finger over a particularly eye-watering amount charged by a local travel agent that the solution began to slowly dawn on him. He flipped the papers over, shifting his attention to the statement address on the first page, and it was only then that he enjoyed a deep sigh of relief, and then a chuckle. "Oh, thank goodness for that," he said, absolutely delighted to note the addressee as one Stanley Sidcup, a minor detail he'd failed to observe while unleashing mini-Excalibur a few minutes earlier.

"Stella's certainly living the high life, courtesy of your credit card, Stanley," he remarked, folding over the pages and placing them carefully back inside the waiting envelope. "Special delivery for Stanley Sidcup!" Frank announced, smiling deviously as he pushed himself back in his chair, the castors gliding gracefully over the laminate floor towards Stan's desk. "Sorry for opening your post, buddy," Frank said to nobody there, placing the hefty bill next to Stan's keyboard for his future consideration. Once he'd wheeled himself back to his desk, Frank clapped his hands together smartly. "Time for a nice brew, Dolly?" he asked of his Alexa-based singing companion. "And maybe a nice chocolate Hobnob or three to keep it company?" he also considered aloud.

But Frank didn't get as far as the kitchen before being startled by the front door opening abruptly and boisterous laughter spilling in, sounding like a hen party being flung out of the pub at closing time. "Is that you making all that racket, Stan?" Frank asked, marching through the hallway to find out for himself.

And his assumption proved correct, because there, standing inside the doorway, Stan was giggling like a schoolgirl, with Edgar appearing to share the joke. "What's tickled you two?" Frank asked. And then, before the pair could answer, "I was just on my way to make a brew, if you'd care to join me?" he offered.

But neither Stan nor Edgar replied, their laughter drying up and the both of them appearing sheepish like they'd just been caught shoplifting. "Ehm... hi, Frank," said Stan, finally answering. "I didn't realise you were in," he added, laughing nervously.

Frank eyed the two with suspicion. "Well, yeah, of *course*, Stanley," he said. "I made a start on the paperwork, remember? The paperwork we were *both* going to clear up before heading off to sunnier climes?"

Stan slapped a hand against his forehead. "Oh, hell. I forgot about that, Frank. Anything you need me to look at?"

"No, nothing urgent, Stan," Frank answered. He could see his mate was in relatively good spirits and what with them going on holiday the following day, he really didn't wish to dampen Stan's mood with current news of Stella's excessively excessive spending. "At least nothing that can't be attended to upon our return," Frank added. "Anyway, what are you pair up to?" he asked with a grin, moving the conversation along. "You've not been on the Pimm's before lunch again, have you?" he asked, in reference to an unplanned and rather boozy brunch earlier that month that had continued until the early evening.

Edgar puffed out his cheeks, looking suddenly queasy, giving the appearance he might see his breakfast reappear. "That was jolly good fun at the time, Frank. But shenanigans I won't be repeating again any time soon," he said.

"So, if not Pimm's...?" Frank pressed, wondering why the two of them weren't moving away from the doorway, and were also acting rather peculiar, having been giddy only a moment ago but now standing there looking slightly guilty or ashamed. "You've not perhaps bumped our two cars together in the driveway, have you, Stan?" Frank asked, suspicious now, and trying to catch a peek at the outside world.

"What? No, of *course* not, Frank," replied Stan, appearing offended at the very suggestion, and yet nevertheless adjusting his position to conceal whatever it was that he was now obviously concealing. "Well if you must know..." he said, first glancing over to Edgar. "If you must know, I've been somewhat impulsive this morning. That's why I was up and out first thing."

"Can we show him, Stan?" Edgar asked. "Let's just show him, yeah?"

"I suppose," replied Stan, as it did seem inevitable. "All right. Close your eyes, then, Frank," he instructed, stepping in close. "You can't see anything?" Stan asked, taking Frank by the arm.

"Not a blessed thing," Frank confirmed, following blindly, allowing Stan to guide him to their home's threshold. "What's all this about, Stanley? I'm not going to find a cardboard box with a Labrador puppy inside, am I?"

"Not with my allergies, I'm afraid," Stan advised, although, aside from the allergies, he did quite like puppies. He then positioned Frank carefully in the doorway. "Ready?" he asked.

"Ready," Frank replied.

Stan released his grip as Frank's eyes slowly opened. "What am I supposed to be looking at?" Frank asked, raising a hand to shield his face from the glare of the morning sun as he glanced about, here and there, though not anyplace in particular, as he hadn't any idea what he was meant to be looking for. It wasn't Easter, of course, so he didn't reckon there were any eggs hidden amidst the grass, for instance. Frank took a tentative step out the door, irrationally wondering if Stan and Edgar were having a laugh at his expense, with maybe a bucket of cold water about to land on his head or some such thing. "I'm not sure what I'm supposed to be..."

"Bloody hell, it's not that hard," Stan suggested with a laugh. "Come on, man."

Frank scanned the area outside the home, but the only thing he couldn't be certain was there before was a flowering plant in a terracotta pot positioned near the front gate. But he soon discounted this as an option, having a vague recollection of a conversation with Jessie about it in which he remembered assuring her that he was listening and absolutely *not* ignoring her for the football match being shown on the telly. Besides, Frank mused, why would Edgar and Stan get so excited about heading out of the house early to pick up a simple plant? "Right, I give up," Frank eventually offered, along with a shrug, as nothing at all was presenting itself as obvious to him.

Stan playfully rolled his eyes, pointing past the garden perimeter wall. "And what about there?" he asked, tipping his head towards the road out front. "Do you notice anything new?"

Frank followed the direction of both Stan's pointing finger and nodding head, but his line of sight was hindered on account of a large motorhome parked directly outside, both blocking access to their driveway and severely limiting his field of vision beyond. "I can't see a thing, Stan," Frank said, still perplexed. "And it's not helping that some selfish pillock has parked that bloody great big shit-heap right outside our house."

Edgar cleared his throat, whilst also suddenly finding something utterly compelling to stare at by his feet.

"Ah," said Frank, successfully putting two and two together. "I don't suppose, Stan, that your moment of impulsiveness was this motorhome itself?"

"Yes," Stan said weakly, and somewhat deflated (just like one of the vehicle's tyres, coincidentally enough, which he'd need to attend to). "Ehm... surprise?"

***

Fortunately, Stan didn't sulk for too long about his big reveal not being ultimately received with the gusto he'd anticipated. That reveal being big in quite the literal sense, as it was a Swift Escape 2010 model motorhome, presently preventing any vehicular access to their driveway.

"It's a six-berth beauty," Stan related, for Frank's edification, running an adoring hand over the side of the vehicle. "Sure, there are a few blemishes on the bodywork..." he went on, beginning to sound like a sleazy salesman in a backstreet garage. "But then haven't we all," he indicated, accompanying this with an exaggerated laugh, which was then followed by a long, lingering sigh. "Here, have a proper look around and familiarise yourself," he suggested.

Frank took a wander around the vehicle, kicking each of the tyres in turn as he circumnavigated the massive beast (as that seemed to be something people sometimes did, although he had no idea why), not really sure what he was supposed to be looking for exactly. Once he'd completed his lap, Frank presented himself back before Edgar and Stan.

"Before you say anything..." Stan said, holding his hands out like a defence lawyer preparing to make one final, impassioned plea on behalf of his client. "It's an impulse buy on my part, I admit. But I was contemplating your bucket list, yeah?"

"My bucket list...?"

"Yeah, the one that brought us to this magnificent isle in the first place, Frank," replied Stan. "You see, it struck me that your bucket list isn't very long. That is, we've never really added too many things to it."

"Okay?" Frank answered, tilting his head. "Go on," he said, receptive to hearing more.

Stan looked across to Edgar for moral support before then continuing. "I thought the motorhome might be a nice idea. I've spoken to so many people who head off into the wilderness for grand adventures, yeah?" he offered, sharing his reasoning. "For instance there's the Scottish Highlands, the Lake District, scenic Wales, and also so many beautiful areas right here in the Isle of Man that we still haven't fully explored," he related, his eyes becoming pleasantly unfocussed as he brought these places to mind. "And there's plenty of room," he added, after catching his breath for a moment, and now reading from the salesman's tick list consigned to memory in his head. "Six berths, as I said, so that me, you, Edgar, and Jessie can head out into the wilds to enjoy all that Mother Nature has to offer."

"And we also thought it'd be ideal for when Dave and Monty are racing off-island," Edgar chipped in. "We could be like groupies following them all around wherever they go."

"So, whaddya think?" Stan cautiously asked.

Frank looked at the new purchase, and then over to the limited amount of available space in their driveway. He walked partially out to the motorhome once again, slowly running his eyes over the gigantic transport that perhaps, being kind, had its best years now visible only through the rear-view mirror.

"I can always look into taking it back..." Stan suggested shortly thereafter, concerned he might have made a colossal mistake. "Maybe it wasn't the best idea I've ever had, but—"

"Stan," Frank gently cut in. "Stan, I'm simply trying to work out how to juggle the vehicles around so we can get this whale of a beast onto our driveway."

"Oh. So you *do* like it, then?" Stan gamely ventured.

Frank approached Stan and Edgar with a broad smile, extending his arms and pulling them in close. "Like it? No, gents, I absolutely *adore* it," Frank revealed, giving them both a generous squeeze.

Frank let go of them both, struggling to contain the moisture that was in imminent danger of being released soon from his tear ducts. "Stan, these last few years, I've come to realise that a successful bucket list isn't just about visiting exotic locales, or doing something that terrifies you, like swimming with sharks, or jumping from a plane with only a thin sheet of nylon or silk stopping you from being pulped." Frank held his gaze for a moment or two. "For me, it's more about the people you surround yourself with," he revealed. "And if that big van—"

"Motorhome," Stan corrected him.

"Sorry, *motorhome*," Frank was happy to concede. "So if this new purchase of yours, that big motorhome, means that I get to spend even more time with the people I care about most, well, in my book, then that's the best purchase, impulsive or not, that money can buy."

Stan bounced up and down like Tigger, from *Winnie-the-Pooh*, excited by all of the grand adventures that would surely await them. "I *told* you he'd like it, Edgar! Didn't I tell you?"

Edgar nodded his head in agreement, smiling warmly. "You did at that, Stan. You did at that."

Stan proceeded to give Frank the full tour of the vehicle's interior, stressing that the shower and related facilities both still required his own special brand of cleaning. Also, there were a few questionable stains on the dated upholstery, Stan noted, but nothing that wouldn't come out with a firm application of elbow grease, he stressed.

After the tour was concluded, the boys decided it would be an opportune moment for a nice cuppa. "You know," Frank thought aloud as they wandered back towards the house, "when we get back from Las Vegas, I might look into taking down a section of the garden wall. You know, remodel things a bit in order to make room for the old girl and welcome her into the family properly."

"*Pfft*," scoffed Stan. "If you recall, the *last* time you'd armed yourself with a hammer, you burst a waterpipe. So maybe best if we get the builders in, yeah? You *do* remember the burst waterpipe incident, don't you, Frank...?"

"Cheeky bugger," Frank said, chuckling at the recollection of the incident he'd chosen to hide away in the darkest recesses of his memory banks. "You won't be quite so jovial when you open your post," he then muttered to himself under his breath.

"What's that? You want me to help you with the post?"

"Nah, you're good. There's nothing important there, buddy. Certainly nothing that couldn't wait for our return, at any rate," Frank answered, smiling serenely. "Anyway, let's get ourselves that nice cuppa, and talk about our first adventure in... in..." he said, looking to Stan for possible answers. "Hmm, what should we call her?" he asked.

"Oh, I hadn't thought of that," Stan said, giving each of his knuckles a crack, as if this would in some way get his creative juices flowing. "What about..." he began. "Then again, no, that's not good," he decided.

Edgar raised his hand. "Considering the bodywork needs a bit of cosmetic attention," he offered, "what about *The Rust Bucket List*? It could be the name of both the vehicle and its mission."

"I love it," said Stan, clapping his hands in delight. "Frank? What about you?"

"Here's to many great adventures in *The Rust Bucket List!*" Frank said in answer, raising an imaginary glass to toast their future travels.

Chapter
TEN

One of the minor niggles at times about living on an island, virtual paradise though it may be, was the fact that you were, well, living on an island, surrounded on all sides by the Irish Sea like an enormous moat. What this meant, in practice, was that any desire or inclination to venture further afield first required either a ferry trip or a short hop on a plane. And it was for this reason that Team Frank 'n' Stan, along with Stella, had been awake since the crack of dawn to commence the first leg of their journey to Las Vegas, which in this instance meant a flight over to the UK.

Because of the early hour, the majority of emotional goodbyes with loved ones had been conducted under a warm duvet. This was not entirely the case with Stella, however, who was quite insistent that the main man in her life be present at the airport to wave her off on her travels. However, that man wasn't, as one might expect, her loving husband Lee, but rather the *other* man in her life — that being Bovril, her cherished cat, who she'd rarely been separated from — with Lee also in attendance and playing second fiddle to their beloved fur baby.

Unfortunately, as it turned out, pussycats weren't overly fond of airports, in particular the noisy tannoy systems and the roar of jet engines. Still, airport security and the baggage handlers eventually saw the humorous side after more than an hour chasing a nervous feline around Ronaldsway Airport, the Isle of Man's only airport, just south of the isle's capital of Douglas. The same could not be said for all the passengers, however, whose flights were temporarily delayed as a result.

As such, just over an hour later than scheduled, Frank, Stan, Dave, Monty, and Stella arrived at London's Heathrow Airport for the next section of their journey...

"I shouldn't be made to wear this!" Stan moaned, crossing his arms like a petulant child. "I'm supposed to be a respected businessman, and yet I look like a drunken lout going to Magaluf on a stag party," he insisted. "I also don't think this is the sort of t-shirt one wears in the executive lounge of an airport. They have certain *standards*, you know."

Frank, sitting beside him, struggled to stifle a laugh, less concerned by their current attire, it would seem, than Stan. "Well, I quite like them, Stan," he remarked, looking over to Dave on the opposite sofa in the opulent lounge.

Dave, for his part, didn't appear to be fussed one way or the other. "It's all right, I suppose," he put forth, taking a look down at himself. "Although a size larger wouldn't have gone amiss," he suggested, cupping his breasts to illustrate the point.

Stan shook his head, annoyed that he was the only one who was presently annoyed. "And it's not just the offensive message printed there on the front, either," he noted. "This horrible colour doesn't even go with my beige *chinos*," he insisted.

The group t-shirts that currently had Stan in such a fluster were a surprise that Stella had arranged just prior to their trip. Resplendent in bright orange (so they couldn't lose each other, according to Stella) each shirt sported the catchy and descriptive logo: TEAM FRANK 'N' STAN'S BUCKET LIST – BELLENDS ON TOUR, along with a printed image of Dave and Monty's most magnificent sidecar.

"And besides," Frank said, after some consideration, "Stella has spent her own hard-earned money providing us with these shirts, yeah? And you could see that she was pleased as Punch when she handed them over to us. You don't want to hurt her feelings, do you, Stan?"

Stan pursed his lips. "We look like a bunch of plonkers," he said, with the tail end of his sentence markedly decreasing in volume as Stella returned with a bottle of champagne in each hand.

"Are you a bit thirsty, Stella?" Frank asked rhetorically, while casting another admiring glance at Stella's audacious mini skirt, its design heavily inspired by the American flag. Where she'd even managed to find such a thing, he had no idea.

"The skinny bloke with the glasses told me it was a free bar," Stella replied, taking a seat next to Dave. "So I thought I'd stock up before he changes his mind," she advised, placing one of the bottles down by her hobnail boots before ripping the cork out of the other one.

Stan leaned forward in anticipation of some possible liquid refreshment, doing all he could not to look up Stella's impossibly short skirt in the process.

"What are you looking at?" Stella asked, her eyes narrowing.

"I was just wondering if and when you were going to pour the champers and get this party started," Stan said, glancing about in an attempt to locate a glass. "I mean, it's still a bit before noon, but still..."

Stella raised the opened bottle to her lips, taking a generous mouthful like an F1 driver who'd just won the Monaco Grand Prix. "Eh? I just told you it was a *free* bar, Stan," she said after swallowing. "So go and get your own if you want some, you lazy get," she instructed. "And stop looking up my skirt!" she added, loud enough for the rest of the executive lounge to hear.

Stan lowered his head like a naughty boy, even though he was completely innocent, all thoughts of complaining about his new shirt appearing to be on hold for now. "Right. I'll go and fetch us a drink, then," he kindly offered, receiving a nod of confirmation from both Frank and Dave. "Has anybody seen our Monty?" Stan asked of nobody in particular, looking around the lounge area to make certain Monty was included in the beverage round.

"He's laid out on one of those massage chairs," Stella replied. "And judging by the stupid expression on his face I reckon he might have enjoyed a happy ending by the looks of things," she added, a bit too loudly, again with no concern as to the other patrons possibly overhearing.

"I'll make sure I get Monty a beer while I'm at the bar," Stan noted, pushing himself up from his seat.

"And a handful of tissues," Stella shot back with a cackle, before returning her attention to the now partially empty champagne bottle.

Stan then came to a sudden halt, half-sitting, half-standing.

"You forgotten where you're going?" Dave asked. "It was the bar, in case you were wondering," he said helpfully.

Stan parked himself back down onto the cushions, a thought appearing to have suddenly occurred to him. "The business class flights so kindly provided to the four of us are the reason we're presently enjoying this luxurious hospitality, correct?" he asked, looking first to Frank and then over to Dave.

"Yep," Dave agreed. "Although… I still appear to be without a drink, Stanley," he remarked.

"I won't be long with this," Stan assured him, before continuing with his previous line of enquiry. "And business class flights are significantly more expensive than, say, economy class flights, yes?"

"Correct again," Dave replied. "Thousands of pounds, Stan, if I'm not mistaken. I must remember to give the responsible party a huge kiss when we land in Vegas to show my appreciation."

Stan turned his attention to Stella, who wasn't showing that much interest in what was being said. "Stella. You know how you used my credit card to purchase both your flight and hotel tickets?" he asked.

"Yeah? What of it?" she answered.

"Well, it's not the Americans who are paying for your trip, Stella. I am. As in, I'll need to pay back what you've spent. So, can I just check something?" he replied. Stan said this in a calm, soothing manner as he spoke, as to raise your voice with Stella was like kicking a bear while it was trying to catch salmon. "Did you book an economy-class air ticket, which would have potentially saved me thousands of pounds?"

"What? Don't be daft," Stella answered, appearing distinctly bored by this line of questioning.

"But that could have saved me an awful lot of money, Stella," Stan pressed, through gritted teeth.

Stella now appeared agitated. "Jesus, Stan! Do I need to do *all* of the thinking for you?" she barked. *"That's* the reason I'm hammering the free bar, yeah? Trying to recoup some of the money you spent on the *flight* tickets."

Stella tapped the side of her head at the temple, like she had all the answers, which, as far as she was concerned, she did. She then tipped up the champagne bottle to demonstrate that its contents had now been successfully polished off.

"That's roughly sixty quid I've already saved you right there, Stan," she pointed out, using her own particular brand of logic, while now reaching for the second bottle. "And I'm just about to save you some more, as well. You're *welcome*, Stan!"

***

A bit later in the afternoon, when their flight to Vegas was eventually called, some of the orange-shirt-wearing *Bellends on Tour* brigade could be witnessed staggering their way towards the departure gate.

"I've never wanted a plane to be delayed more in my life," Frank confessed, feeling giddy from all the free drinks he'd been enjoying, with an arm draped around Stan's shoulders half in camaraderie and half for the physical support it provided.

"Yeah, I reckon I could definitely get used to travelling in style like this," Stan remarked, with all concerns about his offensive t-shirt now drowned in free alcohol. "That executive lounge is a little bit of me."

"It's safe to say Stella has made herself firmly at home here as well," Frank suggested, spotting her up ahead of them trying her damnedest to cram another bottle of unopened champagne into her studded leather handbag. "Here," Frank added, straightening himself up. "We'd better do our best to appear sober or they might not let us on board?"

"Well, if that happens, then I imagine we'll just have to head straight back over to the executive lounge," Stan mused.

But they needn't have worried too much, as the friendly airline staff appeared to take more interest in the Stars & Stripes-themed skirt wrapped tightly around Stella's waist than to be concerned about how much any of them may have had to drink.

Stan took immense delight that his flight ticket permitted him to turn left once onboard the aircraft, towards the *good* section of the plane, as opposed to the great unwashed, the shuffling herd, as it were, sitting over in the opposite direction. "Look at all the plebs sitting in economy," Stan remarked, a little too loudly, as he looked to his righthand side, giving Frank a nudge in the ribs along with a devilish laugh.

"Who are you calling a pleb?" asked a burly chap sitting near and to the right, incensed, and fumbling to remove his seatbelt like he was preparing for a row.

Frank raised an apologetic hand on behalf of his travelling companion. "Huge apologies, sir," he said, acting as the peacemaker. "My friend here is not just an idiot, but he's an idiot who's had too much to drink."

The angry chap scowled at Stan but released his grip on his seatbelt, leaving it fastened for the time being.

"Come on, mate," Frank said, pulling Stan towards the business class section of the plane before any kind of physical altercation might arise.

"Would you look at this place," Stan said, several moments later. "We've each got our own little pods," he remarked, admiring their home for the next eleven hours or so.

"Who let *you* heathens in?" Dave called over, stretched out on his reclining chair with a crystal flute glass in hand. "Honestly, and I thought they had standards," he joked.

But before Frank or Stan could respond, Stella came marching up to them. "Do I need to wait for this thing to take off before I use the loo?" she asked. "Because I've got a turtle head sticking out right now. I can feel it."

"Uhm, I'm no expert, Stella, but I reckon you do need to wait," Frank answered for the both of them. "It shouldn't be too long, though, I don't think?"

"Right, I'll just have to hold it in for now, then," Stella advised, looking around and about her in search of her seat.

"Can I help?" a flight attendant asked, noting Stella's look of uncertainty.

In response, Stella held out the ticket she'd printed at home.

"Oh, I'm sorry, madam," the flight attendant said, once he'd inspected her confirmation. "You're actually not sitting in this section of the plane."

Upon overhearing this conversation, Stan's ears perked up, hopeful that the damage to his credit card wouldn't be quite as bad as he'd first suspected.

"You're actually booked in as a *first-class* passenger, madam," advised the flight attendant. "So if you'd like to follow me and I'll show you to your seat?"

Stan reached over to tap Frank on the shoulder. "Did you just hear that?" he asked, hoping he hadn't just heard what he thought he'd just heard.

"Uhm..." Frank replied, unsure what to really say on the subject, except, "I think Stella's booked herself a first-class ticket?" he offered, shoulders starting to heave through stifled laughter.

The blood drained from Stan's sunbed-kissed cheeks. "Stella, please tell me you've not used my credit card to book a first-class ticket?" he called out.

Stella came to a halt, shaking her head gravely. "You *know* I've recently had major surgery, Stanley," she chided him. "So if you think I'm sitting in an uncomfortable seat for hours on end, well, think *again*, mister. *Honestly*, Stan, you can be such a selfish sod at times!"

"They were haemorrhoids, Stella!" Stan shot back. "And that was nearly two years ago!" he protested. But it was too late, as Stella had already made her way through to the promised land that was the first-class section, which, as fine as business class was, somehow managed to be even *more* posh than that.

Twenty-five or so minutes later, somewhere in the general vicinity of Irish airspace, and Stan was still seething. He'd tried watching a film on his personal entertainment system, but that wasn't taking his mind off of things. Just then, the plane's public address system pinged into life.

"Ladies and gentlemen, this is Kevin, your Flight Service Manager," Kevin, the flight service manager, said in a velvet-smooth, professional manner. "I do sincerely apologise, and regret to advise that the bathroom in the first-class section of the plane is unfortunately out of service at this time. We're working to address this situation and assure you there are plenty of additional facilities located throughout the aircraft. Once again, my sincere apologies, and I, along with my team, welcome you onboard this flight to Las Vegas."

This announcement brought a smile to Frank's face. So much so that he immediately rose up from his executive pod to share the joke with his grumpy best mate sitting nearby. "Did you hear that?" Frank asked, presenting himself before a semi-reclined Stan.

"What's that?" said Stan, removing his earphones.

"Over the tannoy. They said the toilet's out of action in first class," Frank took great delight in telling him, hoping to cheer up his mate.

One corner of Stan's mouth raised up, resulting in a lopsided grin. "Yeah?"

Frank nodded. "Yes indeed. So if you think that you're having a bad day, spare a thought for the poor cabin crew questioning their career choices as they're forced to unblock a toilet, very likely the result of Stella's mischievous bowels."

"And what about all the upper-crust mob sitting at the very front of the plane, having to suffer through Stella's sparkling company for eleven hours straight?" Stan suggested, perking up. "That in *itself* is an Instagram moment or twenty waiting to happen!"

Frank lowered his head a bit further into Stan's pod, so that he could speak more privately. "Listen, mate," he said. "About Stella's credit card bill…"

"Thanks, Frank. And there I was, just starting to enjoy myself," Stan offered.

"I'll split it with you," Frank told him.

"You will?"

"Sure. She's like our adopted daughter, so it's only right that I cover half with you. Besides, it's a small enough price to pay for the laughs."

"Stella really is the gift that keeps on giving," Stan suggested. "Can we sneak into first class to see how her presence is going down with the landed gentry?"

"I thought you'd never ask, Stan. Do lead on, my good man."

***

Just before seven in the evening, local time, the gang touched down at Harry Reid International Airport in Las Vegas, tired, slightly hungover, bursting from a constant supply of exquisite food, and unsure of what time of day it was, exactly, in this new location of theirs.

Walking towards the baggage reclaim area inside the airport terminal, Stan glanced down at his watch to check the time, and was horrified by what he discovered. Not in relation to the time, but rather what he spotted on his beige chinos. "Aww, soddin' hell," Stan moaned, looking across to Dave and Monty on his left, and then to Frank and Stella on his right. "Did none of you think to tell me about the whopping great grease stain on my…" he said, trailing off. And then, after first checking that none of the other passengers were within earshot, "On the *zip* area of my trousers," he specified, applying a spit-covered index finger in an attempt to remove the unwelcome remains of one of the inflight meals. "Oh, that's just made it bloody worse," he observed, after having just made it worse.

"It does look like you've pissed yourself, Stan," Monty offered helpfully, having a look at the offending area.

"Relax," said Frank. "Just shuffle towards the baggage carousel and stand where nobody can see you, Stan. Then, when your luggage arrives, you can pull out a spare pair of trousers and get changed in the loo."

Stan liked that idea, as it was as good a plan as any, and did as Frank suggested, crossing his hands over his groin for the time being and waiting patiently.

For his part, waiting patiently didn't appear to be at the top of Dave's agenda after a boring, overlong flight. "Monty, fancy a race?" he asked, tipping his head towards two currently unused luggage trolleys nearby.

"*Pfft...* yeah!" Monty answered.

"Don't be crashing into anybody, boys," Frank cautioned, like a nervous father, before then turning his attention to a rather subdued-looking Stella. "How was your first taste of first-class travel, Stella?" he asked, by way of conversation.

But Stella didn't seem too terribly impressed by the experience, judging by the shrug of her stout shoulders. "Honestly, I'd rather have a pint and a game of darts," she said, using a tissue to casually mop up some of the excess moisture that had accumulated under her armpits, as it often did. "Although I did quite like the salt and pepper shakers," she revealed. "Solid silver, they were, with the image of a plane stamped into them."

"Ah. They sound nice," Frank answered, pleased to see Stella pleased about something.

Stella dipped her fingers into her handbag, rummaging about inside. "Here, I'll show you," she said, producing the aforementioned salt and pepper shakers for Frank's careful consideration. "You see the stamp?" she asked, thrusting the stolen booty towards his face so he could view them properly. "They match the cutlery," she noted, reaching into her bag once more and exchanging the items in her hand for more of her ill-gotten goods, namely a knife, fork, and a dessert spoon, with remnants of her dessert still visible on the shiny surface.

"You're not supposed to *take* them!" Frank said, whispering so as not to alert the nearby security staff.

Stella lowered her head. "Well I felt bad about using Stanley's credit card," she insisted. "So I thought I'd take these to cheer the soppy old sod up by giving them to him."

Frank rubbed the side of her arm gently. "That's actually very thoughtful, Stella, I think? Although maybe hand them over to him once we're clear of the terminal building, yeah?"

"Right-ho, Frank. I'll do that."

The luggage carousel emitted a beeping noise like a reversing lorry, resulting in the queue of waiting passengers stepping forward a pace or two as the conveyor belt stuttered into life. Gradually, luggage of all sizes started to appear like the weekly shopping heading towards the supermarket cashier. One by one they were retrieved by their owners until the throng in their area of the baggage reclaim hall started to slowly thin.

"Come on, boys!" Frank called over to Monty and Dave, who were currently showing no signs of tiring in their trolley-racing adventure. "I think your cases are on their second rotation and starting to look a little lonely!"

Frank was correct. Though soon enough, he, Dave, and Monty had all collected their luggage, desperate as they each were to get their holiday started. But Stan was still just standing there.

"Come on, Stanley," Dave said, tapping his watch. "We've got a pint of something cold waiting for us."

Stan laughed a nervous laugh, because the beeping noise had long since stopped and the only thing that was now circulating on the conveyor was an empty crate, and a lone abandoned flip-flop. "I'm sure it's just about to come out...?" he said, staring intently at the rubber fringe where the luggage ordinarily made its way through.

"Ah, I shouldn't panic, Stan. Stella hasn't got her luggage yet either," Monty put forth, suspecting that misery might appreciate some company at this stage.

"I've not got any luggage," Stella revealed.

Frank waited for her to offer some sort of follow-up to that statement, but nothing arrived. "Wait," he said, as Stella started ambling away, bored of hanging about it would appear. "What do you mean you've got *no* luggage?"

Stella pivoted, pointing to her handbag, home to her stolen aeroplane inventory, amongst other things. "I've got three pairs of clean knickers in here, a toothbrush, and also a packet of wet wipes for an intimate wash," she replied. "Everything else I buy when I get there. It saves carrying a heavy suitcase or hanging around in places like this for hours."

Frank couldn't fault the logic, even if it was completely bonkers. "And the return leg?" he asked, unsure if she was pulling his leg or not. "How do you get your purchases home?"

"What doesn't fit into my handbag will simply go in the bin," Stella explained. "That way I'll have no washing to do when I get home, and no luggage to hump about."

There was certainly a method in her madness, Frank had to admit. Especially when considering the strain present on poor Stanley's face.

"I hate to say this, Stanley," Dave offered up, several minutes later, upon noticing the conveyor had well and truly come to a complete stop, with absolutely no more motion to be had. "But sadly, I think your suitcase has done a Lord Lucan."

Eventually, Stan had little choice but to reluctantly concede that his baggage would not be coming with him at this late stage of the game. After which, armed with both a missing luggage report and a sour expression, Stan and his band of intrepid explorers successfully cleared customs with nary a rubber glove in sight.

"Nearly there, Stanley," Frank advised, hoping to cheer up his travelling-light companion, pointing to the welcoming *'Arrivals'* sign guiding them to the outside world.

"I'm wearing an offensive, hideously orange shirt, and without my suitcase and thus the ability to change, I look like I've had an incidence of incontinence down below," Stan replied, along with a heavy sigh. "This is not exactly the auspicious welcome to Las Vegas I'd envisaged, Frank."

Frank was the first to approach the automatic doors leading through to the arrivals hall. "Stan?" he said in his chirpiest manner. "Stan, don't worry about it, yeah? We're in a foreign country where nobody even knows who you are and where nobody's going to give your sullied chinos a second glance."

"I suppose," Stan agreed, though he remained none too happy about the situation. "But we're *absolutely* stopping at the nearest shop to buy some new trousers," he insisted, just as the doors parted for them.

"THEY'RE HERE!" came a collective cry, causing both Frank and Stan to stop immediately in their tracks. Waiting behind the barriers in the arrival hall were row after row of people, waving placards and signs as they simultaneously hooped and hollered, excited to greet the new travellers.

"What the flippin' heck?" Stan said, looking to Frank for answers. "Have we taken a bloody wrong turn?" he asked as a gaggle of photographers waved furiously, vying for a clear shot.

"No," Frank said, taking a closer look at the various signs being waved around. "This, if I'm not mistaken, is the *Isle of Man TT Aces* fan club. It would appear the show has received a great deal of advance publicity, if all this hullabaloo is any indication."

In fact the show was generating quite the rabid fanbase, before it had even aired on TV, courtesy of Clifford Tanner's pulling out all the stops in promoting it. Whether it was the British accents (which Americans tended to like), the interesting cast of real-life characters, the extreme racing action, or a combination of all three, Clifford didn't quite know for sure. But whatever the reason, Clifford was certain they had a hit on their hands, and had capitalised on that interest by promoting it even harder... which only served to produce even *more* fans.

Stan slowly eased his hands together, creating a shield of fingers which he placed over the front of his trousers. "I can see you're right, Frank," Stan said through gritted teeth, offering an awkward smile for the TV camera crew approaching them. "And as you'd indicated earlier, it's a good job *nobody out here knows who we are.*"

Stella appeared next, with Dave and Monty arriving shortly thereafter, a sight which produced another bout of fervent cheering. "It's Dave and Monty!" many of the welcoming committee shouted in unison, giving the impression they'd just set eyes on their heroes, which perhaps they had.

"Oh, sod this," Stella remarked, heading straight for the exit. "Frank," she said on the way past, "I'll be outside having a fag."

Chapter
ELEVEN

Two unsuspecting police officers bravely struggled to drag Dave, Monty, Frank, and Stan through the adoring crowd that appeared to be increasing in size by the very minute. Indeed, the last time four individuals from across the pond had received such an ecstatic reception on US soil was when four mop-topped Liverpudlian fellows came over in 1964.

Fortunately, Brad was soon there with the goal of whisking the gang away and transporting them to their hotel. But there was little opportunity for an ordinary welcome with him, what with all the flailing limbs inside the arrivals building desperate for some kind of a small souvenir from their heroes.

"They were tearing pieces off my t-shirt!" Monty complained once in the back of the waiting minivan, pointing to the gaping hole revealing his left nipple for all to see.

Stan collapsed into one of the other rear seats, checking his own shirt for damage. "How bloody typical. I see mine has been left completely unscathed," he said. "How unfortunate."

Chip, who'd been waiting in the van outside the terminal, appeared slightly confused. "Welcome to the—" he began to say.

"Just go! Drive!" Brad instructed, cutting his brother off mid-sentence. "For the love of god, just go."

Once underway and clear of the airport, Brad looked over his shoulder, speaking to his guests. "I'm sorry about that, guys," he said, with some degree of trauma evident in his voice. "That was pretty wild, right?"

"What happened? Did a few people turn up?" Chip asked, filling in some of the blanks for himself.

"Yeah, you *could* say that," Brad replied, pulling down the sun visor and checking to see if the rented vehicle had a mirror on the back of it, which fortunately it did. "Some crazy biker chick elbowed me in the freakin' face during the frenzy," he informed his brother. "I was sure she was gonna break my nose or something!" he added, checking himself in the mirror for any potential damage. "No, looks okay," he advised.

"Wait, so how many people turned up?" Chip enquired.

"Hundreds, I reckon," Dave entered in from the back. "It was carnage in there. Absolute bloody mayhem. I'm sure I even felt some rogue fingers plunging down the rear of my trousers at one point, having a bit of a wander."

Monty held up his hand. "That was me, buddy," he confessed. "When that group of old ladies got their talons into you and tried dragging you away, I thought, *Not on my watch, you don't!* I was only trying to grab you by the waistband, so apologies if I ended up violating you."

"Hey, I wasn't really complaining, Monty, I was just surprised by it," Dave answered. "You have a very soft, gentle touch, if you don't mind me saying so," Dave elaborated.

Monty waved away the compliment, though he did appreciate it. "It's all just down to a careful, regular moisturising regime at bedtime, Dave," he advised. "I'll talk you through it when we return home."

"Carnage, huh?" Chip offered.

Oddly, in Dave's view, Chip didn't appear entirely too surprised by their recent, wild encounter, and Dave was just able to catch a glimpse of Chip's facial expression through the rear-view mirror. "Judging by your smile, Chip, I'm guessing you were behind our little welcoming committee?" he speculated.

Chip shook his head in the negative. "Oh, no, that definitely wasn't us, guys, I promise," he answered. "NBC has been running ads for the upcoming show like crazy, promoting the living shit out of it, releasing clips of it on social media and stuff," he explained. "So now, with the premiere being right around the corner, it wouldn't surprise me if they leaked news of your arrival, hoping to see what kind of reaction there'd be."

"Well," said Stan, "I think you could say the reaction was enthusiastic, to say the least, boys."

"Yeah, and if I was smiling a second ago, that's why," Chip explained. "Because they must've liked what we created, right?"

"And what about you, Frank?" Brad asked, concerned that he hadn't heard a peep from their other guest. "You're not injured or anything back there, are you?"

Frank was still attempting to sort himself out from the previous tumult, taking deep, relaxing breaths, in through the nose and out through the mouth and all that. "No, I'm all present and correct," he answered. "Well, I hope I am, at least. It's just that..." he said. "Nah, maybe I took a bang on the head and just imagined what I saw...?"

"What you saw?" asked Brad, turning in his seat so he could directly address Frank as he was speaking to him.

Frank laughed the sort of laugh which said, *don't think I'm bonkers or anything*. "Well, when one of the police officers was threatening to unleash her pepper spray, the crowd parted a bit. And there, with a view of those standing at the rear, I noticed some of them wearing those funny rubber masks. You know, the ones that look like famous people, like ex-presidents and such."

"I think I may have spotted them too," Stan offered. "But it was difficult to get a clear view, what with the ample bosom my face was pressed into at the time."

"You guys saw people wearing Richard Nixon masks?" Brad asked, likely wondering if their rented vehicle came equipped with some kind of first aid kit.

"No, not Richard Nixon," Frank advised, glancing out at the freeway traffic hurtling by. "They looked like..." he started to say, hesitant in case he was driven straight to the psychiatric hospital. "Well, they looked like none other than bloody Rodney Franks," he revealed, followed by another *don't-think-I'm-bonkers-or-anything* sort of laugh.

Both Brad and Chip, in front, shared a quick sideways glance, panicked that the jig was up. Of course, they both knew they'd have to bring everyone up to speed about the developments on the Rodney front eventually. They just weren't prepared for doing so right now, on the journey from the airport, necessarily.

"Um..." Chip offered by way of a placeholder, thinking about what he might say to them for now. "I suppose... I mean, well, it was a long flight. You're probably just very tired. Plus, I don't imagine you guys were too overly shy with the complimentary champagne, right?"

Frank chuckled. "Guilty as charged," he confessed, holding up his hands to accept his fate. "And I suppose it might just have been the angle I was looking at the masks," he considered. "After all, who would actually spend their own hard-earned money to look like *that* pipsqueak?"

"I know, right?" Brad replied, sharing the laugh but secretly squirming on the inside. "That would be crazy!"

With only a modest commute from the airport, it wasn't long before Chip started the drive up the iconic Las Vegas Strip, with Stan dangling half outside the rear window like a dog enjoying the wind against its face on a long family drive. "It's more than I ever imagined," Stan declared, as the glittering lights reflected against his eyeballs, all of the sights and sounds and smells overwhelming him. "Yeah! Las Vegas, baby!" he called out, throwing his arms out like he was somehow going to give the hotel in front of them a large hug. "Frank, what do you think?" he asked. "Isn't it splendid?"

"Frank's fallen asleep," Monty advised, once Stan returned his head inside the vehicle lest it be removed by a palm tree.

"How could anyone possibly sleep at a time like this?" Stan asked, drinking in the scenery, marvelling at the sheer scale of the place.

"Word of your appearance in town has already reached social media," Brad was happy to reveal, stretching out his arm to pass Monty his phone. "Here, check it out."

Stan and Dave leaned in closer for a view of the video being displayed on the phone's screen, that video being a shaky, hand-held recording of their arrival captured by one of the welcoming committee back at the airport and subsequently uploaded for all to see.

"Oi, those biceps curls you've been doing are really paying off, Dave," Monty observed. "You can really see the gains."

"No pain, no gain, Monty," Dave sagely advised.

Just then, the camera in the video they were viewing started to zoom in, with whoever was filming it clearly getting buffeted by those around them, resulting in the image bouncing all over the place. Indeed, the recording was starting to resemble one of those found-footage type horror films, the ones where the camera never sits still.

"Jesus, this is making me dizzy," Monty remarked, preparing to return the phone to Brad.

Dave grabbed Monty's arm. "Wait, where are they going with this?" he asked, chuckling away to himself, as he already seemed to know the answer. "Oh, look out, Stan. Your chinos are about to go viral," he warned.

"Stop them!" Stan cried out, waking Frank from his nap in the process. "Monty, they're zooming in on my damp patch!" he protested, telling Monty what he could now plainly see for himself. "Delete it, Monty!" Stan demanded. "There are some things the world is not meant to see!"

"How am I meant to delete it?" asked Monty, thoroughly perplexed. "Someone's uploaded it to Facebook. So unless you've got Mark Zuckerberg on speed dial, there's not much to be done." And with that, he returned the phone to its rightful owner.

"Lovely. Isn't that just bloody marvellous," Stan complained, shooting his crotch an evil look. "Brad, you don't know if there's anyplace around here to buy new clothes, do you?" he asked.

Brad nodded. "Are you kidding? You could get married to a camel at three in the morning in this town if you wanted to," he declared. "So getting just a simple pair of pants shouldn't be too much of a problem. I'm sure there's someplace nearby, and the store at the hotel might even have something."

Chip slowed the vehicle to a halt outside the Venetian, the resort hotel that was their destination. "Here we go, guys," he said, rolling down the window to speak to the valet. "Brad can get you inside while I get this thing parked, okay?"

Once outside their vehicle, Stan's mood immediately lifted. "Oh, yes!" he said, slowly raising his head to appreciate the entirety of the magnificent building before them. "Oh, Frank," he exclaimed, placing an arm around his mate's shoulder. "Whaddya reckon to this?"

"It's not half bad, Stanley. Not half bad," Frank commented, as the group stood on the sidewalk staring up at the hotel like the tourists they obviously were. "I think I'm going to like our little vacation to Sin City, Stanley."

"Can I borrow a pair of trousers once we get inside, Frank? Or even a pair of shorts, now that we're here in Vegas?" Stan asked. "I don't think I've really got it in me to go clothes shopping just now."

"Sure. They might not be as stylish as you're used to. But no problem," Frank answered. "Oh, and don't forget, you'll have a shopping buddy to help keep you company when you do decide to go," Frank reminded him.

"I will?" Stan asked, assuming Frank was kindly offering himself up for the position.

"Yep. Stella will also need to top up her wardrobe," Frank advised. "Honestly, who goes on holiday without a suitcase?" he said with a chuckle, in reference to their dear companion mentioned.

Both Frank and Stan continued to take in their surroundings for a bit longer. Sure, they were absolutely shattered from their journey. However, the giddy excitement from finally being there kept tiredness at arm's length for now.

After their brief period of quiet appreciation, Stan returned his attention to ground level, at which point he placed a hand to his face. "Frank," he whispered softly. "Frank, there's something I need to say, and I don't want you to panic."

Frank's cheery demeanour hardened. "Eh? What's up, Stan?" he asked. "You're not unwell, are you?"

"I'm fine, Frank," Stan quickly assured him. "It's just... well... erm, you know in all the kerfuffle at the airport?" Stan asked, lowering his hand.

Frank scanned his friend's face. "Yeah?"

"I think we've forgotten something," Stan gravely advised.

In response, Frank quickly patted himself down, checking his pockets for his passport, wallet, and other personal possessions. And it was at that precise moment the horrifying realisation hit him like a bolt of lightning. "Oh, bloody hell, you've got to be kidding me, Stan. We *haven't*, have we?"

Stan chewed down on his bottom lip, slowly nodding along. "We have," Stan confirmed, swallowing so hard his throat appeared like he'd sucked in a golf ball. "We've only gone and left Stella at the bloody airport!"

Chapter
TWELVE

L as Vegas was hot. Not hot like the current group was used to on the warmest of summer days on the Isle of Man, but the sort of arid heat one might experience if you were, say, a stoker in a Victorian ironworks. Though, fortunately for our crew, there was such a thing as air conditioning indoors.

Up early after a fitful night's sleep, Stan parted the curtains of the twin bedroom he was sharing with Frank. "Holy Moses, Frank," Stan marvelled, looking down onto the sprawling metropolis below. "It looks a bit different in daylight, but still, what a city!"

"Sorry? Was that you talking to me all the way over there?" Frank said, cupping his ear as he wandered over. As he'd joked with Stan the previous evening, the room they'd been provided was so spacious that they could likely stay there for the entirety of their vacation without ever even bumping into each other.

"Blimey," remarked Frank, upon arrival to the window of their room on the sixth floor, a window which offered visual access to a breathtaking vista. "It's bloody big."

"It's bloody big?" Stan scoffed, underwhelmed by his friend's wordsmithing abilities. "You know I've always felt you should be a travel writer, Frank. And that impressive assessment you just provided of our current sublime, panoramic view only confirms my beliefs."

"Cheeky bugger," Frank said, giving Stan a friendly elbow in the ribs. "For that, I'm not lending you a pair of my shorts."

"How about if I treat us to a sumptuous breakfast here on Las Vegas Boulevard?" Stan proposed.

"Pancakes, bacon, and the full works?" Frank asked, hopeful, and definitely liking the sound of what he was hearing.

"Throw in a clean t-shirt and you've got a deal," Stan said.

"So does that mean you shan't be wearing your *Bellends on Tour* number today?" asked Frank. "Stella might be offended."

"No, that thing will be consigned to the very bottom of my suitcase, I can promise you that," Stan insisted, cinching up his complimentary luxury bathrobe. "Once my sodding suitcase decides to turn up, of course. And on the subject of Stella being offended, I still can't believe she *wasn't* offended that we'd buggered off without her, leaving her back at the airport in all the confusion."

"Right? I thought she was going to punch my lights out when we finally went back to retrieve her," Frank replied. "But when I found her there outside the terminal building, she didn't seem the least bit bothered. I suppose, judging by the huge pile of discarded cigarette butts by her feet, she was content to just watch the world go by for a bit. She did make one comment to me, however."

"Oh? What's that?" Stan asked.

"She told me the Americans hadn't reacted well when she'd said to them, *I could sure murder a fag right about now*."

"Oh dear."

"Yes. The only thing she could conclude, she told me, was that Americans didn't care much for smoking."

"Right. Anyway," Stan remarked, clapping his hands together and appearing ready to take on the world. "We're meeting the rest of them at, what, noon, did we say?" he asked, to which he received a nod of confirmation in response. "Excellent. Plenty of time to have a bite to eat and replenish my wardrobe. I'll go and jump in that spacious shower, Frank, and then we can be off."

***

Even though there were still a couple of hours until the midday sun, traipsing around Las Vegas with several bags of shopping was, perhaps, not Stan's wisest decision.

"I've got jetlag, the onset of a hangover, and now I think I've got a blister on my toe from these new deck shoes I'm wearing," Stan moaned, struggling to place one foot in front of the other.

"Don't forget the whopping great sweat patch on your back."

"Oh, I've not, have I?"

"I'm afraid so. For someone who spends so much time on a sunbed, Stanley, I thought you'd be rather accustomed to these tropical conditions."

"I am, Frank. Well, when I'm sitting around the pool drinking a mojito cocktail, that is."

In truth, Frank was also slightly flagging by this point, certain he could hear rumblings coming from the direction of his belly. "Maybe we should have eaten first, as we'd planned," he commented. "How about that fine breakfast you promised me, Stanley? Although, by now, I suppose it'd be considered brunch."

"Righty-ho, Frank. Any ideas where?"

Frank came to a halt, performing a lingering, 360-degree turn, surveying his surroundings with hands rested on hips. "Hmm, how about that place on the corner?" he proposed, tipping his head in the appropriate direction.

"You reckon they do food?" a weary Stan asked.

"I dunno, Stan. That twenty-foot-tall plastic cheeseburger on their roof might just be there to confuse hungry tourists?"

Stan allowed the gentle sarcasm dripping from Frank's words to wash over him. "Lead on, my good man. Lead on," he said.

Once inside the diner — an homage to the celebrities who'd eaten there if the extensive wall art was anything to go by — Stan stood with his arms outstretched, allowing the air conditioning unit to work its magic. "Oh, Frank, this is glorious," he said, spinning like a dreidel, allowing the cool air to caress as much of his skin as was decent and legal.

A minute or two later, a refreshed Stan joined Frank at the counter that ran through the length of the establishment, hopping up on one of the swivel stools.

"Feeling better now?" an amused Frank enquired, brandishing a menu for Stan's consideration.

"Like you wouldn't believe," said Stan, giving the menu only a cursory glance before placing it back down on the countertop. "I think I already know what I'm having."

"Hey, guys," said the server, a muscley fellow in a tight-fitting t-shirt who was sporting the most splendid, extravagant moustache Stanley had ever seen. "What can I get for you?"

Stan marvelled at the man's facial hair, as well as his bulging physique, staring perhaps a little longer than was necessary.

"Ready?" the server asked, trying again, tapping his pencil on his little white notepad.

"Oh, yes. Sorry about that," Stan eventually replied, slightly blushing. "May I please get a big stack of fluffy American pancakes, with plenty of maple syrup, along with a pile of your finest American streaky bacon?" he asked, looking over to Frank for his approval.

"Same here," Frank advised, closing over the menu he'd just read from cover to cover despite having already decided much earlier at the hotel exactly what he wanted. "Two of those, if you wouldn't mind."

"Oh, and can we also have some coffee?" Stan added. "Freshly brewed?"

"Of course. No problem," said the man with the splendiferous moustache, scribbling on his pad. "I'll bring the coffee right over, and then..." he added, although trailing off and never finishing his sentence. He stood there staring at them, first at Stan, then at Frank, and then to Stan again. It was unnerving for the hungry duo, the kind of look one might receive after having just offended the virtue of someone's mother.

Stan offered a polite smile, wondering if he'd somehow managed to insult the man without realising it. Was it the fact that he'd asked for freshly brewed coffee, for instance? Perhaps the fellow didn't know that where he and Frank came from, instant coffee was much more common, and that he was simply looking forward to the freshly brewed variety for a change. "Is, ehm... is everything okay?" he asked, starting to worry, as with the addition of a few tattoos, Stan could now easily imagine this rather intimidating fellow being part of some sort of outlaw biker gang on the weekends.

"You two look kinda familiar," the server said, using his pencil and notepad like a drumkit once again while tilting his head as he considered them. "Do you guys hang out at the strip club over on Western Ave, by any chance?"

Stan looked over to Frank for help, but no help was offered just yet. "Erm, that's not an establishment we're familiar with," Stan offered. "We're new in town, you see."

"We've only arrived just last night," Frank finally chipped in. "We're here on holiday."

"Huh," said the server, still wracking his brains, if the contorted expression on his face was anything to go by. "Well, you should definitely check out the club before you head home," he advised. "I think I've got some leaflets in the back for a two-for-one dance offer. Remind me before you go."

"Thanks, very kind," Stan answered, having no wish to offend their gracious host.

"Wait, hang on," said the server, starting to walk away but then stopping in his tracks. He turned back around to face Stan and Frank, tapping the side of his head with his trusty pencil. "I think I remember, now, where I know you guys from," he said, his emerging smile revealing a perfect set of chompers that sent a brief shiver down Stan's spine. "You're part of that motorcycle racing thing, aren't you?" he asked. "Those bikes with the funny-looking sidecars, right?" And then, looking specifically at Stan, while pointing to his own crotch for emphasis, "You're the guy from the airport. The one with the wet spot on his pants?" he said.

Stan didn't know if he was being subjected to a gentle ribbing or the sort of cruel teasing he received as a youngster at school. Either way, he wasn't too happy about being recognised the way he was currently being recognised. "Yeah, that's me. And that's us," he conceded, letting out a sigh, suddenly not feeling all that hungry anymore.

"I knew it!" said the moustachioed man. "Mikey!" he added, addressing his colleague flipping burgers further up the diner. "Mikey, we've got a couple celebrities in the house!"

"I don't think I like being a celebrity just now. Not like this," Stan whispered through the side of his mouth, to Frank, while their server was momentarily distracted. "Can we just go?"

"Breakfast on the house for my new friends!" the server announced, appearing genuinely thrilled to have such esteemed guests in his humble establishment.

"Then again..." Stan remarked, his appetite quickly returning, "I suppose being well-known might come with certain added advantages? What do you reckon, Frank? Now that breakfast is free, would it be terribly rude to add a couple of orange juices to our original order? And I don't suppose they've got a desserts menu?"

***

Soon fed, watered, and in possession of several two-for-one dance vouchers for Little Darlings, the aforementioned strip club over on Western Avenue, Frank and Stan made their way to their next appointment, an informal press conference the TV network had arranged.

"We should go back for breakfast tomorrow," Stan suggested, his voice cheerful as he climbed out of the taxi that'd delivered them to their destination.

"I'm not sure the offer of free food extends to the duration of our stay, Stanley," Frank pointed out, after handing over some cash to the driver and telling him to keep the change. "Or is that because of the rugged waiter with marvellous, manicured facial hair?"

"I'm happily spoken for, Frank, as you well know," Stan replied with a sniff. "I just thought the pancakes were to die for, that's all, and I think they served real maple syrup there, as opposed to the cheap imitation kind."

"That *was* a good breakfast. Even if the bacon is different over here," Frank was happy to agree, checking his handwritten itinerary for about the third time. "Right, this is us," he said, indicating towards the conference centre next to the Las Vegas Motor Speedway. "Shit," he added, as he glanced at his watch. "We're running a bit late, Stan. We need to pick the pace up."

"Sod that, Frank. I've only just dried out my last sweat patch, so I've no intention of picking up any pace," Stan answered.

The destination the boys were sedately ambling towards was a media event that Brad and Chip had casually dropped into the conversation the previous evening like it was no big deal. Obviously, NBC Boston was eager to take advantage of Team Frank & Stan's presence in the US to promote the release of the new show, hence squeezing in as many such events as time should permit. And it's not as if the Manx contingent could complain, really, considering the whole reason they were there to begin with was because of the network's generosity.

This first press conference was pitched as an informal affair, designed to largely introduce Dave and Monty to the American audience. In addition, Brad and Chip, as the creators of the series, would bring their personal experiences of the iconic sporting event to life, along with Clifford Tanner, the network head who'd rubberstamped the project, sharing his views as well.

"Where's the bloody entrance?" a panicked Stan asked, surrounded by towering concrete buildings in every direction and now acutely conscious of the time, as Frank had warned.

Frank gave a slight tug on Stan's shirt. "Follow me, Stanley," he said.

"You know where you're going?" Stan asked, following as instructed.

"Not at all," Frank responded. "But when lost, I often find that smoke signals will lead the way."

The smoke signals Frank was referencing belonged to Stella, who had arrived with Dave and Monty, and who was currently standing outside the required entrance enjoying a fag or three in the early afternoon sunshine.

"Hiya, Stella!" Frank called out as they approached, receiving a scowl-cum-smile in response.

"I thought you were heading out clothes shopping, same as me?" Stan asked, once they were standing before her, noticing she was dressed in exactly the same clothes as the previous day.

"Eh? Why?"

Stan looked her up and down. "Well, by your own admission, you didn't bring any luggage along with you on the trip," he said. "Remember?"

"Yeah, of *course* I remember. I'm not daft, like you," Stella remarked, rolling her eyes. "I *told* you, I've brought three pairs of clean knickers. Plus, this t-shirt's still got a bit of life left in it," she said, giving her left armpit a quick sniff, just to be sure. "I dunno, maybe I'll go shopping tomorrow. We'll see," she added with a shrug, dropping her spent fag to the ground and using the heel of her hobnail boot to extinguish it. "So are you pair coming in, or what?"

The auditorium where the press conference was being hosted was the same venue for the celebratory premiere of the show, which was scheduled to be held the following evening. And while there'd been no obvious advertising placed on or about the outside of the building just yet, it soon became clear that the network's PR machine had gone to town, starting quite a bit of work inside.

Frank and Stan strolled through the sprawling lobby of the building with their jaws hanging low. Atmospheric black-and-white action photographs adorned every available wall space, showcasing the Isle of Man's famous Tourist Trophy races in all their glory, including shots of machinery hurtling down Bray

Hill, leaping over the iconic Ballaugh Bridge, and one particular image that caught Frank's eye of the TT grandstand area, with his and Stan's house partially visible in the background, no less. Fast-paced radio commentary from past races was being piped through the venue's sound system, making it easy to believe you were sitting right there on a grassy bank, beer in your hand, just inches away from mighty machines hurtling by.

And it didn't end there. Lifesize cutouts of some of the great names to grace the famous track were positioned around the lobby, thus introducing themselves to the Americans, including, for example, Mike Hailwood, Giacomo Agostini, Joey Dunlop, John McGuinness, the Birchall brothers, Dave Molyneux, Jenny Tinmouth, and Maria Costello. All of them held court, with several other distinguished motor racing royalty presenting themselves in cardboard form as well.

"Look over there!" Stan said, moving towards the set of elaborate auditorium doors, upholstered in tufted leather. Just before them, two rows of sidecars were laid out on either side, performing a sort of guard of honour to welcome their adrenaline-fuelled guests.

"I'm starting to feel homesick," Frank confessed, retrieving his mobile phone to capture a photographic memento. "Hang on, Stan," he added a second or two later, his attention drawn to the resplendent outfit parked up closest to the doors. "That's not…?" he asked. "It bloody *is*, as well," he said, quickly answering his own question.

"It's the Big Blue Boiled Sweet!" Stan observed fondly. "How the hell did they—?"

"It must be a replica," Frank put forth, kneeling down to run an appreciative hand over the bodywork. "And it's a damned good one, at that," he added, noting the precision application of the sponsor's stickers, and even splattered flies on the fairing for good measure and a degree of authenticity.

"Jayzus, will you two dickheads hurry the hell up?" Stella moaned, stepping forward and holding open the auditorium doors for them like the world's grumpiest lobby attendant. "I've not got all day, you know."

The interior of the auditorium was impressive, home to a little over one thousand seats with an uninterrupted view of the central stage area which, according to Brad and Chip, would be packed to the rafters for the premiere event, if the juggernaut that was NBC Boston's advertising campaign had anything to say about it. For now, however, it was a rather more subdued affair with maybe thirty or so journalists and other assorted people in attendance, some of them even wearing the *Isle of Man TT Aces* promotional t-shirts provided by the event organisers.

There, standing towards the front of the raised stage, both Dave and Monty appeared visibly nervous, allowing a sound engineer to connect a wireless mic to the collar of their shirts.

Spotting Frank and Stan's arrival, Dave offered an amiable wave. "You're not joining us?" he asked, looking down from the stage. "There's plenty of room up here!" he added, indicating towards the row of available chairs the production crew had laid out for the interviews.

"That's very kind!" Stan replied, cupping his hands around his mouth to amplify his voice. "Although we're quite comfortable down here, thank you very much!" he said, settling himself down on a padded velvet seat. "Good luck!"

Dave and Monty were first up in the running order, directed to their proper positions on stage by an industrious production assistant's guiding hand.

"I'll just need you to say a few words first, before we actually get this thing started," the assistant said, once Dave and Monty had taken their places. "The sound crew just needs to test the sound levels to make sure everyone can hear what you're saying, all right?"

"What should I say?" Monty asked. "I'm not very good when I'm put on the spot, you see. I never know what to say, and I just tend to clam up, if you know what I mean? Now that I think on it, I suppose it's something of a nervous affec—"

"Perfect," the assistant cut in. "That's all we need," she said, having received the required thumbs-up from the sound booth in indication that the volume was at optimum levels.

"You're very good at this, Monty," Dave observed, impressed by his buddy's ability to ad-lib on request.

Monty, for his part, wasn't sure what he might have done to warrant the compliment, but he was happy enough to receive it nonetheless. "Thanks, Dave," he replied, now looking all warm and snuggly.

Waiting in the wings, both Brad and Chip hovered, appearing anxious and uncomfortable. "You need to tell them, Brad," Chip whispered. "You need to tell them *now*, before this thing begins. It's almost about to start!"

"Why me?" Brad protested.

"We played rock-paper-scissors, and you lost," Chip had to remind his brother. "So fair's fair."

Brad sulked for a moment, like a child whose mum had just hidden away the biscuit tin (or, in Brad and Chip's case, whose mom had just hidden the cookie jar). *"Fine,"* he said eventually. "But you're doing the *next* crappy job."

"Go get 'em, tiger!" Chip said by way of encouragement, giddy with relief that he wasn't the one who had to do the deed. "I'll go and make sure we've got a first aid kit somewhere on hand. Oh, and remind me what blood type you are, just in case?"

"Same blood type as yours, Chip. We're *identical twins*, in case you forgot," Brad shot back, although knowing full well that his brother was only teasing about the possible need for any blood. Or so he hoped.

Brad emerged from the darkened area at the side of the stage and was immediately flooded in harsh, artificial light from the spotlights trained on the area. He squinted, wandering towards Dave and Monty with the hesitation of a man taking his final steps to the gallows.

"Oh, hey, guys," Brad offered to the seated Dave and Monty. "Uh..." he added, and then nothing.

"Eh, you, okay?" Dave eventually asked. "You're plucking up the courage to ask me on a date, is that it?" he joked. "Only now is probably not the ideal time, what with all the cameras here and such."

But Brad looked to be distracted, appearing to temporarily hold his breath while nodding his head, like he was counting down from ten. Eventually, he exhaled. "Okay," he said. "I'm just going to come right out and say it..."

Monty returned a blank expression. "Erm... come out and say *what*?" he asked. "Have I missed something?" he added, looking to Dave for answers, although Dave didn't appear to have any either, as near as Monty could tell.

"Okay, so you guys promise me you won't get angry?" Brad asked, taking a cautionary step backwards before beginning to say whatever it was he was about to say.

"Just so you know, I already have a significant other," Dave cautioned. "But assuming that's not it, and I'm fairly certain it isn't, just spit it out, man!"

Brad took another deep breath, before reciting, at a considerable rate of speed, what was on his mind. And the small matter that appeared to be troubling him so, as it should happen, involved the subject of one Rodney Franks. Brad started out by first positioning the very real possibility of a potentially lucrative whole new set of episodes for the television docuseries, but outlined that the network had certain conditions, those conditions being that Rodney Franks and his race team were to feature much more prominently than they had in the first series.

Brad didn't allow Dave or Monty the opportunity to interject as he continued onto the second half of his verbal download. That particular doozy of a topic being the head of the network, Clifford Tanner's, audacious masterplan to promote the TV series — a winner-takes-all sidecar race between Dave and Monty and Rodney's team at the nearby Las Vegas Motor Speedway racing circuit.

"So... what do you think...?" Brad asked at the conclusion, taking an additional step back, just to be on the safe side.

Dave released the sort of half-hearted laugh you'd offer your poor gran after she'd told you the most rubbish joke you'd ever heard. "What is this?" he asked, looking around and about him. "Is this an episode of Candid Camera or something, or whatever it is the kids are watching these days?"

"Oh, no, this is no joke," a nasally sounding voice offered from the opposite side of the stage. "I can only imagine that the people in charge finally found their senses and realised who the *real* star of this production actually is," Rodney Franks said into his wireless mic, his voice being amplified around the auditorium. "And that person is yours truly, of course," he added, taking a bow in the middle of the stage, looking rather flamboyant in a bespoke blazer, crafted with a casino-inspired print made up of playing cards, poker chips, slot machines, and finally the image of a large roulette wheel on his back, all in honour of the present location, Las Vegas.

With an entrance a pantomime villain could only aspire to, Rodney sauntered over towards a still-seated Dave and Monty, his Cuban-heeled boots echoing off the wooden floorboards of the stage as he was followed a few paces behind by his racers, a smug-looking Andy Thomas and Jack Napier.

"Brad, this is like a performance from WWF WrestleMania," Monty offered. "Is Hulk Hogan going to appear in a minute and break a chair over our heads?"

"Oh, I'll break a chair over your head, if you like?" Napier suggested.

In response, Dave reared up out of his seat. "Brad, if you think for even a moment that I'm working with this snivelling little cockwomble, you can, quite frankly, kiss my arse. And as for the idea of us racing against those two knuckle-dragging neanderthals... well, again, you can kiss my arse."

"Who are you calling a neanderthal?" Thomas responded, grunting and posturing rather like, one would imagine, the actions of a Neanderthal.

Several seconds later and the stage was now resembling the previously mentioned WWF contest, with arms flailing in every direction, expletives exchanged, and flying kicks administered with abandon.

"Should we go and help them out?" Frank asked Stan, unsure what to do, exactly, but thinking they ought to do something. But by this point, stage props were being chucked from one side of the stage to the other, and neither Frank nor Stan were what could be considered fighters by their own admission.

"Hold my fags!" Stella growled, leaping over the row of chairs in front, with little regard to her skirt riding up during the manoeuvre.

"This should be interesting," Stan remarked as Stella climbed onto the raised stage, after which she immediately secured Rodney in a vice-like chokehold, while administering several quick jabs to the area of his kidneys.

"Stan?" a concerned Frank said. "Stan, I've got a sneaking suspicion that any plans for series two might now be on hold…"

Chapter
THIRTEEN

Little did the catering team know that the champagne buckets they'd laid out in the hospitality area would be called upon for medical purposes, with one of them being appropriated for such application by Stella, who groaned in relief as she dipped her hand into its icy interior. "You'll need to get me a pair of tweezers, I reckon," she said in Stan's direction. "I believe there's a fragment of somebody's tooth currently embedded in my knuckle," she explained, along with a contented *job-well-done* sort of smile. "I think it's either Napier's or Rodney's. Not sure which."

"I think we should just go," Stan cautioned. "I'd imagine the police are already on their way here, and if so, we're all likely to be deported," he advised, as any of the press or other attendees there were escorted from the auditorium.

Frank was in complete agreement. "Here's your fags, Stella. Let's aim for a sneaky retreat before anybody notices we're still here." But someone *had* already noticed, if the finger pointed in their direction was anything to go by.

"I was promised there'd be no battering of the facial area!" an indignant Rodney Franks protested, still stood up on stage, and presently rubbing his sore cheek. "And that's precisely what that lumbering ox over there has done! And as if that weren't bad enough in itself, my underpants are also torn from when she administered a wedgie!"

"What the hell's that idiot talking about?" Frank wondered aloud. "Promised by *who*?"

Stella removed her hand from the ice bucket, ready for round two. But before she could commence a further assault, a smartly dressed man wearing a broad-brimmed cowboy hat appeared on stage, with an equally broad grin and confident swagger.

"That was even better than any of us had planned!" the man boomed. And then, lowering his voice, "Wait, hold on, the press has already been escorted from the building, right?"

"Yes, Mr Tanner," someone replied. "You can speak freely."

Now satisfied there were no prying eyes or ears from the media, Clifford circled the stage, offering everyone still up there a generous helping of applause. "All of you deserve an Oscar for that performance," he declared, shaking his head in joyful disbelief. "Hell, considering you had little time to rehearse, that sure was convincing. In fact, I'm going to have our feature film division sign each and every one of you up!"

"Performance?" remarked Stan. "He thought that was some kind of *performance*?"

"Uhm," said Frank, from the comfort of their padded velvet seats, his hand raised. "What on earth is going on?"

Clifford Tanner adjusted the brim of his large cowboy hat — which he'd purchased specifically for the occasion of his trip to Vegas — using it to help shield the glare of the spotlight from his eyes as he looked out into the audience seating area to see who was talking. "Is that Frank out there? Frank from our show?" he asked of Clara, his personal assistant standing nearby.

Clara squinted her eyes against the harsh light. "Yes, I believe so, Mr Tanner. And Stan, also," she answered. "Although I'm not sure who the woman is with them. But she was the one throwing most of the punches, from what I could see."

Clifford offered a friendly wave to Frank and Stan, who he'd only previously seen onscreen and not yet met in person. "Come on up here, guys," he offered. "And bring your lady friend, too, since we're celebrating!"

"Have we entered The Twilight Zone?" Frank asked, turning to the others beside him. "Because if we haven't, then what the devil is going on?"

"Only one way to find out, I suppose," Stan said with a shrug, before then taking to his feet. "You coming?" he asked of the other two, as he started off towards the stage.

Stella shook her head. "Sod that, I'm going for a fag," she said, heading in the opposite direction, with her punching hand still held submerged in the bucket.

Frank took Stan's lead, following a few paces behind. "Dave!" he called out in advance of their arrival. "Dave, as you can imagine, we're a tad confused over here. So, if you'd be so kind as to fill in the blanks, that would be marvellous."

Dave, with Monty in tow, climbed down from the stage to do just that. "Remind me to buy Stella a pint," Dave said fondly, before starting to fill the guys in. "The way she sucker-punched that tosspot Jack Napier was sheer poetry."

"Dave...?" Stan pressed. "Any chance...?"

"Sorry," Dave responded. "Well, it all began with a phone call Monty received when I was out shovelling pig shit. It's funny, these types of calls always seemed to happen when I was out shovelling pig shit. Anyway, on this one particular occasion..."

Dave spent the next minute or two veering off on a tangent, admonishing Monty for always going AWOL whenever the pigs needed mucking out, before Stan's timely and strategic cough steered Dave back on course. Dave then revealed how Brad and Chip had both called on speakerphone, speaking with Monty about an offer they hoped the boys couldn't refuse: the potential of a second series of *Isle of Man TT Aces* episodes. Dave went on to reveal that there was, as was now apparent by the present company in the room, something of a cravat-wearing curveball thrown into the mix. Of course, Dave and Monty's immediate reaction had been to tell them to stick their offer right where the sun doesn't shine, as when it came to Rodney Franks, all bets were off as far as they were concerned. That was, however, until

Brad revealed how much cash they could expect to receive if they were willing to go along with things. Further, Brad decided to strike while the iron was hot, according to Dave, by relaying Clifford Tanner's desire for a showstopping PR stunt: a winner-takes-all exhibition sidecar race with $50k prize money on offer.

Apparently, Brad had gone on to talk about the obvious tension that existed between the two race teams, as evidenced in series one. This had been a major hit with focus group viewers, a plot point they'd particularly enjoyed. So Clifford Tanner, in his wisdom, had suggested playing that aspect up, stoking the fire, in future episodes, confident the audience would lap it up. And that's also how the idea of a staged barroom brawl was first conceived, with, of course, assorted members of the press to be conveniently in attendance to witness, although Dave and Monty weren't aware of this specific part of the plan until the very last second.

"And we *wanted* to tell you," Dave said, with Monty nodding along. "But Brad and Chip swore us to secrecy for fear that the entire thing would fall apart."

"They made us cross our hearts and everything," Monty advised, looking deadly serious. "And that's as good as a signed contract written in blood in my book."

"So let me get this straight," Stan said, trying to digest what was, after all, a fair bit of information he'd just heard. "You two," he said, looking to both Dave and Monty, "are now best mates with that odious little turd and his two equally odious riders?"

Dave laughed at the very thought. "Bloody hell, of course not! Make no mistake, they're the biggest pack of wankstains I've ever had the misfortune to come across. In fact, I'd rather muck out the pigs with my bare hands than spend time in their company. But, if dealing with them means I'll be able to provide a dream home for Becks and Tyler… well, it's a no-brainer."

"I did accidentally connect with Napier's chin at one point in the scuffle," a sheepish Monty confessed. "Although I reckon he thought it was Stella and thought better about retaliating."

Dave looked like a proud parent viewing the collection of top marks received on his child's school report. "Well done, Monty. Terrific job."

Frank caressed his chin between his thumb and forefinger. "So, just to be clear, we don't need to exchange pleasantries with Rodney Franks...? There'll be no inviting each other to tea? We can still—"

"*Hell*, no," Dave was quick to confirm. "The network wants to portray him and his team as the pantomime villains. As long as we don't kill them or seriously maim them or anything, it's fine. So, you know, you can simply carry on and keep right on hating them as usual. It's all good."

"How did they manage to ship the Big Blue Boiled Sweet over without us knowing?" Frank asked, pointing in the general direction of the lobby area. "Or is it a—"

"Yeah, it's a replica," Monty advised, guessing at what Frank was going to say. "With a twist, though. See, Clifford's production company purchased two similar sidecars, one for us and one for Rodney's team. But mechanically, they're identical. Unlike at home."

"Oh?" Frank asked.

"Yep," Monty replied. "Obviously, back at home, Napier and Thomas race on a no-expense-spared factory-works-built machine, which we couldn't compete with in a zillion years. This way, with the same spec sidecars, we're racing on a level playing field. So it's all down to talent alone."

"But what are the other eight sidecars for?" Stan queried.

"Eight American teams have also been invited along to bolster the starting grid, in order to make it better viewing for the spectators," Dave entered in. "Although we're all under strict instructions that this is purely an exhibition race, so under no circumstances are we to take any unnecessary risks."

"American sidecar racers?" Stan asked. "I didn't even know there was such a thing."

"Yeah, I don't reckon they'll pose too much of a challenge to us," Dave said with a chuckle. "But, you know, they're just there to improve the spectacle."

"Fifteen thousand tickets have been sold in less than twenty-four hours!" Monty was delighted to reveal. "But the stands can hold nearly eighty thousand, so, who knows? It should be quite the atmosphere."

"Jesus, are you still talking?" Stella said, having successfully replenished her nicotine levels. "Honestly, you're like a bunch of old women gossiping down at the bingo."

Frank smiled, looking down at the champagne bucket full of ice Stella was carrying under her arm like a set of bagpipes, her injured hand still stuffed inside of it. "Monty and Dave were just telling us all about the—"

"Absolutely not interested," Stella snapped back. "We need to go and eat, because I always get a ravenous appetite after I've been fighting. You coming or what?"

Meanwhile, attending to his wounds up on the stage area, Jack Napier ran an exploratory tongue over his left canine tooth. "Andy?" he said, opening wide and thrusting his face in Andy's direction. "Andy, av I bust me toof?" he asked of his racing partner, using the aforementioned tongue to highlight the area of impact, his opened mouth and occupied tongue having a serious adverse effect on his ability to speak clearly.

Andy took a look, before immediately recoiling in horror. "Jesus, Jack. That's awful."

"Ith it bwoken?" Jack asked, releasing a generous spray of spittle in the process.

"No, it's fine," Andy advised. "But your breath, man... it smells like boiled cabbage."

Jack closed his mouth and returned his tongue to its normal position. "Thank god for that," he replied, now able to converse without any obstruction.

"Thank god you smell like cabbage?" asked Andy.

"No, cabbage is lovely," Jack answered matter-of-factly, not the slightest bit worried about his oral hygiene it would appear. "But I meant the tooth," he clarified. Jack then looked across the room towards his assailant, who was currently making her way out of the auditorium. "You know, there's something very sexy about a voluptuous woman who isn't afraid of getting into a bit of a scrap," he confided, casting an amorous eye in the exiting Stella's direction. "And that leather skirt…"

Andy grinned, certain he was being teased. "Wait, you're being serious?" he asked after a moment. "Here, is there any possibility you might've received a concussion? Do you need to get yourself checked over?"

But any possible answers to those questions would need to wait for now, as Rodney headed over, having just concluded his conversation with Clifford Tanner.

"I'm disappointed boys, I won't deny it," Rodney revealed, attempting to discreetly adjust his damaged underpants, the result of his recent wedgie.

Andy and Jack exchanged a blank look. "Disappointed about what, boss?" Andy then asked.

"That–that… absolute *brute* of a woman," said a furious Rodney, struggling to get his words out.

"You mean Jack's girlfriend?" Andy asked with a schoolboy smirk.

"She bloody humiliated us," Rodney insisted. "The fight we'd planned out beforehand was supposed to portray me as an elegant brawler. But with her unexpectedly jumping into the fray like that, unscripted, everything was left in tatters. She punched me, she… did other things to me, and worst of all, I was even being choked by her at one point. I could feel my eyes start to water, and it must have looked like I was bloody crying, right there in front of all the cameras!"

"Oh. You mean you *weren't* crying?" Jack asked. "Because it honestly did look like you were. Didn't it look like he was crying, Andy? Andy…?"

But Andy decided it wasn't worth picking away at that recent scab, thinking it wiser to move the conversation in a different direction. "So, the tickets for this exhibition race are selling well, boss," he offered, saying something he hoped might help to raise Rodney's spirits.

Rodney's expression hardened as he pushed himself up on his toes, wishing to appear taller than he actually was. "This is *not* an exhibition race," he declared through clenched teeth.

"It's not?" Andy asked. "But I thought that the bloke from the network said—"

"I don't care what the bloke from the network said," Rodney shot back, mocking the sound of Andy's voice. *"Exhibition* is another term for *loser,*" he barked, shifting his attention between his two racers. "Did you not watch Rocky Four?"

"Erm, is that the one with Mr T?" asked Andy.

"Nah," Jack jumped in. "Rocky Four was Ivan Drago."

"Yes," said Rodney, placing his heels back down on solid floorboards. "And what happened in Rocky Four...?" he asked, sounding like he perhaps already knew the answer.

Andy wracked his brains, having only watched the film one time, many years earlier. "Did Apollo Creed not have an exhibition match with Ivan?" he suggested, it coming back to him a bit. "Erm... but then what?" he asked, his memory failing him as to how the storyline eventually played out.

Jack now appeared somewhat concerned. "Apollo got killed," he advised gravely. "Boss, you don't want us to beat Dave and Monty to death, do you? Because they're big lads. And if that woman friend of theirs is also in their corner, then I'm not sure we're up to the job, to be quite honest."

Rodney sneered at the blatant stupidity of what he was hearing. "What? Don't be daft. Of *course* I don't want you to beat them to death," he assured them, before glancing about, making sure nobody was earwigging into their conversation. "No. Apollo Creed thought he was getting involved in an exhibition match, and look how that turned out for him, yeah?"

"So what exactly are you saying, boss?" Andy asked, as he remained not at all clear on what Rodney was attempting to get across.

Rodney planted a weary hand against his forehead, massaging his temples with the tip of his thumb and ring finger for a moment. "What I'm saying is that while this is technically an exhibition race, I want you two..." he said, pointing to them each in turn, "to pull out all of the stops and win this race at any cost."

"Any cost?" said Jack.

"*Any cost,*" Rodney reiterated, using his best sinister tone, missing only a crack of thunder to complement his evil genius. "If there are fifty thousand American dollars on offer for the winning team," he continued, "then you can bet your house that Dave and Monty won't be taking things easy. And so we won't either. Rodney Franks's team are *winners*. What are we?"

"Winners!" Andy and Jack replied, feeling a little awkward about the high-five that Rodney insisted on administering like an uncool uncle trying his best to be cool.

Rodney offered an indignant sniff. "We'll show those fat loser bastards who the real stars of this TV show are," he said with an exaggerated, villainous laugh.

"But no killing, right...?" Andy asked, as he wanted to be absolutely clear on this one particular point. "Rodney? No killing, right...?"

Chapter
FOURTEEN

It's often been said that America is the land of opportunity, a country in which your aspirations are limited only by the scope of your dreams.

Indeed, as travellers to the great nation have noted for years, everything appears bigger, bolder, and brasher. Whether it's taking the family for a wallet-denting vacation to one of Walt Disney's namesake resorts, or perhaps a city expedition to admire the towering New York skyline, or even here, in Sin City, where you'd be forgiven for thinking you were caught up in some kind of surreal dream, enjoying opulent Roman-style hospitality at Caesars Palace one minute and navigating your way through the Venetian's canals in a gondola the next.

And rather like the Isle of Man TT races, the Sin City experience was difficult to describe to the uninitiated unless you'd experienced it yourself, for to do so, you'd likely fall significantly wide of the mark. It was simply mind-boggling.

Moreover, something else bigger, bolder, and brasher for the Vegas virgin to enjoy was the scale of the many all-you-can-eat buffets, one of them presently being considered by a rapacious Stella...

"Look at her, Monty, trying to balance a beef shish kebab on top of that already-huge pile on her plate," Dave remarked, having just returned to their table with his own assortment of goodies from the BBQ section.

Monty offered an amused glance in Stella's direction. "It's like a teenager who can't be arsed emptying the bin, so they just keep balancing stuff onto the quivering stack."

"There's no way she's making it back to the table with everything still on her dish," said Dave, unable to take his eyes off her.

Frank, already seated and enjoying his late lunch after witnessing the earlier altercation between Rodney's crew and his own, lowered his Szechuan sticky rib. "You'd be surprised," he said, looking across to Stan for validation.

"She's the master," Stan proudly advised. "Stella once ate a large doner kebab on the roller coaster at Alton Towers without spilling a single drop of sauce."

"Not one single drop was lost," Frank confirmed, in fond recollection. "Ten bucks she doesn't drop even a crumb now?"

"Deal," Monty immediately replied, happy to accept the wager.

By now, Stella had conceded that she couldn't continue to wear her *Bellends on Tour* t-shirt indefinitely, especially considering it was hot enough outside to fry an egg on the pavement, resulting in her shirt getting rather ripe. As such, she'd since been and purchased some additional items, including what she was presently wearing — a white, sleeveless t-shirt with the image of a casino chip cleverly placed over each nipple, accompanied by the snappy logo GET YOUR CHIPS OUT FOR THE BOYS. Add to this a pair of sequin hot pants, so tight they looked like they'd been painted on, which perhaps they were.

As Stella returned to their table, it wasn't clear if some of the other patrons were also watching her every move because of her quirky dress sense or, like Dave and the others, to see if she was able to navigate the short walk without spilling her food all over the patterned carpet.

"I told you," said Frank, the moment Stella joined them without so much as a morsel out of place, gratefully accepting the cash from Monty. Then, turning his attention towards Stella, "You do know it's a buffet," he said, very gently, so as not to cause offence. "So you can come and go as you please, without, you know..." he pointed out, motioning towards her heavily overburdened plate.

Stella placed a large bratwurst close to her lips. "I *know*," she snapped, holding the sausage like a microphone as she spoke. "And that's why I went easy on the seafood section," she said, nodding towards what appeared to be the rear end of a solitary prawn poking out from between its meatball neighbours.

Stan nibbled on his watermelon slice, strangely drawn to the tubular portion of meat Stella was now making short work of. However, his attention was soon diverted by the sound of his mobile phone vibrating against the table in front of him. "What the dickens?" he said, staring down at his phone like it was the first time he'd ever received a call on it.

"Uhm, you answer it, and then you put it by your ear?" Monty helpfully pointed out. "And then you usually say hello."

"Thank you so much for your technical assistance, Monty," Stan remarked, along with an eye roll, cautiously picking up his phone like it was going to explode in his hands or something. "But if I answer that, will I not get hit with hundreds of pounds in Roman charges? And why doesn't the display tell me who's calling?"

Monty couldn't resist a chuckle. "It's *roaming* charges, Stan. Not *Roman*. And you'll be fine, as long as you don't have one of your usual calls that go on for several days."

Stan scowled at Monty as he answered the call, but he wasn't being serious in his displeasure. "Hello," he said, now adopting his posh accent reserved for phone conversations with callers unknown. "Yes, this is Mister Sidcup," he acknowledged, though remaining sceptical, in case this was one of those scam calls he'd received on previous occasions. "Ah! You've located my missing suitcase?" he said, repeating back what the caller had just said to him, his demeanour immediately brightening. "Yes, that's definitely some splendid news," he continued. "You see, I'm attending a rather plush event tomorrow night, and my tuxedo is hopefully uncreased inside that case, because at this event—"

Monty smirked, tapping his watch as the conversation continued. "This is costing you money," Monty reminded him.

"Ah, right," Stan said to Monty, pulling up short, deciding the caller didn't need to know the entire details of his personal engagement. "So... you'll drop my case off?" he asked of the airline representative on the other end.

Frank raised a thumb, pleased his friend's luggage had been located.

"It's where?" Stan asked, tilting his head, as if this would in some way change his perception of what he was being told. "My suitcase is in Madagascar?" he said, uncertain how to process what he was hearing. "I'm not familiar with that hotel. So if you could have it delivered to our suite at the Venetian?"

Stan returned Frank's raised thumb, sensing that he was one step closer to regaining his belongings. "You what?" he then said, his optimistic expression suddenly souring. "What do you mean, *Madagascar the country*? You're telling me my tuxedo, along with all my other belongings, is presently on an island in the middle of the Indian Ocean?" Stan listened intently for several more seconds, the colours in his cheeks turning redder than the sequins in Stella's hotpants. "Well that simply will not do," he advised sternly. "What am I meant to be wearing for the celebratory premiere of the television series I'm soon to be appearing in?" he asked, loudly enough for the rest of the dining room to be impressed, right before hanging up, as he was conscious that the call, as concerning as it was, was also likely costing him a fortune in 'Roman' charges.

"So who was that calling?" Dave asked, struggling to stifle a smile. "Anybody nice?"

"Wait, hang on," Monty interjected. "Are we supposed to be wearing tuxedos for this shindig tomorrow...?"

***

"So not *one* of us, aside from myself, considered what we were going to wear for such a formal, swanky, important affair?" Stan asked, just to be clear on that particular point, walking ahead of the group like an unhappy parent with his grumbling kids trailing behind. "And Frank," he added over his shoulder, "I can understand *Dave and Monty* not giving it any thought, but *you*?"

Frank bowed his head, his hands tucked into the pockets of his shorts, following as Stan traipsed at speed along the sidewalk of Las Vegas Boulevard and doing his best to dodge the array of pushy leafleters trying to stuff flyers for X-rated services into the palms of passing tourists. "No, thank you very much," Stan said, firmly declining the latest offer and holding his hands above his head like he was surrendering to the police.

"Erm, Stanley?" Monty called out from behind. "I just wanted to point out that although we didn't think about what to wear, we're still in precisely the same position as you, who *did* think about it. As in, we've got bugger-all also."

"Well at least I have an excuse," Stan commented. "As in, *my* luggage is in bloody *Madagascar*." Stan took a moment to try and calm his mind, while glancing down at the directions he'd been so kindly provided, on short notice, by their obliging hotel concierge. "Anyway, I think what we're after is right up this street...?"

Fortunately, according to Deontay — the impeccably helpful concierge at their hotel — there were several formalwear shops within walking distance of the Venetian that should be able to kit the gang out so they wouldn't be wearing shorts, t-shirts, and flip-flops. Unfortunately, Stella couldn't be convinced to join them, suggesting she'd sort out her own outfit and instead opting, for the time being, a recce of the nearby Bellagio Hotel and, specifically, their lauded fountains.

However, Deontay was also quick to point out to the lads that most folks attending formal functions in town opted to rent their outfits, just like they were preparing to do now (as opposed to bringing it with them in their suitcase, as Stan had attempted to do). As such, demand could in his experience raise prices, or on some occasions even completely outstrip the available supply — information that did very little to ease Stan's already elevated blood pressure.

"This is it," Stan advised the group, coming to a halt outside a glass-fronted shop with what appeared to be a well-presented security guard stationed outside on sentry duty.

Dave placed a hand over his mouth, leaning in close to Monty. "If there's a security guard outside of any sort of place, it usually means it's bloody expensive inside," he whispered.

Once through the entrance, it was evident the boys were in the correct place, what with row upon row of suits of all shapes, colours, sizes, and designs on display. However, at first glance, they didn't appear to be the traditional James Bond style of tuxedo, but rather a mix of options you'd wear to a fancy rodeo, perhaps, if there was such a thing, or, say, a Liberace reunion party. All of this was fine in its own right, if these were the sorts of clothing items you were looking for. It just didn't match up very well with what the current group was after.

Aware of Stan's heightened anxiety levels, Frank suggested he admire a group of decorative, sparkly suits he thought might prove a pleasant, temporary distraction, while he went over to make enquiries at the sales desk. Monty and Dave, for their part, just stood there looking awkward, unsure of what to do with themselves.

Frank approached the counter, behind which was a view into the rear of the shop. There, dozens of suit bags could be seen dangling from an array of coat hooks, with all items presumably hanging at the ready, just waiting to be picked up. And it was certainly an elegant establishment, Frank observed, with polished white tiles, classic art adorning the walls, and fine stone carvings standing atop marble columns. Yes, this was, by some distance, the most upmarket suit hire establishment he'd ever frequented.

Frank waited, offering a polite cough in the hopes of attracting a sales assistant he assumed to be busy somewhere in the rear of the shop, just outside his available line of sight. Hoping Dave and Monty were keeping themselves out of mischief, he turned for a moment to check on them. He should have known.

"Don't touch that!" Frank whispered, finding them groping the stone bosom of what looked to be the depiction of some Greek goddess or another, probably Athena or Aphrodite. "Honestly, how old are you two?" he admonished them, along with a vaguely amused grin.

By the time Frank had turned back to his original position, a rather suave-looking gentleman of a certain vintage, with greying, slick-backed hair and a well-tailored suit, appeared as if by magic. "Oh!" Frank remarked, clutching his chest. "You gave me a bit of a start," he said, catching his breath.

"Sorry to have kept you waiting, sir," the man offered, accompanied by a humble bow of the head.

This fellow oozed classical sophistication, Frank considered, like a butler from *Downton Abbey*. Harold was his name, Frank could see, according to the gold-plated name badge pinned to the man's lapel.

"How may I help you?" asked Harold.

Frank warmed to this chap immediately. "Ah, an English accent?"

"Oxford born and bred, sir."

"Marvellous, Harold," Frank said, addressing the fellow by name. "It's a pleasure to meet you," he went on, laying the charm on thick. "We're all in town, visiting from the Isle of Man, for a formal event to be held tomorrow evening. The issue, however, for one reason or another, is that none of us has a dinner jacket or tuxedo, or however they refer to them this side of the pond."

"I see, sir," Harold replied, reaching for and then opening what appeared to be a well-thumbed order book.

Frank leaned slightly over the shop counter, conspiratorially. "And as much as I can appreciate the more flamboyant type of outfit you have on offer here…" he said, tipping his head towards what appeared to be an Elton John collection, "I wondered if you might have four of what might be considered a more traditional ensemble?"

"I see, sir," Harold said again, gently closing the order book over and returning it to its original position.

This action didn't go unseen by Frank. "It's really important, Harold," Frank stressed, pleading his case. "You see, we're involved in a TV series which is having its premiere event tomorrow evening, and at this rate we're all going to be turning up in shorts and a t-shirt, if you know what I mean?"

Harold tilted his head, just a touch, almost imperceptibly. "A television programme?" he asked, raising Frank's hopes a notch or two. "And *they're* also involved in this programme of yours?" Harold asked, indicating towards Dave and Monty.

Frank turned, his eyes following the direction that Harold's well-manicured fingernail was pointing to. "Bloody hell! Stop touching them!" Frank chastised the unruly pair, the two now taking selfies with the busty Greek goddess's bust. "I'm sorry about them, Harold," Frank apologised. "But, yes. And believe it or not, they're the stars of the show, actually."

"Sorry, Frank!" the two perverts said in unison.

"Apologies, sir. But the reality is that we only have so many fittings available, and what we have are fully booked," Harold insisted. "If you'd considered something more... flamboyant, as you had put it, I might have been able to accommodate. Sadly, I can only now offer my humble apologies."

"No joy, Frank?" Stan called over, as he wasn't so far away that he couldn't get the gist of the conversation.

But Harold, upon hearing Frank's name again, narrowed his eyes like he was trying to place the name with a face. "Frank?" he said, reaching for his order book once again. He then wet his thumb, flicking through the pages at pace. "Ah, I thought the name sounded familiar, sir!" he said, tapping his finger on the page he'd arrived at. "And I *knew* I'd spoken to an English chap about some sort of television premiere or other."

Frank nodded politely, offering a hopeful smile.

"Ah, I didn't expect you and your party until tomorrow, Mr Franks," Harold offered, sounding entirely more congenial now.

"And I have the fitting booked in for three, rather than four," he politely noted.

"Mr Franks?" replied Frank. "Oh, I think there's…" he began, before immediately trailing off, catching up with the direction of the current conversation pretty darn quickly. "Uhm, the booking you have, Harold. That's for Rodney Franks, correct?"

"Yes, Mr Franks. That's correct."

Frank clapped his hands together smartly. "Excellent, Harold. Do you think you could squeeze one extra suit in for my good friend, plus get us in today, if that wouldn't be too terribly much trouble?"

"No trouble at all, Mr Franks. We'll certainly see what we can do," Harold assured him. "If you'd like to follow me through to the fitting room…?"

Frank nodded compliantly, first walking over to speak to the rest of his group. "Right," he said, pulling Dave, Monty, and Stan into a tight huddle, "I don't have time to explain right now. But until further notice, while we're in this shop, my name is Rodney Franks, okay?"

Frank received nods of acceptance in return from everyone, and then Dave whispered, "I don't know what's going on. But I've got a sneaking suspicion I'm going to like it!"

Chapter
FIFTEEN

Later that same evening, Frank pressed a cocktail glass to his curious lips, blowing gently to ensure that the previous flame had indeed petered out. "What's this one called?" he asked, slightly slurring his words, his eyes glassy.

Stan glanced down at the cocktail menu resting before them on the bar countertop. "A Flaming B-52, apparently," he replied confidently. And then, not quite so confidently, "Or is that what we just had? If so, I think this one's a Flaming Lamborghini."

"Whatever it's called, it's flaming loverly," declared Frank, licking his top lip to mop up any overspill left there. "Did I just say *loverly*? I think I did. Anyway, I'm fairly certain the flames have burnt away my excess nasal hair, which is an added bonus."

The cocktails, whatever they should be called, were, by Stan's reckoning, their fifth of the evening. Propped up at the hotel bar, it was just the two of them for right now, with Dave, Monty, and Stella trying their luck at the roulette wheel, popping back periodically like excitable children to show mum and dad how much they'd won (if children gambled, that is). According to Monty, Stella hadn't quite grasped all of the game rules, getting protective over certain numbers and pushing away any other player's chips that encroached on her selections. But the dealer was patient enough, he related, kindly asking security to stand down when they arrived mob-handed, assuring them that Stella was just confused rather than a troublemaker as initially suspected.

"I was just thinking," Stan commented, as Frank returned from the loo a short time later.

Frank raised his hand towards the bartender, which he hoped very much would not look like a Nazi *Sieg Heil* salute, as that was precisely the way it looked, he realised, though he by no means intended it that way. "Two more of your choice, please," he said, leaving the final decision to the professional. "Sorry, Stan. You were saying?"

Stan appeared contemplative, staring at his empty cocktail glass. "I was just thinking about how far we've come," he said after a moment. "Maybe it's because I've had several or more cocktails, but I was thinking about how we first met, all those years ago," he revealed.

"At school?" Frank asked. "When you were getting picked on by that complete arsehole, what's-his-name...?"

"Wayne Stanhope," Stan answered with a shudder. "He went to jail for robbing a post office, years later, as I recall."

"What made you think of him?" Frank asked, nodding in polite thanks to the barkeep as their latest round of alcoholic concoctions were delivered.

"I dunno, Frank. I suppose I was just reflecting on how we've been together, through the various ups and downs, through a number of businesses, and how, through it all, we've always remained the best of friends," Stan remarked, accepting his drink, and raising it to toast that fact of them remaining friends for so long, as he'd just said. "And now look at us, Frank. We're sitting in Las Vegas, ahead of the premiere of a television series we're both going to be featured in. It's all a bit bizarre."

"It's been a rollercoaster ride, all right, that's for sure, Stanley," Frank agreed, reaching down to give Stan's knee a gentle pat as they both enjoyed a moment of quiet introspection. Then, Frank laughed to himself. "Oi, you'll never guess who I was just thinking about on the way back from the lav," he said, clearly amused.

"Go on," said Stan.

"Rodney Franks," Frank answered.

Stan simply rolled his eyes.

"I know, I know. But I was just thinking back to all the lovely, unfortunate incidents that we've been an instrumental part of, where ol' Rodney's been concerned."

"Such as?"

"Well..." Frank said, taking a sip of his drink. "The very first time we met the guy, in the space of two hours, if you recall, we managed to destroy his fancy designer sunglasses, we successfully covered his blazer in warm milk, resulting in him looking as if a baby had spit up all over his back, we surreptitiously planted my prescription medication upon his person—"

"And got him pulled aside by the Isle of Man airport customs agents for a strip search as a result!" Stan cut in, fondly remembering the details of that whole medication incident.

"Oh, yes. And then we stole his taxi, which meant he was late for the auction of the TT Farm property. Back before it was the TT Farm property, of course."

"Poor old Rodney," Stan offered, letting out a chuckle. "And there's been a few more, ehm, *misunderstandings* since, for lack of a better word," he added, along with a mischievous grin. "It was unlikely that our friendship, if you could call it that, was going to flourish following that unfortunate introduction."

"It was the tuxedos that got me thinking about him," Frank noted. "I'd love to be a fly on the wall when he rocks up with his team for a fitting with Harold tomorrow and there's no room at the inn, so to speak." Frank then sighed the sigh of a man quite content with his lot. "Stan?" he said, raising his glass for a toast.

"Yes, Frank?"

"The rollercoaster ride I mentioned a moment ago? You do know I couldn't think of another person I'd rather have joining me on that ride than you."

Stan chinked his glass against Frank's. "Back at you, buddy. Back at you."

Just then, Monty came sprinting over, grinning from ear to ear. "Frank! Stan!" he said, slightly out of breath. "You need to come!" he insisted, cocking his thumb over his shoulder. "Stella's ended up in a high-stakes poker game with a group of Chinese businessmen, and she's not got the faintest bleedin' clue what she's doing!"

Frank drained the contents of his glass and jumped down from his barstool. "How much has she lost?" he asked, inviting Monty to lead the way.

Monty shook his head. "That's just the thing, Frank. She's not lost. She's actually on a roll. There's a crowd of people standing behind her like something out of a Hollywood film. When I left to come and get you, she was about six thousand dollars up!"

**

Following a boozy evening — at least on Frank and Stan's part, where they'd proudly reached nearly three-quarters of the way through the alphabet with the names of the various cocktails they were imbibing — a lazy morning by the hotel was the order of the day. With the special event for the TV show being later that same day, Stan was also eager to top up his Isle of Man fake tan with the real thing, commenting on how a bronze glow accentuated the luminosity of his recently bleached teeth.

The other members of their travelling party weren't quite so keen to spend their time lazing away on a sun lounger. Dave and Monty, for instance, had been invited on a tour of the Las Vegas Motor Speedway ahead of their exhibition race, while Stella had opted to spend some of her recent gambling windfall searching out an appropriate souvenir for her cat Bovril, and perhaps even something for her husband Lee as well.

Although, as it was later discovered, Stella wasn't quite the poker ace that Frank and the others had first assumed her to be. Apparently, as Dave learned from speaking to the croupier, the wealthy Chinese businessmen incorrectly assumed Stella to be an Eastern European hooker and were eager to avail themselves of her services. So when Stella, having not one clue about poker, rapidly burned through her own stake money, the businessmen — charmed by both her peculiar ways and unique dress sense — didn't wish for her to get away from them so easily. As such, they were only too pleased to slide an impressive stack of chips in her direction, hoping to curry favour and, perhaps, a down payment on services to be later rendered. Of course Stella didn't appear to perceive any of this generous behaviour to be in any way unusual, happy as she was to continue gambling with the amorous strangers' cash. But such was her erratic, nonsensical approach to playing the game, coupled with her unusual demeanour, that hotel security — who'd been keeping her under close scrutiny since the roulette wheel encounter — eventually suspected her to be the leader of a card-counting betting ring that'd been operating around the various Vegas casinos for the past week or so.

Fortunately, Stella had only ended up being questioned and detained for no more than a half hour or so, during which it became abundantly clear that she didn't know a royal flush from a full house, and explained that she thought she'd been playing blackjack rather than poker the entire time. Still, despite not knowing her arse from her elbow in the game, she did manage to leave the casino floor with the tidy little sum of just under three thousand dollars. Also, the timely intervention of hotel security likely saved the Chinese businessmen a furious beatdown from Stella, as they no doubt had been expecting, at some point, a services-rendered type of return on their lavish investment.

Back over beside the bustling and expansive swimming pool, Frank and Stan were sprawled out like two contented walruses basking in the early afternoon sun.

"Right. I'm turning over onto my belly now," Stan announced.

Frank peeled his face off the fabric sun lounger. "I'm not surprised with all of these scantily clad beauties about, Stanley."

"You know what I mean," Stan replied, shifting his position and rolling over onto his front. "I need you to apply the Hawaiian Tropic to my back and legs, Frank. And don't be frugal with the cream because it's a hot one today."

Frank moaned like a teenager wanting another ten minutes in bed, or, in this particular case, more like a walrus wanting another ten minutes of dozing on the beach. "But I'm comfortable and tired," he complained, a sleepy trickle of saliva pooling under his chin.

"Frank, you didn't complain when I glazed you like a ham earlier, did you?"

Frank begrudgingly pushed himself into a seated position, enjoying a good stretch as he surveyed his surroundings. "You really do have the hands of a masseuse, Stanley," he said in reply to Stan's remark, giving Stanley his due. "Edgar is a lucky man," Frank added, in reference to Stan's magic hands.

"You're not wrong there," Stan answered, happy to agree.

Swinging his legs off his lounger, Frank reached into their bag for the suncream, as requested. A few moments later, he loomed over the recumbent Stan, giving the plastic bottle of Hawaiian Tropic suntan lotion in his hand a firm squeeze. "Oh, excuse me," Frank joked as the cream loudly erupted from the bottle, a huge dollop heading directly towards Stan's back. "That must be the salmon I had for breakfast, as too much of it always makes me gassy," he explained, for extra comedic effect.

"Bloody hell!" Stan exclaimed, arching his back as the lotion hit his skin. "You're *supposed* to warm the cream in your hands before application, like I lovingly did for *you*."

"Was I?" Frank asked, not sounding particularly bothered, as after all, it wasn't his skin the cream had just hit. Frank then began rubbing the protective salve into Stan's back, with one eye on the game of water polo taking place in the pool. "Here, we should give that water polo a go," Frank suggested. "It looks like a right laugh."

"No thank you, Frank," Stan replied, not being impressed by the sound of all the splashing and frivolity. "A swimming pool on holiday is to float in or cool down. Not for exercise," he insisted. "Are you covering all of the bare flesh?" he added.

"Yessir," Frank responded, squirting another large glob of the chilly cream directly onto Stan's left leg, resulting in some instant squirming from his client below. "Oh, sorry, Stan," he offered, without too much conviction, chuckling to himself until he felt something strike him on the ankle. He looked down but could not see any obvious culprit.

"Hey, mister!" someone from the swimming pool called out. "Will you pass our ball back?"

Frank looked behind him, now spotting a yellow ball rolling slowly away. "No problem," he said, resting the plastic bottle next to Stan's unattended leg and heading off in pursuit of the wayward ball.

With his right palm still slightly covered in suncream, Frank didn't feel confident throwing the ball, suspecting it'd likely end up going in the opposite direction and strike some unsuspecting sun worshipper in the face. Instead, he held the escapee in his hands, escorting it over to the pool edge. "There you go," he said to the expectant group whose game was temporarily on hold.

"Come in and join us," the grateful lad in the pool suggested.

Frank waved away the suggestion. "Thanks, but I've never—"

"*C'mon*, don't be a party pooper," the lad persisted. "We're one player down, and it's a lot of fun!"

Frank brushed his hand clean and then tightened the pullcord on his shorts. "You know what, why not," he said. "It does look like fun," he decided, jumping into the pool with as much grace as he could muster.

It took Frank a few minutes to get the hang of his soon-to-be favourite sport, but his fellow players were patient teachers. And soon enough, he was having a whale of a time, having even managed to score a goal. Moreover, as the game was conducted in water, there was limited impact on his often-temperamental joints. In the moments celebrating his goal, Frank took a mental note to seek out and join a water polo club the instant he returned home, assuming such clubs existed on the isle. Indeed, he could have quite happily continued for the rest of the afternoon if he'd not seen Dave and Monty returning from their recent excursion.

"Dave!" Frank called out, now waving his arms above his head. "Will you throw my towel over?" he asked, once he'd attracted both Dave's attention and most of those lying around the perimeter of the pool.

Dave nodded, heading to the sun lounger that Frank was now pointing a water-wrinkled finger towards. Then, like a diligent pool attendant, he returned with it held out in front of him like he was preparing to personally towel Frank down.

"How was the grand tour?" Frank asked once he'd said goodbye to his water polo chums and emerged from the pool, gratefully wrapping himself up inside the fluffy towel.

Dave looked at Monty with a fierce expression. "It's not like I'd imagined, Frank. I won't lie to you."

Monty shook his head in solidarity.

Frank plunged the corner of the towel into his ear canal. "It's just a racetrack, isn't it?" he asked, not really sure what the issue was.

Dave and Monty followed Frank as he returned to the now-sleeping Stan. "It's not just a racetrack," Monty advised. "We thought it would be a fairly modest affair. You know, like our Jürburgring back home."

"You didn't think to Google it first?" Frank asked. "That's what I'd have done," he offered with a shrug. "So, it's big, then? This Las Vegas Motor Speedway?"

"Big?" Monty scoffed. "It's a freakin' *monster*, Frank. They race NASCAR there."

"Eighty thousand capacity," Dave said. "Frank, that's more than the entire population of the Isle of Man, give or take."

Frank didn't have a single clue as to what NASCAR could possibly be, but he didn't wish to reveal his ignorance on that point. "NASCAR, eh? *Impressive*," he replied, trying his best to make it sound as if he knew what Monty and Dave were talking about as he commenced with drying off his legs. "Well, I've scored a goal playing water polo while you two were gone," he advised, hoping for a congratulatory pat on the back in response, though it was a response that didn't arrive.

Instead, Monty had turned his attention to Stan, who was still face down in the prone position on his sun lounger and snoring softly like a kitten. "Uhm... Frank? What the hell has happened to Stan?"

Frank ceased his drying operations, turning and looking down at his horizontal friend. "Oh, shit!" he said, dropping his towel. "Shit, shit, shit!" he said, hopping from one foot to the other as he placed a hand against his mouth.

Stan hadn't moved at all during the time Frank had been gallivanting with his new polo friends — maybe an hour or so, by Frank's reckoning. As a result, both of Stan's legs now were flamingo-pink on account of the intense rays bearing down from the Las Vegas sun.

Dave grimaced, taking the palm of his hand and hovering it over one of Stan's legs. "Sweet Jesus, you could cook a steak on that," he remarked. "Did he forget his suncream?"

Frank mirrored Dave's actions, hovering his own hand above Stan's other leg, detecting, even inches away, the hot plate that was Stan's skin. "No, I did," he whispered, biting down on his lip for a moment in deep anguish. "I was just preparing to apply the cream on his legs, but then the water polo ball hit my ankle and diverted my attention. And then I ended up being invited to play a game. And that's when he must have fallen asleep."

"Any good?" Monty enquired.

"His nap?" Frank answered, misunderstanding. "I imagine so, as he still hasn't woken up yet, even after being burnt to a crisp."

"No, I meant about the game," Monty clarified.

"Oh!" said Frank, happy there was now some interest shown in that regard. "Yes, as I said earlier, I scored a goal," he declared proudly, inflating his chest.

A clearly impressed Monty raised his hand for a high-five, which was immediately accepted with equal enthusiasm.

And then, turning his attention back to the sleeping beetroot, "I must have missed a bit when I was applying the cream," Frank confessed.

"A *bit*?" Dave scoffed, although not entirely unsympathetic to Frank's situation. "A bloody *lot*, you mean. His legs look like crab sticks. Except for that one spot on his left leg, oddly enough, just there."

"I'd got as far as squirting some gloop onto the back of one thigh," Frank explained. "But then never got a chance to spread it around and rub it in."

"Is that you, Frank?" Stan asked, roused by the chatter, and lifting his head slightly from the folded arms he was using as a pillow. "I must have nodded off," he remarked sleepily, without rolling over.

"Em, everything okay there, Stanley?" Monty asked. "That is, you're feeling okay, mate?"

Stan didn't immediately reply, giving the impression he may have fallen back asleep.

"My legs do feel kind of funny, now you mention it," Stan answered eventually. "I think I might have been bitten by a mosquito? I'm still too lazy to move, Monty. Will you be a dear and have a look for me...?"

Frank swallowed hard. "I played water polo!" he blurted out, hoping to distract Stan from the current situation. "And guess what, Stan? I scored a goal! Stan, what do you think about that, Stan? Stan...?"

Chapter
SIXTEEN

A few minutes before six p.m., Dave and Monty were both standing outside of the hotel at their previously agreed rendezvous point, looking like a pair of right handsome bastards according to Monty's critical assessment.

"You know how these tuxedos we've got on are rented?" Monty commented, fidgeting with his dickie bow.

"Yeah," said Dave, unsure where Monty was going with this.

"Well, just imagine who may have worn these suits before us, Dave," Monty continued. "This close to Hollywood, *movie stars* could have once climbed into the trousers we're currently wearing. You never know."

"Or a corpse?" Dave wondered aloud, randomly shifting the direction of an otherwise reasonable conversation.

Monty's optimistic demeanour soured. "A corpse?" he asked, while dusting down his lapels. "But how could a corpse climb into anything? And why would a corpse rent a tuxedo?"

"I dunno, Monty. Maybe someone drops dead of a heart attack after having lost all of their life savings in the casino, yeah? And the gambler, never expecting to die, hasn't brought a suit to be buried in so the casino rents one on their behalf."

Monty gave Dave the sort of look you'd offer a drunk who'd wandered into your house by mistake thinking it was the local chippy. "I'm no expert on dead people, Dave, but wouldn't they just ship the corpse home and leave it for the person's loved ones to sort out? And even if that weren't the case, in this grim scenario of yours, how would we be wearing tuxedos that have already been put into the ground?"

Dave shrugged, as he never claimed to have all the answers all of the time. "Oh, wait, hang on," he then offered, in a moment of clarity. "Maybe they'd whip the suit off the corpse just before it goes in the big oven or gets dropped in the dirt? After all, it's a rental, so the casino wouldn't want to pay for the suit forever."

"I think the heat's starting to get to you, Dave, I really do," Monty put forth.

But before Dave could defend his way of thinking, an elderly couple presented themselves before the smartly dressed duo. "Would you mind calling us a taxicab?" the woman asked, in what sounded to Dave like a South African accent.

"A cab?" Dave asked, scanning their faces.

"Yes, if you please," the lady confirmed, smiling kindly. "We're going to watch Celine Dion this evening," she added, before retrieving and then carefully placing a monetary note of some kind in Dave's breast pocket. "That's for your trouble," she said.

Dave threw Monty a quizzical glance.

"They must think we work here at the hotel?" Monty said in response, whispering it from the side of his mouth. "Probably because of the corpse suits?"

Dave dipped his fingers into his pocket, intending to return the cash that had been teased in there. "No, I'm sorry, we don't actually..." he started to say, until his eyes clocked that it was a twenty-dollar bill. "Ah! One taxicab coming right up," Dave then promptly announced, helpful sausage that he was. "Celine Dion, you say?" Dave asked by way of conversation, before stepping out to hail one of the many passing taxis.

But their taxi-hailing duties didn't end there, as it should happen, because the moment the elderly Celine Dion fans were dispatched and on their way, another family, impressed it would appear by Dave's successful ability to summon transportation in short order, were eager to avail of his services as well. "Where to?" Dave cordially asked, in response to another generous tip being thrust his way.

With a modest queue forming, and over sixty American dollars already in his possession, Dave could quite happily have continued with his new enterprise for the foreseeable. That was, however, until the hotel's concierge service appeared, looking somewhat irate by the interlopers encroaching on their turf. As such, Dave and Monty were told in no uncertain terms that if they raised another arm to hail another taxi, the concierge team would snap that arm off and beat them with it, or similar words to that effect.

Indeed, it was fortunate that Dave and Monty quickly painted themselves as confused hotel guests — whilst also making it a point to mention that Frank and Stan, who were in their group as well, were already friendly with their colleague Deontay — or they'd have likely been driven out into the desert and interred there, Dave commented to Monty. But at least, if that were to happen, then they would already have their nice suits on, Dave added, as the two of them made sure to keep their taxi-hailing hands securely holstered in their pockets.

Fortunately, Dave and Monty didn't have to wait for the rest of their party too much longer, as Frank and Stan emerged from the hotel lobby, with Stella following a few paces behind.

"Over here!" Dave had to call out, as he and Monty had been moved by the concierge team to an area a little further afield from which they could not easily interact with any other hotel guests seeking transport. "Frank, we're over here!" Dave shouted a little louder. And then, "It's okay, they're with us," he promised the watching concierge. "We're absolutely *not* poaching them from you, I swear," he advised with a plucky wave.

"What have you two been up to?" Frank asked upon arrival, noting the stern expressions being cast in their direction.

However, neither Dave nor Monty responded, as they were instead captivated by the outfit Stella had picked out for the evening's event. Their eyes were initially drawn to the familiar hobnail boots, accompanied by a pair of fishnet stockings that looked like they'd recently been to work hauling walleye pollock from the Bering Sea. Further up, her figure-hugging mini skirt enjoyed various printed images of the band One Direction festooned all over it. Complementing the overall look was a white, cropped tank top which was waging a serious, tenacious battle to contain Stella's ample, curvaceous bosom. And finally, the finishing touch on her ensemble was a black dickie bow she'd acquired, fastened around her naked and prodigious neck.

"You're looking, erm..." Monty started to say, trying to think of something positive to offer, ever the gentleman. "I, ehm... I didn't know you were a One Direction fan, Stella?"

Stella rummaged around inside of her shirt, offering Monty a chilling scowl. "What?" she said with disdain, removing a packet of Camel no-filter ciggies (the *good* kind, that you couldn't easily get back in the UK) that'd been concealed somewhere within the depths of her cleavage.

Monty panicked, concerned he'd managed to cause offence. "I just noticed the picture of..." he said, pointing a cautious finger towards Stella's skirt.

"What, them?" she asked with a cackle. Stella took a lungful of her now-lit fag, blowing the exhaust fumes in Monty's direction. "Don't be daft. That's the Beatles," she insisted. "Bloody *One Direction*? Honestly, Monty, sometimes I do wonder about you," she said, shaking her head.

Monty cast another look southward at Stella's skirt, making it only a quick glance, as he didn't want to be accused of leering. "But that's Harry Styles?" Monty gently suggested, turning to Frank and Stan to back him up.

Stella responded with a disappointed sigh. "Harry Styles isn't in the Beatles, you silly muppet," she said.

Rather than backing Monty up, Frank, sensing or fearing this could go on all evening, gave Monty a gentle tap on the arm. "You need to know when to walk away," he whispered, speaking with the wisdom of years of experience in such matters. "Learn to just walk away, mate."

Monty did as advised, and just in time, as it should happen, because just then an expensive-looking SUV with heavily tinted windows slowed to a halt beside them like a mob hit was about to go down. Fortunately, however, no asses were capped this fine night, as the occupants of the plush motor were soon identified as Brad and Chip, there to whisk them away to the evening's engagement.

"Your chariot awaits," Brad invited, once the passenger-side window was rolled down. "Climb on in!"

Stella extinguished her fag on the back of her hand, waiting impatiently for someone to open one of the vehicle doors for her. Dave eventually took the hint, skilfully averting his eyes as Stella hitched up her already meagre and restrictive skirt, showing a generous selection of her cheese wire thong for all and sundry as she climbed inside.

"That's a vision that I'll never... ever unsee," Frank remarked from behind. "And I mean, ever."

***

If Team Frank & Stan (plus Stella) thought the reception they'd got at the airport was lively, then they were about to receive something of a wake-up call. Both Brad and Chip, who'd been working at the venue for most of the day, tried to prepare the gang about what to expect in advance of their arrival. But their words couldn't quite convey what Frank and the others could soon see for themselves.

After a short drive, a harried-looking policewoman directing traffic held out a hand. With the SUV at a halt, she approached Chip in the driver's seat. "VIPs only in this lane, sir," she announced in a firm yet cordial voice. "Do you have a pass?"

Chip presented his laminated credentials for consideration. "There you go, officer. We're the directors of the show, and the guys in back are the stars of it," he explained, hoping this would expedite things.

The officer peered through the opened driver's window into the rear of the vehicle, appearing a bit unimpressed. That is until she noticed Stan grinning back at her. "Oh!" she said, her professional expression giving way to something much more cheerful. "I *do* recognise *you*."

Stan's grin widened. "A pleasure to make your acquaintance, officer."

The policewoman removed her head from the front window, now looking to her colleague thirty or so feet up the road. "Let this one pass through, Steve!" she announced. "It's the guy from the airport who pissed his pants!"

Waved through by the welcoming committee, Chip turned off the main road towards their destination. And it was once they turned the corner that the scale of their reception became apparent to the others. "Christ on a bike!" Monty exclaimed, with his nose pressed up against the glass. Because there, on either side of the road, were crowds several heads deep waving from behind safety barriers.

"What did we tell you?" Chip replied, waving out his opened window as he crawled along. "They *love* you guys. And it's a good thing the glass is tinted, because if they knew it was you back there, they'd probably attack the vehicle."

Brad looked over his shoulder from the front, eager to see the reaction of Dave and the crew, and he wasn't disappointed. "It's wicked cool, right? And word on the street is that a few A-listers are going to show up, which I'm sure didn't hurt the crowd size either."

"A-listers?" replied Stan, interest piqued, considering his rather extensive experience in the performing arts (that being the egg commercial, seen by at *least* four thousand people). "Anyone we'd know?"

Chip cleared his throat. "George Clooney and Brad Pitt, from what I hear. Both serious racing fans."

Stella, who'd appeared bored throughout the commute, suddenly leaned forward. "Brad Pitt?" she asked, with hope-filled eyes. "Brad Pitt's going to be here tonight?" she said, exhibiting a rarely witnessed flurry of enthusiasm.

Chipped nodded his head as he steered the vehicle, making his way towards the team of valet parkers waiting to assist the various new arrivals. "That's what people are saying, yeah. Are you gonna hunt him down for an autograph?" he asked.

But Stella didn't immediately answer, instead reaching for her handbag. Then, after extracting what she'd been looking for, "Do you think he'll sign this for me?" she asked, waving around an eight-inch battery-operated provider of pleasure.

"You brought that *with* you?" Frank asked, gobsmacked.

"I never travel anywhere without Brad, Guy, or Idris Elba," Stella advised. "So what do you think, Chuck?" she asked, tapping the aforementioned sex toy on Chip's shoulder.

"Holy shit, I'm trying to drive, here!" Chip protested. "And it's *Chip*, actually, not Chuck," he advised.

"No, I reckon your name is Chuck, and the other one's name is Brandon," Stella answered, deciding that's what she was calling the two of them for now. "Though I can never tell which one of you is which."

"Stella, can you not keep that thing on my shoulder, please?" Chip pleaded. "It's making me kind of uncomfortable."

But Stella wasn't listening, resting the well-used Mr Pitt on Chip's shoulder, just as she imagined she'd do if she met the real Brad Pitt, introducing the two Brad Pitts to each other.

The walk from the valet parking spot to the venue entrance wasn't all that long. However, when you were in a procession of other guests on the red carpet, stopping to have their pictures taken, signing autographs, or speaking to the assembled throng, progress was decidedly slow. Not that neither Dave nor Monty minded too much, however, as they were rather quite enjoying the attention lavished on them, particularly when an enthusiastic brunette revealed her finest assets for a signature *on* each, *by* each of them. "A couple of tits signing a couple of tits," Dave was heard to quip as he set to work with the felt-tip pen, finishing his turn before the lovely woman was escorted away by security staff. "Our better halves wouldn't mind, I'm sure of it," Dave assured Monty, along with a wink, once business was concluded.

And someone else having an absolute blast was Stan, who made a point of chatting to any journalist who wished to speak to him and even several of those who didn't. In fact, it was only Frank's guiding hand that stopped Stan from doubling back on himself so he could saunter up the red carpet for a second time.

"This is a bit of me," Stan said, striking a pose each and every time a camera was pointed in his general direction.

Frank was a bit less involved, instead offering a simple, understated smile on each occasion. "You've certainly mastered your pout, Stanley," he remarked, happy because his friend was happy.

"When we get back home, I'm going to look into resurrecting my acting career, Frank," Stan decided.

Now Frank was no theatrical agent, but even he knew that appearing in an advert for eggs wasn't really the foundation of an acting career. But Stanley was proud of his accomplishments and Frank was there to support him. "You should, pal," he said. "I reckon you'd be a natural treading the boards."

Once inside the venue, both Frank and Stan had dry teeth from smiling so much. Fortunate, then, that a team of greeters were on hand with amply stocked trays of liquid refreshments. "A glass of shampoo, Stanley?" Frank asked, reaching for two flutes.

"Rude not to, Frank," Stan answered.

Even though they'd visited the venue previously, both Frank and Stan couldn't help but be impressed by the staging the production company had accomplished. And the invited guests appeared to appreciate the effort as well, captivated by the atmospheric images of the Isle of Man TT races displayed throughout the lobby, along with the audio backdrop of racing commentary being piped in over the speaker system. Also proving to be particularly popular, judging by all the attention it was currently receiving, was the replica of the Big Blue Boiled Sweet, parked up in the lobby with the paintwork shimmering in the overhead lights.

"All right, then?" Frank asked, as Dave and Monty appeared, both with a bottle of beer pressed to their lips.

"I was just listening to the commentary," Dave remarked, tilting his head for better reception into his ear hole. "I have to say, I think I've got a bit of a lump in my throat."

"Me too, Dave. Me too," Frank replied. And then, "Blimey, to think that we're suited and booted, together in Las Vegas," he added with a chuckle. "It really doesn't feel like that long since we first landed on the Isle of Man."

"Remember our first night, Frank?" Stan asked in fond recollection. "Me and you waking up in the back of Dave's van using his armpits for a pillow?"

"Kicked me out of my bloody place to sleep, as I recall," Monty reminded them, recalling the time he spent on the flea-infested couch under his and Dave's awning instead of the van.

Frank raised his glass. "Right. Here's to Team Frank 'n' Stan's Bucket List, then," he said, proposing a toast. "And what a hoot the journey's been so far!"

But before anyone could raise their own glasses or bottles, Dave, glancing over Stan's shoulder, could witness someone approaching at speed. "Ding-dong! Knobhead at twelve o'clock!" he quickly alerted the others. "And what on earth is that knobhead wearing?" he added.

"Twelve o'clock?" Stan asked, glancing at his watch to check the time, not really taking Dave's meaning.

"Oi!" a nasally, angry voice called out. "I've been *searching* for you lot!" it stressed.

Frank and Stan spun around, whereupon they were greeted by the furious and runty vision of Rodney Franks glaring up at them. "I know what you've done," he said, stamping his foot on the patterned carpet. He looked like a child as he did this, which was perhaps appropriate given his diminished stature.

"Nice suit, Rodney," Frank commented, struggling to stifle a laugh.

Rodney's cheeks were puce, which was a stark contrast to the bright white of his questionable suit, so blazingly white that it almost made your eyes hurt. It also had lapels that were far too wide, and the trouser legs flared out at the bottom, like it was something straight out of the 1970s.

"You look like some rubbish entertainment director at some equally rubbish holiday camp," Monty pointed out, much to the amusement of the others. "Are you here to tell us what time the bingo starts?"

Rodney reared up. Or at least he reared up as best he could, considering. "You boorish louts have stolen our tuxedo rentals!" he roared, jabbing an accusatory finger into Stan's chest, as poor Stan just happened to be the closest. "And this suit I'm wearing was the last turkey in the shop, as there wasn't enough time for us to go anywhere else!"

In such circumstances, Stan would ordinarily try and offer a denial for fear of inflaming the situation. But not this time. "Yep, we sure did, Rodney," he boasted, pressing his shoulders back to showcase the sartorial elegance of his dinner jacket. "And what are you going to do about it?" he said, first checking that Dave and Monty were still standing close enough to defend him if need be. "Huh?" he then added, fearlessly returning a jabbed finger into Rodney's own chest.

By now, Rodney was incandescent with rage. "Well I hope you didn't pay too much of a deposit for your rental," he said, tightening his fingers into a fist, giving Stan the impression he was about to bop him squarely on the chin. "Because they don't take too kindly to any damage," Rodney added, reaching for the area of Stan's handkerchief. But rather than stealing the handkerchief as Stan might have imagined, Rodney yanked his hand down in a sharp movement, ripping the front portion of Stan's breast pocket away from the rest of the suit.

"Oh, dear!" Rodney offered. "What a clumsy so-and-so I am," he declared with a frown, tickling the flap of fabric now hanging down from Stan's chest.

Stan stood rooted to the spot, unsure what to do or say next. Fortunate, then, that Stella should return from her celebrity-hunting quest at that very moment.

"I've looked everywhere for Brad Pitt — the *real* one, I mean — but bugger-all," Stella complained, taking another cursory glance around.

"Stella," Stan pleaded, in a high-pitched warble. "Stella, he's ripped my pocket," he protested, like he was grassing up a classmate to the teacher.

However, Rodney did his best to retain his air of bravado, despite the current threat of Stella's sudden presence. "Oh, marvellous," he said, looking Stella up and down. "And what exactly have you come as...?" he asked with a sneer.

"I wouldn't poke that particular bear," Monty cautioned. "I don't think it will end well for you."

But Rodney wasn't in the mood to listen, it would appear. Instead, he pointed towards the black dickie bow secured around Stella's neck. "I suppose you stole that from the suit hire shop as well?" he asked. "Although I wasn't sure they rented clothes out to frizzy-haired oxen in that establishment."

Stella, having just arrived, wasn't privy to all of the details as to what was going on at the present scene. But it didn't matter. "Who are you calling an ox?" she said, in a tone suggesting that Rodney should *seriously* consider the next words to come out of his mouth.

Unfortunately for Rodney, he didn't. "Are you stupid as well as deaf, or is—"

But Rodney didn't get to finish his sentence. With the speed of Clint Eastwood reaching for and using his pistol, Stella thrust her hand into her bag, retrieved Brad Pitt, and then proceeded to beat Rodney Franks about the head with her silicone phallus. She did this with little regard about damaging her favourite toy, as she knew from experience that it could withstand loads and loads of abuse.

"I told you it wouldn't end well for you, didn't I?" Monty helpfully pointed out, a moment before the security staff arrived.

Chapter
SEVENTEEN

There weren't too many people in Las Vegas who could lay claim to being floored by an eight-inch dildo, but Rodney Franks could now boast of that dubious privilege.

Fortunately, the security staff were eventually able to see the humorous side of things, with Brad and Chip on hand to calm the situation and offer assurances that there wouldn't be any repeat performance from Stella, and with most people present just assuming this had all been for show and simply a colourful promotional stunt anyway. And aside from some temporary redness to Rodney's temple, cheek, and forehead, nothing appeared to have been broken. Well, apart from Brad Pitt, that is, whose battery housing cover had broken loose during the kerfuffle, spilling its AA batteries out amongst the dumbstruck bystanders.

Later, after a few glasses of fizz and a delightful finger buffet, all of the assembled guests were invited into the auditorium to take their seats. Unfortunately for Frank and co, they were sat directly next to Rodney and co (with Rodney's two riders looking precious in their matching 1970's-style groovy white outfits, same as their boss). But as the event was a sold-out affair, there was no option available to juggle around the seating plan and they were all stuck with each other.

But Rodney, nursing his injuries, was in no mood for a further scuffle if his browbeaten demeanour, along with his browbeaten brow, were anything to go by.

The house lights soon dimmed, and the room sat in hushed silence. Until, that is, Stella decided this to be the ideal time to get stuck into the packet of crisps she'd brought along to watch the presentation. Several seconds of crunching and packet rustling elapsed before the venue's sound system erupted, blaring out the thunderous noise of a motorcycle engine roaring into life, moving up through its gears, and scaring the hell out of most who weren't expecting it.

Then a beam of light from the overhead spotlight burst forth, illuminating a pair of feet, just visible, off to the side of the raised stage. The feet started moving, the spotlight of concentrated artificial light now encompassing the entire figure, revealed to be the smartly dressed form of Clifford Tanner, the bigwig from the show's network, NBC. He confidently walked out, clapping as he made his way to the centre of the stage like an accomplished politician on the campaign trail. Once in front of the microphone stand the speaker system silenced, allowing him to appreciate the generous applause being directed his way.

"I'll bet the sound of that engine had the hairs on the back of your neck standing up, didn't it?" he offered, receiving relieved laughter from the audience as the shock of the recent sonic assault wore off. "For those of you who don't know me, I'm Clifford Tanner," he continued, bustling with energy. "And I want to extend a big thank you for coming here to tonight's sneak preview of our latest programme, *Isle of Man TT Aces*. Now, as you might be aware, the first series will consist of eight episodes. And tonight, we're overjoyed to be able to present to you a special, advanced showing of the first, one-hour-long pilot episode."

Clifford paused, allowing the subsequent round of applause to abate before continuing. "As you can imagine, in my line of work I have a lot of ideas for TV shows pitched to me. With some of them good, and some, not so much. And I'm sure they won't mind me sharing with you all, but Brad and Chip Freestone, the creators of tonight's show, originally came into my office with a couple of real stinkers." Clifford glanced down at Brad and Chip, sitting near Frank and the others in the front row. "Something about one-legged nuns crossing the Atacama Desert was one of those clunkers, am I right, gentlemen?" he asked, along with a wry smile, raising a giggle from some of the audience.

"That's still going to be a hit!" Brad shot back. "And the price to buy it has just gone up!" he joked.

Clifford offered the boys a friendly wink before turning his attention back to the rapt audience. "It's a good thing I've brought my chequebook along then, folks. But in all seriousness, Brad and Chip did eventually pitch an idea to me that ended up sending shivers up and down my spine. They played me a video featuring action-cam footage from a racer named Guy Martin, who was blazing around the Isle of Man TT racecourse, and it's one of the most incredible things I've ever watched."

Clifford shook his head in disbelief, recalling the first time he'd seen it. "And many of my executive team, who are here with us tonight, were convinced the Freestone brothers had either sped up the footage for dramatic effect or were showing us a clip from some videogame. But they hadn't! And I won't lie, but like many on this side of the Atlantic, I'd never really heard of the Isle of Man TT races until these two brought it to my attention and spoke so passionately about it. But after being blown away by their video, when they told me they wanted to create a series about the unbelievable characters who come together, sacrificing their time, money, and sometimes their sanity, just so they can compete in what's been described as the greatest road race on earth, well, who was I to stand in their way? Ladies and gentlemen, it's with immense pride and pleasure that we give to you... *Isle of Man TT Aces*."

With that, a production assistant briefly came on stage to remove the microphone stand, with the spotlight disappearing and the stage curtains parting ways to reveal a massive video screen. A moment later, a small white dot appeared at the centre of an otherwise blackened image, the dot steadily increasing in diameter like a sleeper opening their eyes following an extended afternoon nap, revealing, eventually, a swath of clear tarmac stretching out into the distance ahead.

The sound of a beating heart, faint at first, gradually increasing in both volume and tempo, now accompanied the image on the screen. Slowly, the camera angle panned down, just slightly, granting the audience a glimpse of a yellow printed splodge on the front of a shimmering blue sidecar bike's nosecone, familiar to many as being that of Dave and Monty's magnificent beast. But there wasn't time to dwell, as a split second later, the noise of a race-tuned engine screamed into life, propelling the camera, and the sidecar fairing it was mounted on, hurtling away from the Isle of Man TT grandstand area and down Glencrutchery Road towards St Ninian's Crossroads.

The audience, sat there mesmerised, could now likely understand Clifford Tanner's earlier comment about being shown a video game, as it was difficult to imagine that what they were watching could be anything other than computer-generated wizardry. Even Stella, rarely too enthusiastic about anything, appeared captivated, edging forward in her seat, her right hand poised above her half-eaten packet of crisps.

Positioned closely above the track by virtue of its position on the sloping, aerodynamic fairing, the GoPro camera bounced along with the movement of the bike, capturing a unique perspective. And it was from this unique, street-level POV that one could appreciate just how quickly these machines tore along the same roads used by the public only an hour or two earlier.

Crowds of cheering spectators were visible — albeit slightly blurred at warp speed — watching the action from behind the safety barriers as bikes hurtled down the daunting descent of Bray Hill at impossible speed. At the foot of the hill, with the suspension in danger of bottoming out, the camera mounting shuddered as Dave kept the throttle pinned, the 600cc engine screaming in horse-powered fury as it propelled the bike towards Ago's Leap, a well-known area of the course named after the charismatic Italian racer Giacomo Agostini.

It was about this point that a racer likely started to think about the integrity of their brake pads. Because following a flat-out dash across Quarterbridge Road, it was time to shift down the gearbox, applying the anchors for the first time since you'd left the grandstand, hoping to sufficiently reduce your speed to negotiate the upcoming sharp right-hander. And, if you didn't, there were usually dozens of spectators enjoying a pint at the Quarterbridge Pub to witness the ensuing turmoil if your brakes weren't quite up to the job.

Then, on the giant video monitor, the onboard camera cut away, now showing Dave and Monty's ass-end accelerating at speed towards Braddan Bridge — an enviable view of which was enjoyed by those watching on from the nearby pub, pint in hand.

Amongst the throng of spectators who'd taken up position at the Quarterbridge Pub for the day were a group of three twenty-somethings from Runcorn, a town near Liverpool, who Brad had spoken to earlier in the day. Apparently, two of the group were desperate for the Ibiza sunshine and senoritas in bikinis, but they'd been persuaded by their mate that a trip to soak up the action at the Isle of Man TT races was a much better option instead, even if there wasn't quite as much sun, or, for that matter, scantily clad ladies in bikinis.

The passion for the Isle of Man TT was something Brad and Chip, as documentarians, desperately wanted to convey in their feature. Not just in relation to the racers, whose personal sacrifice to participate was significant, but also in regard to the motivation of the spectators, who arrived in their thousands each and every year from across all four corners of the globe. And what better way to achieve this than by filming the reaction of a couple of raw recruits — in slow motion — the very first time they clapped eyes on the bikes in action. As Brad had considered at the time, a picture really does paint a thousand words. And the intense, dramatic, and visceral reaction of the Runcorn lads was cinematic gold and the perfect way to introduce the *Isle of Man TT Aces* to the uninitiated.

Attempting to condense days worth of gripping footage into a one-hour pilot episode that held the audience's attention and encouraged them to continue viewing had been a considerable challenge that both Brad and Chip remained acutely aware of. And while now, at present, they were enjoying seeing the fruits of their labour being presented up there on the large auditorium screen, mostly, they were busy stealing furtive glances around the auditorium, hoping folks were both laughing when they were supposed to and engrossed when the action dictated. And from what they were able to see in the darkened room, that certainly did appear to be the case.

The two brothers had agonised for weeks, knowing that the initial episode was their first chance to make a good impression on the viewing public. To achieve this, they knew they needed to skilfully weave a mix of action, emotion, personal conflict, relationships, and passion into every frame, hopefully whetting the viewer's appetite for more and leaving them desperate to watch the rest of the series. Their work had to convey a story the audience felt immersed in, and ultimately cared about. If they could do this, then they knew their project had been a success, and one that the Nielson ratings (which tracks TV viewing habits in the US), plus streaming figures, would hopefully confirm.

In the closing minutes of the episode, Rodney Franks finally made his eagerly awaited appearance onscreen (and with no one more eagerly awaiting it than him). "What a handsome devil!" Rodney called out, disturbing the rest of the auditorium in the process. But Rodney didn't appear too concerned, taking to his feet and removing his phone to capture a shot of his debut with the phone's camera. Again, he did this with no regard to those sitting behind him whose view he was presently obstructing. He looked particularly enamoured with himself, watching as his onscreen representation was captured marching through the TT paddock area, barking orders at his weary-looking and long-suffering underlings.

Most of the audience, many of whom had already enjoyed brief snippets of the show over YouTube and the like, instantly knew who this small man in the funny white suit was. Some in the audience cheered at him as he stood there creating a disturbance, while others in the crowd booed. But whether cheers or jeers, it sounded like it was all delivered in good spirits, rather like the moment the Wicked Queen character first appears onstage to a UK audience in a yearly Christmas panto. Indeed, it was just as Clifford had suggested, insisting the public would love a cartoon villain. And if the enthusiastic love/hate reaction Rodney Franks was receiving from the room was any indication, then Clifford Tanner had been exactly correct in his assessment.

Like many iconic TV programmes over the years, you knew the episode was soon coming to an end when the cameraman zoomed in on one of the characters in that scene, ready to capture whatever important, dramatic line they were about to deliver, setting things up for the next episode. And this was no different. The footage onscreen, previously unseen by anyone in the audience, players in the show included, showed the camera zoom in on an unsuspecting Rodney Franks, who was still mic'd up and in deep conversation with Vince (with Vince being the stocky, shaven-headed brute who, amongst other job responsibilities, was also Rodney's chief henchman).

The camera, clearly handheld on account of the shaky image, captured Rodney first looking over his shoulder, and then leaning closer to Vince's cauliflower ear. "That idiotic TV company have signed up those two cretins, Dave and Monty, as the poster boys for their new series," Rodney revealed to his trusty servant.

"That's not good, boss, is it?"

"You're correct, Vince. That's not good. Not good at all."

Vince cracked his knuckles, appearing both agitated and in a state of readiness. A state of agitated readiness, one might say. "What's the plan, boss?"

The onscreen Rodney turned, glancing to the distant camera like he was inadvertently staring straight down the lens. "We can't let that happen, Vince," Rodney insisted. "We need to do anything in our power to oust those two pillocks from this TV show, along with that pair of imbecilic sponsors of theirs, Frank and Stan."

"Anything...?" Vince asked.

Rodney nodded his head. *"Anything*, Vince," he said, narrowing his eyes.

But the audience would need to wait until episode two to find out what happens next.

Of course, as these were historical events having just been depicted onscreen, those involved in them certainly knew how things had all turned out in relation to the show, as well as to that year's set of TT races. Although watching this footage must still have been fairly awkward for them, especially considering that the two 'pillock' riders in question, along with their pair of 'imbecile' sponsors, were presently sitting in the same row of seats as Rodney Franks. Indeed, many would be rather embarrassed by the chilling words that had just been revealed to the great and good in attendance.

Not Rodney, though. Oh, no. Rodney was the first person on his feet again, whooping and hollering, cheering his own evil brilliance. With arms outstretched, he turned to face the audience. "Who loves Rodney Franks?" he asked, cupping one of his hands and pressing it to his ear. "I said who loves Rodney Franks?!"

Several seats away, an inflamed Stella reached for her handbag. "If that little dipshit doesn't shut his piehole," she said to nobody in particular. "Then bloody Brad Pitt is coming back out to finish what's already been started..."

Chapter
EIGHTEEN

"Move over, JR Ewing, there's a new badass in town and his name is Rodney Franks!"

"Action, intrigue, and did I mention action?"

"Book me up! I'm going to the TT races!"

"The perfect cast, the perfect location, the perfect event – Five out of five stars."

"I didn't hear the last one!" Stan shouted over from his seat under the shade of a towering palm tree. "Frank, I said that I didn't—"

"They gave it five stars!" Frank said a little louder, his nose still pressed up close to his iPad. "Look, why don't you come over and join me on the sun loungers? That way, you can read the assorted reviews for yourself?" he offered, indicating towards the empty lounger positioned next to his.

Stan appeared for all the world like a little boy lost, sitting sheltered and alone at a small table, while everybody else in the pool area was enjoying the glorious sunshine. "How can I sit directly in the sun when I've got bloody third-degree burns all over most of my body?" he asked.

Frank didn't even bother to look in Stan's direction. *"Pfft,"* he said dismissively. "Your legs are a little bit red, Stan. Nothing the aloe vera gel you had me apply earlier won't sort out."

Stan wrapped his fingers around his tall glass of iced tea, using it to chill his fingers as best he could. "I'm sure it's starting to blister, Frank," he suggested, before putting his cold digits on a section of the afflicted area, moaning in relief.

"Do you want me to slap on some more of that aftersun gel for you?" Frank offered.

Stan forced a smile through his grimace. "Would you mind terribly?" he asked. "And let me read the rest of those reviews while you're busy doing it."

Frank couldn't help but oblige, considering the redness on Stan's legs was technically his fault in the first place. "You know, if I didn't know you better, Stanley, I'd say you were just wanting me to give you a good rub-down," he said with a smirk.

"Oh? Don't flatter yourself, Frank," Stan said with a chuckle, moving into a position to grant Frank better access to the affected region. "And this time, try and cover the whole fleshy canvas instead of splattering it on like Jackson Pollock."

"I don't know what that means, Stan. But rest assured you'll have my full attention this time."

As Frank began working wonders with his soothing hands, Stan set to work scrolling through the particular article Frank had last been reading on his iPad, a news piece detailing the various reactions to the show so far. "Ooh, a bit more just there, if you wouldn't mind, Frank," Stan instructed.

"Very good, sir."

Stan absorbed the details of the article like his skin was absorbing the healing salve. "The press certainly appear to have liked what they saw," Stan remarked, telling Frank what he already knew. Although this information wasn't exactly all that much of a surprise to either of them, really. Because the moment the preview had concluded the previous evening, the entire auditorium took to their feet to show their appreciation, including those invited guests from the various media outlets.

"I don't get what they see in that offensive little oaf, though," Stan complained. "Honestly, the way the press is gushing over him, you'd be mistaken for thinking he was some loveable rogue, rather than just a complete—"

"Arse?"

"Yeah, that sounds about right, Frank."

"No, I mean how far up your legs do you want me to go, Stan?" Frank clarified. "I'm getting close to your arse area now, so I reckoned on stopping soon."

"It does feel a bit warm around there, now you mention it," Stan offered. "Just go as high up as you can," he advised. "Better safe than sorry, I say."

"The things I do in the name of friendship," Frank muttered under his breath, applying another splodge of aloe vera gel to his already greasy fingers.

Fortunately, as Stan was presently discovering, it wasn't just Rodney Franks receiving all the plaudits from the press in their reviews. Reviewers were also captivated by the stunning Isle of Man scenery, amazed by the spectacle of the TT, and charmed by the quirky cast of real-life characters featured in the show. "One of these writers describes me as being delightfully eccentric," Stan said a moment later. "That's good, right?"

"Sure is, buddy. And sums you up to a tee."

The writer of the article went on to describe the bitter rivalry that existed between Team Frank 'n' Stan and Rodney's crew, building it up into something it really wasn't, in Stan's opinion, which Stan was quick to mention. Yes, there was a strong dislike for each other as individuals, but to say there was intense professional rivalry... well, that wasn't really the case, because they were never directly competing with each other. Not exactly, at least. Not precisely. Because those with any real knowledge of the TT knew that Andy Thomas and Jack Napier were in a different league to Dave and Monty, a fact that Monty and Dave were happy to concede. But it wasn't that Andy and Jack were head and shoulders above them on the talent stakes, necessarily. Rather, it was the fact Napier and Thomas had top-flight machinery (along with a team of expert mechanics to keep it operating) beneath them that was impossible to compete with on a shoestring budget. To use a different sort of racing analogy, it was, quite simply, like a talented jockey entering the Grand National on a seaside donkey hoping to compete with a thoroughbred. So for the reporter to build up the competitive rivalry to such a fever pitch, in Stan's view, was something of a stretch.

"Hmm, so the sidecars the boys are competing on tomorrow are all essentially the same?" Stan wondered aloud, finished with the article now.

"Apparently so," Frank answered. He wiped his hands clean on Stan's towel, his mission attending to Stan's legs having been accomplished.

Stan returned his friend's iPad. "I don't really know about all this," he said with a solemn expression.

Frank nodded in agreement. "Yeah. The exhibition race, you mean?"

"Yes. Reading that article, you'd think it was a kind of Battle of the Titans or something, rather than just a friendly outing."

Frank took a seat next to Stan, offering a polite hand to the passing poolside waiter. "Two more of those, whatever they are, if you please," he requested, motioning towards Stan's beverage.

"Iced tea," Stan offered helpfully.

"Coming right up, sir," the friendly waiter advised.

Frank returned to Stan's point. "Well, I don't know. I do think the friendly exhibition element may have gone out the window when they threw a cash prize into the mix, don't you?"

"Exactly. And I just don't trust Rodney Franks, or those lads he's got racing for him," Stan revealed. "I mean, you just needed to watch the first episode last night to see what a devious, conniving little wretch Rodney Franks is."

"So what is it you're saying, Stan?" Frank asked, feeling like Stan was leading up to something.

"I don't think I want Dave and Monty entering this exhibition race, Frank. That's what I'm saying. I just don't have a good feeling about it. Do you know what I mean?"

"I do," Frank readily agreed. "Because that's the exact same thought that I've been having. But what are we supposed to do about it now, at this late stage so close to the race?"

***

At Stella's request, lunch was a particularly meat-filled affair, at a nearby restaurant she had discovered called For Pete's Steak. Apparently, she'd chanced upon it when out purchasing knickers, later commenting that the aroma wafting out of the place was fookin' stupendous. And as they'd soon discover, the taste of the food was equal to the fookin' stupendous aroma.

It was only Frank, Stan, and Stella together for lunch, however, as Dave and Monty had been invited for a race suit fitting over at the track, and then an open practice session to get to grips with their new sidecar around the circuit. The exhibition race was scheduled for 3 p.m. the following day, and according to Brad and Chip, ticket sales had been moving along at a fairly good clip. And with the first episode of the show due to air on TV that same evening, there was hope amongst the organisers of a last-minute rush on tickets as well.

"Oh, I think I'm having a cheeseburger baby," Stan moaned, after lunch, running a paternal hand over his swollen belly as they rode in the back of a taxi towards the racing circuit. "I should've gone back up to the room for a lie-down after eating that lot."

"It was good, wasn't it?" remarked Stella.

"I think they put half the bloody cow into it," Stan replied.

"I'm going back there later," Stella commented, brandishing a menu she'd acquired during their visit. "They do a thirty-two-ounce ribeye which I reckon has got my name written all over it."

Frank, who appeared to be suffering from meat sweats if his glistening forehead was anything to go by, waved away the idea. "For me, I think it's a brisk walk and a salad for tea tonight," he advised.

Upon arrival at the racetrack, Stan started to panic, wondering if they'd perhaps arrived on the wrong day. "Uhm, today *is* just the practice session, isn't it?" he asked, climbing out of the taxi and concerned by the presence of hundreds of people milling about in the area of the exterior concourse.

"Well, the practice session has been advertised on the radio for the last week or two," the helpful taxi driver advised, holding his hand through the opened window as he waited for payment. "So I figure that's probably why they're here?" the man put forward, suggesting what might be described as the obvious.

Stan handed the driver some cash, still surprised by the volume of people congregating around, with some enjoying a beer, and others taking advantage of the food trucks (or some availing themselves of both, of course).

"Ooh, hotdogs," Stella remarked, her nose alerting her to their nearby presence. *"Now* we're talking."

Frank and Stan watched as Stella made a beeline towards the hotdog vendor. "Where the hell does she put it all?" Frank wondered aloud, still struggling to digest the huge lunch they'd consumed only thirty minutes earlier.

Stan extended a discreet finger, aiming it at a group of what appeared to be college-age kids, all of whom were busy being equally discreet as they worked on finishing their beers without being seen by any security personnel or other authority figures on hand. "Here, have a look at that," Stan said.

"Eh? What's that?" Frank said, directing his eyes where indicated. "Ah, they're only having a good time, Stanley," Frank offered, casting Stan a mildly disapproving look. "Don't tell me you didn't snaffle a few sneaky underage beers in your time."

"Rather more than a few, Frank," Stan answered. "But I don't mean that, silly. Check out their t-shirts," he clarified.

"Their t-shirts? Why do I..." Frank began. "Wait, that's us!" he was delighted to report, grinning from ear to ear. "Some of them have got images of our mugs on their shirts, Stan." Frank stared over at the group longer than was probably advisable, bearing in mind their young age. "I see they've also got ones with Dave and Monty on them, and some featuring the Big Blue Boiled Sweet," he fondly observed.

"Eh, let's move on, shall we?" Stan suggested, aware that the teenagers were now looking back in their direction. But they didn't need to walk too far to discover where the group's t-shirts had originated. Outside the main venue, near the food vendors, were positioned a half-dozen or so stallholders selling all sorts of motorsport-related merchandise, t-shirts included.

Frank and Stan approached the closest stall in wonderment, amazed to see their faces staring back at them in printed form on some of the goods for sale. "They've even caught my eyes perfectly," Stan noticed, already reaching for his wallet.

"Hey, guys, what can I get for you?" the plucky vendor asked, sensing an easy sale.

Stan ran his eyes around all the items on offer, counting no less than five different products with his likeness on them. Why he wasn't receiving any royalty payments for this was perhaps a question for another day. For now, he was just delighted to be so highly thought of.

"Yes, my good man," Stan offered, pointing an inquiring finger towards the t-shirt selection. "I see you have separate images of both Frank and Stan."

"Great. Which ones do you want, and what size?" the chap asked, fidgeting with his money belt.

Stan couldn't resist a devilish smile. "I just wondered which one was more popular out of the two designs?" he asked, throwing a sideways glance at Frank.

The seller tilted his head, as this was an unusual question and one he'd not encountered so far. "Which is most popular?"

"Yessir," Stan confirmed.

"Hmm, I'm not sure," the fellow replied with a shrug. "I don't think I've really kept track, to tell you the truth." The seller, as polite as he was, didn't seem so certain of making a sale as he'd initially been, and peeked behind Stan and Frank to see if there were perhaps any other customers waiting to be served, customers who might be more inclined to spend some actual money, as opposed to just standing there asking questions.

But Stan pressed on, as this was clearly important to him. "Yes, which designs have you sold more of today?" he asked. "The ones with Frank on the front, or the ones with Stan?"

The seller was about to tell Stan to step off to the side when he spotted a wad of notes in his new friend's hand. "Hmm, well I guess I'd have to say this one," he replied, perking up again as he pointed to a t-shirt with Frank's image on it.

"Ha!" Frank offered smugly. "These Americans are no fools, Stanley."

"Just how many are we talking about, sir?" Stan asked, peeling one of the notes out of his hand, ready to skew the results more in his favour.

"I'm not certain. I guess I've probably sold about eleven of him since I set up shop here."

"Eleven! And what about the other image?"

"Uh... maybe one? Or possibly two?"

Stan shook his head in disbelief. "No accounting for taste," he said with a sniff.

"So, anyway. You wanna buy something, or...?"

"Do I get a discount for being on the shirt?" Stan asked. "Because that's my face on there."

"Is it?" asked the seller. "Ah, I *thought* you looked kinda familiar. Anyway, dude, sorry, but it doesn't matter if you picked the cotton and constructed the shirt yourself, you know? A guy's gotta put bread on the table. So I don't really give discounts, is what I'm saying, since my profit margin is slim enough as it is, unfortunately."

"Oh," said Stan, his ego somewhat deflated.

"Yeah, so..." the seller replied. "No offence, buddy, but do you want one or not?"

"Yes please," Stan answered.

"That'll be twenty bucks, please," came the response, along with a shirt thrust Stan's way.

Stan examined the shirt. "But I don't want *this* one," he said with a laugh. "Why would I want one with *Frank's* image on it?"

Frank cocked his head. "Eh? Well, why would you possibly want one with your *own* image on it? Is that not even weirder?"

Stan handed the t-shirt back across the countertop. "Be that as it may. But I'd like one of the versions with *my* face on it."

"How many?" the seller cheekily asked, neatly folding up the shirt that Stan had just unfolded.

Stan considered the question for a moment. "I'll take twelve," he settled on eventually.

"Twelve?" the seller asked, spirits instantly raised again now that it became clear he would be able to put plenty of bread on his table. "You want to buy twelve?"

Stan counted out the required amount of cash. "Yes I do, sir! And if anybody else asks which of the designs is most popular... well, you'll know the correct answer."

The cash was gratefully received by the seller, and twelve t-shirts were duly distributed to the customer. "It's a good thing you didn't ask me how many shirts I sold with that *other* guy's face on it," the man remarked.

"The other guy?" Stan replied. "You mean Frank? My good friend here?" he asked, indicating his mate beside him.

"No, I mean that funny guy with the cravat. Because I'm completely sold out of everything that has him on it."

"Come on, Frank. I think our business is done here," Stan insisted, taking up his goods and bustling off.

***

By the time they'd found their seats inside the mahoosive racetrack, Stella had already polished off several hotdogs she'd purchased, along with a good portion of the three-pint stein of strong Bavarian lager she was carrying with her. But she'd not forgot about her travelling companions, offering them a single packet of dry roasted peanuts that she'd recovered from the darkest recesses of her handbag, with strict instructions that the peanuts were to be shared between them.

For the main event the following day, Dave had secured VIP pit passes for them all to enjoy the action from the trackside.

But, for now, they'd need to slum it up in the cheap seats which, in their favour, did offer a rather spectacular bird's eye view of proceedings.

"Monty wasn't wrong when he said this place was huge," Stan remarked. He was just about to open the packet of nuts Stella had given him as he said this, but decided against it, with neither he nor Frank having any more room for food at this point. "You'd probably get about twenty of our Jurby racetrack in here," Stan observed.

"Oh, and then some," Frank agreed.

The oval-shaped track, one point five miles in length for each lap, truly was an impressive affair. And in addition to the main circuit, there were also several infield tracks and even a drag strip. It was no surprise to anybody that this place was regularly packed out with eighty thousand petrolheads craving their fix of horsepower, drawing racers in from all over the planet.

Indeed, having done some research, Dave and Monty were eager to test their racing skills in this striking theatre. And while they had every confidence in their own abilities, there were two slight hurdles they'd need to overcome. The first was that they'd not personally prepared the machine they'd be racing on, which was not ideal. And the second was that the circuit, designed for auto racing as opposed to bikes, was banked at about twenty degrees in the turns and up to twelve in the straights. And while this resulted in perhaps a less challenging course, overall, than they were used to, it was simply an experience neither of them had previously encountered or were accustomed to.

"There they are," Frank pointed out, giving Stan a nudge.

Stan squinted his eyes. "Which one?" he asked, unsure, as the swarm of sidecars coming out onto the track appeared like toy motorbikes from their seats up in the gods.

"Second from the back, Stan. You can just make out the yellow splodge on the front."

"Oh, yes. There they are," Stan answered, waving, for some strange reason, as if Dave and Monty could possibly see them.

"Someone's pointing at you, Stan," Stella said, aiming the last of her hotdogs towards the fellow in question. "Stan!" she said, competing against the sound of the revving engines way down below, as even from this distance they were loud. "Someone's *pointing* at you."

"They are? Who?" he asked, squinting his eyes even squintier in order to get a better look at the track down yonder.

"Not there. *There*," Stella advised.

"What? But I *am* looking there," Stan answered, still looking there, but not the *correct* there.

"There!" Stella shouted in frustration, as Stan continued to look the wrong way, completely oblivious to the hotdog she was so helpfully aiming. "The big unit coming up the *steps*, Stanley," Stella indicated. "The bloke who's as wide as he is tall."

"Oh," said Stan. "*Oh*," he said again, as he was now seeing, at last, who Stella had been referring to. "Do you think maybe he wants an autograph?" Stan asked, smiling nervously at Frank after getting a proper look at the fellow in question.

Frank had a sly glance over. "Oh, he's coming up, Stan. And with the bloody size of him, I'd be inclined to give him what he wants, whatever that might be."

The large gentleman, wearing faded denim shorts and a well-worn t-shirt with an image of an articulated lorry on the front, struggled up the long, steep set of steps, stopping partway to wipe a steady stream of sweat from his brow. "Stan, it's me!" the fellow shouted over.

"Help me, Frank," Stan implored. "He looks a bit angry."

"I think he's struggling to breathe, rather than angry," Frank countered. "Wait," he then added. "Is that not..." he said, shielding the sun from his face for an improved view. "Stan, is that not Tank?"

Stan scrunched down a bit in his seat, almost like he was trying to take cover behind Stella, which in fact he was. "Don't be bloody stupid, Frank. What on earth would..." he started to say. But, then, "Hang on, Frank. I think you're correct."

And Frank *was* correct. Because the girthsome chap slowly heading their way was none other than Tony Murphy, an ardent fan of and regular visitor to the Isle of Man TT. Aged fifty-seven going on twenty-one, Tank, as both his friends and enemies affectionally called him, had been a regular at the TT for much of his life. Indeed, such was his devotion to the isle's Tourist Trophy races that Frank had previously suggested to Brad and Chip that they really ought to keep him in mind for inclusion into any future series episodes.

Frank and Stan had first crossed paths with Tank and his friends during an impromptu and rather boozy session in the beer tent at the TT grandstand area, several years back, a session which had culminated in Tank and Dave engaging in a bout of topless wrestling. The victor on the evening in question hadn't been clear, but the drunken crowd who were on hand to witness it did appear to appreciate the unusual, unexpected spectacle.

"What the hell are you doing here?" Frank asked, rising up out of his seat to greet their guest. He then offered Tank a hearty embrace, which wasn't exactly an easy thing to do given Tank's overall circumference.

"I know, what are the chances, right?" Tank responded. He took several deep breaths to regain proper function of his lungs, and then several more. "One of the drivers at the truck depot is getting married," he continued, pointing to the articulated lorry on his t-shirt with the phrase WANNA COME FOR THE RIDE OF YOUR LIFE? printed invitingly underneath it.

"Ah, a boozy stag do," Stan remarked. "And what better venue than Las Vegas?"

"It's actually a hen do," Tank revealed, with a what-can-you-do sort of shrug. "Irene is actually the driver that's getting married, and she somehow convinced me to attend. Honestly, guys, you think drunk blokes are a rowdy bunch? Well, *this* lot are on another planet."

Frank puffed out his cheeks in sympathy, letting out a heavy exhale. "You're a braver man than I am, Tank," he said.

With his heart rate now away from critical and moving back towards normal levels, Tank spotted Stella's excessively large beer mug, regarding it with thirsty, longing eyes. "I don't suppose I could...?" he asked, pointing first to the mug, and then to the stream of sweat still running down his cheeks.

Stella looked at her oversized stein, with perhaps a mouthful or two of its contents remaining, all backwash at this stage and hardly worthwhile for anyone else to wish to drink. "Five bucks," she said without too much thought.

"Done!" Tank immediately agreed, reaching for and retrieving his wallet. With the transaction swiftly concluded, Tank polished off the rest of Stella's beer in short order, wiping the froth away with the back of his hand. "I couldn't believe it when I heard you lot were in town," a now-refreshed Tank said. "So I checked Monty's Facebook page and read that they were practising here all day, which is why I'm present."

"And to escape from the hens for a while?" Frank ventured.

Tank raised his empty mug to toast that point. "Yep. Amen to that," he joked. "I saw you and Stan down on the concourse before and tried to catch you up."

"That about half an hour ago?" Stan asked, wondering if Tank had lost his way.

"Twenty-two stone of prime Oldham beef doesn't move too quickly in the Las Vegas sun, I can tell you that," Tank advised. "But as good as it is to see you both, there's a reason I wanted to catch up with you."

"You haven't found Stan's suitcase, have you?" Frank joked, receiving a vacant expression in return, as obviously their friend Tank was clueless about that. "Never mind. You were saying...?"

"Well, we're staying in a really swanky hotel," Tank offered. "And you'll never guess who's also staying there."

"Tom Jones?" Stella chipped in, appearing interested for a moment.

"Ehm, no, not Tom Jones. At least not that I know of," Tank replied. "Is he even still alive?" he wondered aloud, before shifting his attention back to Frank and Stan. "No, it's your *best mate*," he told them, in a tone suggesting he wasn't perhaps actually talking about their best mate.

"Our best mate?" Frank asked, looking puzzled. "Who would that be?"

"The little twerp."

"Little twerp? Not Rodney Franks?" Stan suggested.

Tank nodded his humungous head. "The very same! One of the single girls on the hen do even tried it on with him, without much success."

"Oh dear. You didn't have the pleasure of socialising with him, did you?" Frank asked.

"Good lord, no. After what I know about Rodney Franks, and especially from everything you've told me about him, I wouldn't urinate on him if he was on fire. But I was drinking nearby in the hotel bar last night when him and his boys returned wearing the most peculiar white suits, really odd, like they were something fifty years out of date."

Frank and Stan both chuckled to themselves.

"Anyway, I overheard our Rodney carrying on about you lot," Tank continued. "And boy was he pissed!"

Frank rubbed his hands in delight. "Yes? Keep talking," he encouraged.

Tank's jolly expression hardened. "No, what he was talking about was no laughing matter, Frank," he advised gravely. "Now, granted, he'd downed a couple of glasses of fizz, mind you, so it might have been the alcohol talking, but..."

"Will you just spit it out!" Stella snapped. "Honestly, how long does it take to tell us?"

Having not met Stella previously, Tank didn't know how to respond to her. He decided it best to simply forge ahead. "Erm, yeah, anyway, the long and the short of it is that Rodney was furious, telling his racers the whole world would be watching, and that under no circumstances were they coming in second place to... well, that's actually when he descended into a prolonged, expletive-laden tirade directed towards you lot. It was rather impressive in its vulgarity, actually."

Stan didn't appear overly concerned by this. "It's good of you to share this with us, Tank. But it's really nothing he hasn't already said to our faces," he said. "Several times, in fact."

"No, this is bad," Tank pressed on. "Really bad. He was telling Jack and Andy that he'd give them an additional bonus if Dave and Monty didn't finish the race!"

"*What?*" Frank said, aghast. "What the hell is *that* supposed to mean?"

Tank shrugged. "I dunno, but I thought I'd better come right over and tell you. Because whatever he meant by it, it sure didn't sound good."

Frank patted Tank on the arm. "Thanks, mate," he offered, turning to look wistfully at the sidecars circulating out on the track, down below. "We've both, Stan and myself, had a bad feeling about this exhibition race. But that *bad* feeling is starting to turn into a bloody *awful* feeling."

Chapter
NINETEEN

I f Clifford Tanner wasn't the successful head of a major TV network, he'd likely have been just as comfortable as a carnival barker, or perhaps promoting boxing matches. And that wasn't an insult or a slur on his personality. Far from it, in fact. Rather, it was just a reflection that Clifford was simply an excellent showman and, as a result, his marketing team were also masters of their craft.

As such, wherever you looked around Las Vegas, promotional videos for the new docuseries were playing on every available advertising screen, along with posters and placards and such on view at every turn and on every available surface. And one could only assume that the network had arranged similar large-scale ad campaigns in other key US cities as well, such was their desire to have a smash-hit programme on their hands. It was only after seeing how much effort had obviously been invested into the promotion that one might begin to wonder just how much it all actually cost.

Indeed, both Frank and Stan struggled to comprehend how Clifford and crew could have gone to all the trouble of renting a particularly large racing circuit at presumably eye-watering expense, and then casually throwing in a $50k incentive for the winning team as well. But when Brad advised that the exhibition race had sold over forty-thousand tickets at sixty bucks a pop, things started to make financial sense, as far as recouping that huge investment. Especially when you factored in the revenue that was sure to be had from the massive food and drink sales, along with the purchase of a vast array of licenced merchandise – caps, badges, key rings, coffee mugs, t-shirts, et cetera – all of which would generate a certain percentage for Clifford and the gang, with NBC Boston taking their suitable cut of the proceeds. And when you had silly plonkers like Stan, who were willing to buy twelve overpriced items at a time, that certainly didn't hurt matters either.

And then there was the principal reason for the network's generous budget, and that reason was of course to simply raise awareness. If they wanted to sell prime advertising slots for the commercial breaks, or even rake in serious cash by broadcast syndication, selling the rights to other TV distribution channels globally, then that proposition was significantly more attractive when you had a tremendous hit on your hands. Which, fortunately, certainly appeared to be the case, if the early interest being shown was anything to go by.

Meanwhile, after the exhibition race's practice session had concluded for the day, the first episode of the new show was to be broadcast across the nation to the general public, at slightly staggered times, depending upon what time zone folks should find themselves in. So, following a bite to eat at Stella's now-favourite restaurant, For Pete's Steak, Frank and co headed to a nearby sports bar to watch the initial episode for a second time. Although, as they had already seen it previously, Frank and Stan ended up spending most of the time watching the other punters in the pub rather than the screen, hoping to gauge their reaction. And if a crowded pub packed with sports-mad Americans were largely ignoring the football game being shown on a number of the screens, in favour of watching *Isle of Man TT Aces* on the other available screens instead, then it was a good barometer that the audience very much liked what they were seeing.

Of course, for Frank and the others, having the TT course literally on their doorstep, it was perhaps a bit easy to become a little jaded as to just how unique and special an event the TT really was. But if any reminder were required, they simply had to enjoy the astonished reaction of the crowd in the sports bar who were appreciating it for the first time, rather like the captivated Runcorn lads featured in the show itself.

However, even though spirits in the camp were generally high, it was obvious from their demeanour that Frank and Stan perhaps had something on their minds.

"Everything all right?" Dave asked, when he noticed the two of them had shifted their attention from watching the crowd at the pub and were now focussing on staring at him instead.

"Ah," Frank responded. "So, ehm… are you and Monty feeling any better?" he said, swirling around the remnants of beer in his nearly empty glass, easing into a bit of small talk first and not really coming to the point just yet.

Dave considered Frank's question, tilting his head like he was emptying water from his ear. "Well, I reckon I do still feel a bit seasick," he advised, which was slightly ironic considering they were still a fairly good distance away from the nearest ocean (not to mention Dave, being from an island and quite used to the sea, never really got seasick anyway). "I suppose we're just not used to racing on a banked circuit, Frank. It makes you feel a bit woozy, like you've been drinking whisky on a rollercoaster."

To underscore Dave's analogy, Stan aimed a finger at Monty, who was presently making his way back from the bathroom. Despite not a drop of alcohol having passed his lips (as he and Dave were abstaining ahead of the big race held the following day), Monty's gait was curiously lopsided, as if one leg were shorter than the other, giving the impression he was about to keel over at any moment. "Maybe we should give Monty a hand?" he said, half-joking. "He looks like the Leaning Tower of Pisa."

However, aside from a bit of wobbling, Monty did manage to make it back to their table relatively intact, without the need for any assistance. "Uhm…" Frank offered a moment or two later, staring now at both Dave *and* Monty.

"Everything all right?" Monty asked, same as Dave had done.

"Uhm... the thing is... well, you know how the two of you are... ehm, tomorrow, that is... how you're..."

Stan raised a hand, indicating he was going to pick up where his friend had so eloquently left off. "This sidecar race... well, the fact of the matter is... erm..." Stan started to say, but then falling by the wayside, just as Frank had.

Stella shook her head in dismay, throwing the contents of her glass straight down her gullet. "You!" she said to Stan, now that her throat was well lubricated. "Go and get this replenished!" she barked, passing him her empty glass. Then, turning her firm gaze towards Dave and Monty, "And *you* pair," she said. "The Soppy Bollocks Brothers here don't think you should be risking your necks racing in this shitshow tomorrow."

"I'll, ah, just go and get the drinks in," Stan remarked, rapidly leaving Frank to answer the inevitable follow-up questions.

However, after Stan had left, Stella decided she wasn't quite finished speaking. "And for once, I have to agree with them," she continued, raising a knowing finger. "And I'll tell you why, yeah? Because Rodney Franks and those two miserable sods racing for him are not to be trusted. You mark my words. They're what's known in the taxi trade and elsewhere as *wrong'uns*. And aside from that, don't for a moment think that any of these TV people currently fawning over you gives a rat's ass about either of you, okay? Because the moment you're not the flavour of the month or you don't make them any money, they'll all drop you like a hot spud."

Frank sat there with his mouth wide open, like he was trying to think of something else to add. "You know," he eventually offered, "I don't think I could have put that any better than Stella."

"That's because Stella is spot on," Dave was happy to agree, throwing Frank off track with his confirmation. "And anything you're thinking about this stupid race? That's only what me and Monty have been thinking since we arrived here."

"So you're not going to race?" Frank asked hopefully. "I mean if you both think that way, you'd be daft to, right?"

Monty looked across the table to Stella. "Thank you for looking out for us," he said with a friendly wink. "The TV work is just a bit of fun, and we'll milk that cow while people want to watch us," he went on, addressing the larger group now. "But we both know the moment that stops, then it'll all come crashing down. That's why we're happy to cash their cheques while we can. To be clear, Chip and Brad have been nothing but good to us. But we know that what's popular today doesn't mean it is tomorrow."

"A tough industry. And the public is fickle," Dave suggested. "But this race tomorrow, Frank? We can win it. Genuinely, we can win it."

Frank appeared unconvinced. "I thought you said this replica sidecar was slower than yours back home. So...?"

Dave spotted Stan returning from the bar and drained his glass of Coke in anticipation of its impending replacement. "It is slower, Frank. Quite a bit slower, in fact," he told Frank.

"And the suspension is like a bouncy castle," Monty pointed out. "However, if ours is like that then it's a safe assumption that Rodney's team is faced with the same shortcomings. After all, we've been told that they've all been built to the same spec, which appears to be the case from the rather average speeds we witnessed during the practice session today."

"The other sidecar teams invited to participate?" said Dave. "They're all competent racers. But, without being big-headed, I don't know if they're going to pose any real challenge for the top step, from what I could see. And in the case of Thomas and Napier, while me and Monty are used to riding with slower engines and sloppy suspension, Andy and Jack definitely aren't. You see, they've been spoiled by the quality of the expensive, fine-tuned machines they're used to racing on. Granted, they're talented riders, that's for sure. But throw in the banked track, which they're not used to either, and a slower machine, and I'd say that the advantage is with us."

"It's a bit like Manchester United having to slum it, playing a cup tie on a swampy pitch in the arse end of nowhere," Monty suggested. "It rarely ends well for them."

Stan placed the tray of drinks down on their table, finally making his way back. "Sorry for the delay, folks, but I just got nabbed. I was recognised by a few ladies at the bar, and they each wanted to take some selfies with me," he explained. "They told me they loved my English accent," he added, looking back to his gaggle of adoring fans. "Anyway," he said to Monty and Dave. "About this race. How about we just forget all about it, and head to the nearby waterpark instead, yeah? I hear they've got some wonderful slides that—"

Dave gently interrupted Stan, taking hold of his and Frank's hands, offering them both a sincere smile. "I know you're worried," he said, giving their fingers a squeeze. "But we'll be fine."

"We'll be fine," Monty added, placing his hand on top of the pile. "No unnecessary risks, we promise."

"Oh, for fucksake, you lot," Stella said, adding her own hand to the already crowded stack. "Ride carefully tomorrow," she said, giving Dave and Monty a scowl. "While you might be a couple of bellends, you're *my* pair of bellends, yeah?" she remarked. Stella then glanced down at her watch. "Oi, we're going to have to down these drinks," she advised.

"Oh, is that the time already?" Stan said, happy to down his gin and tonic in one. "And you know where you're going, Stella?"

Stella offered a thin smile. "Oh, I *certainly* know where I'm going, Stanley. You just make sure you're ready with the camera!"

***

Frank, Stan, Dave, and Monty watched and waited. Along with dozens of others, they'd been standing there for about twenty minutes or so, having arrived early to obtain a primo viewing spot for the world-famous, massive fountain display. Although, unlike the others who were patiently waiting, our group had assembled for a slightly different reason.

"I don't know about this," Stan said, reading one of the many warning notices strategically placed at regular intervals around the huge landmark. "Stella does know that this is completely illegal, doesn't she? Not to mention dangerous, according to the warning signs. She could drown."

Frank scratched his chin, appearing uncertain about any of Stan's points. "Now you mention it, Stan, I'm not sure she does," he said.

Dave leaned in closer, having been listening in. "I reckon she doesn't," he offered. "You see, just before we left her, she made a remark to me about how surprisingly *empty* the fountain's pool looked to her. I thought she was only joking, so I didn't comment either way."

"How will we know when she's going in?" Monty asked, surveying the area.

"I suspect you'll see security guards sprinting in from every direction and hear horrified gasps from the crowd," Frank suggested. "And then you'll know."

However, five or ten minutes later and there was still no sign of activity they could notice. And while Frank and Stan were always supportive of Stella, happy to see her try and fulfil her dreams (such as, in this case, swimming naked in famous hotel fountains), they couldn't stop themselves from thinking that this wasn't just a *bad* idea, it was an absolutely *ridiculous* idea.

"So, if Stella doesn't think it's illegal and ill-advised, necessarily, then why is she sneaking about like a cat burglar?" Monty wondered aloud.

Dave raised a finger, suggesting he knew the answer to this question as well. "Apparently, she'd spoken to a bloke in the café back at home who was under the impression you could swim in the fountains, but it cost you a fortune to do so. You know how you always meet the wisest owls in your local greasy spoon."

"And that's why Stella thinks it's legal, although expensive, to swim in the fountains?" Frank queried. "Because some bloke in the café told her so?"

"Yep," said Dave, leaning on the railings, simultaneously anxious and yet intrigued by what he might shortly witness emerging from the shadows.

Stan gave a tug on Frank's arm. "Come on, Frank," he said. "We're going."

"Going where?" Frank asked. "We've got a cracking spot to watch the display."

But Stan was insistent. "We're going to stop Stella from getting herself arrested, Frank. That's where we're going."

"Yes, but..." Frank answered, not yet entirely willing to give up his prime viewing spot.

Conscious the spectacle could start at any minute, Stan urged further. "Come *on*, man," he said, looking over to the side of the magnificent hotel, back in the direction of where they'd parted company with Stella earlier. "If we hurry, we might be able to stop her from getting locked up."

However, raised voices in the vicinity suggested that their rescue mission might, unfortunately, be too late. Hearing something of a rumpus, Frank looked through the railings, worried he'd soon be greeted by the vision of Stella's naked form taking a swan dive (or belly flop, as the case might be) into the fountain's large pool of water. But there was nothing. Or at least not yet. "Where's that noise coming from?" he asked.

But the answer to that particular question was about to become abundantly clear, as...

"Stop her!" yelled an urgent, authoritative voice. Up ahead, the crowd of people on the busy sidewalk parted ways, leaving a narrow gap through which Stella, wearing only her skimpy underwear and boots, the rest of her clothes tucked under her arm, came sprinting through, huffing and puffing. How she was still wearing her boots if she'd already stripped down to her underwear remained unclear.

Trailing behind her, several security guards were in hot pursuit, although they appeared to be losing ground despite their obvious exertion.

Frank and Stan pressed themselves up tightly against the metal railing, mindful that getting in Stella's way would be like getting struck by a herd of stampeding bison.

"You know..." Stan remarked as Stella hurtled past, with Stella appearing in imminent danger of being knocked out by her own unruly breasts. "You know, for a lady of a generous build she can't half move when she needs to."

"You're not wrong, Stanley. The way she's powering through puts me in mind of Jonah Lomu in his prime."

Chapter
TWENTY

The day of the exhibition race...

"Excuse me! Hello! Mr Sidcup, sir? Hello!"

A daydreaming Stan walked through the hotel lobby, completely oblivious to the receptionist doing their best to attract his attention.

"Oi," Frank said, giving Stan a gentle nudge, "I think one of the hotel staff is wanting to speak with you."

The lobby was jam-packed with new arrivals pausing to check in, all lined up like famished school kids waiting in the lunch queue. "Me?" said Stan, looking through the crowd to the receptionist Frank appeared to be indicating towards. But all the fellow was doing at the moment was merely smiling in their general direction. "Can't be," Stan told Frank, before turning to continue on his way.

"Mr Sidcup! Hello, sir!" the persistent staff member shouted, now out of his seat and leaning over the counter, waving furiously in hopes of catching Stan's eye or ear. As a result, the waiting guests all pivoted round, wondering who this Mr Sidcup person could possibly be.

"I'm telling you, Stan, the receptionist *really is* shouting your name," Frank insisted. "Look."

"But what could they want from me?" Stan asked, still not convinced, for whatever reason, that it was him they were after.

"It's probably to tell you off for all that dodgy porn you've been watching in your room!" Stella put forth, loudly enough for the majority of the lobby to hear. "Or the state of your bedsheets because of it!"

"I have *not* been watching porn in the hotel room," Stan said in protest, offering an embarrassed smile to those judgemental guests watching on. "Frank, will you tell her that I've not been watching porn in our room?"

Frank took a strategic step to his left, while looking over his shoulder, giving the impression he had absolutely no idea who this Frank chap was that the pervert next to him was talking to.

"I've not been watching anything in my room other than an instructional video on how to play baccarat!" Stan said for the benefit of anybody still listening. "And my bedsheets are *immaculate*," he added, marching through the small army of guests with his head held high, giving the impression he had absolutely nothing to be ashamed of. "You wanted to speak with me?" Stan whispered upon his arrival at the front desk, addressing Santiago, the chap Frank had been pointing out.

"Yes, sir," Santiago advised, flashing Stan a winning smile now that he was finally being acknowledged. "It's in regard to your missing luggage, Mr Sidcup. You spoke to me about it when you arrived?"

A knowing and relieved expression washed over Stan's reddened face. "It's about my missing *luggage*," Stan said loudly, over his shoulder, for the benefit of those standing behind him. "*Nothing* to do with the state of my bedsheets."

Santiago, for his part, didn't appear the least bit fazed. He worked in a busy Las Vegas hotel, so he had certainly seen and heard it all before. "That's good to hear, Mr Sidcup," he offered, before extending a helpful finger towards another section of the hotel lobby. "Anyway, you'll be pleased to know that a representative from the airline has arrived with some assorted articles of missing luggage. It appears that you weren't the only passenger to be separated from their suitcase, sir."

"Thank you, Santiago," Stan replied. "I'll be sure to go and retrieve my *missing luggage*," he added. Again, loudly enough that those standing around could clearly hear.

Stella was still chuckling happily away to herself when Stan rejoined them.

"Honestly, Stella," Stan admonished, "I was running around the Las Vegas Strip last night picking up the items of clothing you'd dropped amidst your great escape, and this is how you repay me?"

"Yeah, and my bra that popped off during my getaway still hasn't turned up," Stella remarked. "That's a mystery, isn't it?" she added, eyeing him with suspicion.

"What are you looking at *me* for?" Stan countered. "Knowing you, you probably took it off on purpose and threw it to one of the onlookers."

"Come on, you two," Frank interjected, playing dad to the two bickering children. "People are still looking over at us."

Fortunately, the queue for the airline employee was considerably smaller than the one for the hotel reception team.

"I'm Mr Stanley Sidcup," Stan announced, when he was motioned forward for his turn. "I believe you might have my missing property?"

The woman ran her finger down a checklist of names. "Ah, yes, Mr Sidcup, I do see your name here on the list. Please accept our apologies for the unfortunate situation," she offered, appearing genuinely sincere, although that was perhaps of little comfort to Stan at this late stage in the game. "Just a moment, please," she added, before spinning around to attend to the large pile of lonely luggage just behind her, checking the tags on each item as she searched for Stan's particular possessions.

"Stan," Stella whispered in his ear, as the airline lady continued her search.

But Stan was in no mood for Stella's antics, it would appear, as he didn't respond.

"Stan!" Stella whispered a little louder.

"Can't you see I'm busy, Stella?" Stan asked with a sigh.

"We go home tomorrow," Stella pointed out.

Stan turned to face her. "Yes, I know that. And...?"

"And you've already purchased enough clothes to keep you going, yeah?" Stella continued. "So you don't actually need your suitcase on this holiday anymore, do you?"

Stan rolled his eyes. "Of *course* I need my suitcase back, Stella. It's got my *belongings* in it."

Stella tapped the side of her head in a *think-about-it-for-a-minute* sort of way. "Stanley," she pressed on. "You've already said you've bought enough clothes to last you until you get home, so what's the point in taking your luggage back on the very last day of the holiday? It just means you're going to have to schlepp a heavy suitcase all the way home. My point is, the airline lost it in the first place, so let *them* hump it back for you."

Frank couldn't help but admire the logic. "You know, Stella, that's actually pretty clever," he noted.

"Here we are, Mr Sidcup," the airline rep said a moment later, with a particularly heavy-looking suitcase by her side. "I'll just need you to sign this form, if you please," she said, presenting her clipboard to him. "After that, you're good to go."

Stan took the pen but didn't appear to be in too much of a hurry to use it just yet. "Say, for example..." Stan began. "Say for example Mr Sidcup was unavailable. Then what would happen to his luggage? Hypothetically speaking."

"Uhm," came the confused reply. "Usually our passengers are very happy to receive their misplaced luggage."

"Just for the sake of argument, though," Stan pressed. "What would happen to it?"

The uncertain lady had to consider this for a moment before answering. "Hmm," she said. "Well, I imagine the airline would be obligated to return the property to the customer's home address."

Stan handed the clipboard back to her. "Marvellous," he said. "Because the airline lost my luggage, I couldn't change out of my stained chinos at the airport and I became a laughing stock," he advised, reliving that painful memory briefly. "So, under the circumstances, the least you can do is ship it back home for me."

"So, you're *not* signing for your luggage, Mr Sidcup?"

Stan shook his head. "No, ma'am. Mr Sidcup is not presently available."

***

The scheduled starting time for the exhibition race was three o'clock that afternoon. But when Frank, Stan, and Stella arrived by taxi just after twelve, it was already busy, and ridiculously so. The concourse where Stan had purchased his twelve t-shirts on their previous visit was teeming with motorsport fans eagerly handing over their cash for souvenirs of their visit, and the food vendors were also doing a roaring trade by the looks of things.

It wasn't just the official refreshment stands dishing out delicious items either. Because throughout the nearby jam-packed parking area, many of its occupants had arrived armed with their own portable grills, cooking up a treat, and filling the air with a tantalising aroma. And they were a fairly sociable bunch, these American motorsport enthusiasts, shooting the shit with each other (to use their vernacular), sharing a beer, and happy to invite anyone walking past to stop by for a hotdog and such and a friendly conversation. Indeed, such was the party atmosphere outside that one could easily assume this to be the reason they'd arrived in their thousands, rather than the main event later that afternoon inside at the track.

"Oh, yes," Frank said, inhaling deeply and filling his nose with the delightful smells. "You know, I watched a show about American football fans who put on social events before the game in the parking lot," he commented. "That's the way they say it over here, by the way. *Parking lots*. Anyway, I think they called these events tailgate parties, or something similar."

"Well whatever they call it, I reckon I like it," Stella advised, following her beak as it led them towards the parked vehicles.

And Stan was happy to be led. "Ooh, I think I just spotted one of my t-shirts," he said, puffing out his chest so all could appreciate his own recent purchase he was currently sporting.

It didn't take too far before they fell victim to the generous American hospitality. "How about some chicken?" a fellow with a ZZ Top-inspired beard asked Stella, as he attended to the grill resting on his truck's tailgate. "I've got wings, drumsticks, a few thighs, and more wings. You name it."

"I can't tell you how much I want some," Stella answered, wiping the drool off her chin.

"Cool. Coming right up, my dear. And what about your two buddies?"

"Greatly appreciated," Frank offered on both their behalf. "And very kind, too."

"Grab yourselves each a brewski from the cooler," the man suggested.

Stella dipped her hand into the ice-filled chest. "Bloody hell, I think I've died and gone to heaven."

The bearded chef worked his magic with the serving tongs, pressing down on the grilling meat, which angered the flames beneath. "Okay, grab yourselves a paper plate and dig in," he soon suggested, with the sort of contented smile that made it clear he was glad to be alive. "Hey, I love your shirt, there, buddy," he told Stan, having only just noticed the design printed on the front.

Stan waved away the compliment. "You can buy them outside the stadium," he was quick to advise. "Although I'd suggest haste, as I believe this particular design is selling *exceptionally* well."

"Thanks, I'll keep that in mind," came the cheerful reply. "You know..." the man added, bouncing his eyes between the image on Stan's t-shirt and Stan himself. "You know you kinda look like the guy on your shirt," he observed.

"That's because it *is* me," Stan proudly confirmed. "I'm Stan, and this is my good friend Frank."

Chef ZZ Top took a moment to register what he was being told, running his eyes over his guests enjoying his culinary fare. "You're sure? I mean, you're *the* Frank and Stan?"

Frank nodded. "Quite sure," he said.

"Ha! That's awesome! I love you guys," the man answered. Then, waving to his friend flipping burgers from the rear of his own pickup truck, "Randy, get your ass over here, buddy! You're not gonna believe who's eating my chicken wings," he said.

Considering the majority of folks in attendance that day were fans of the show, Frank and Stan were recognisable faces (even if, in some cases, recognising them took a moment or two). As such, they couldn't move more than two or three parking spaces before they received another beer thrust in their direction and the friendly offer of more grilled food. Of course, this was most welcome for the first hour or so, but after several or more beers, there was the concern that they wouldn't be able to remember much about the actual reason they were there.

Not that Stella minded, of course, as this car park was her utopia and she could quite happily have soaked up the generous hospitality for the remainder of the day. Nothing made her more pleased than to hold a good hunk of meat with one hand while washing it down with a nice cold beer held in the other. However, conscious that time was ticking on, Frank made the sad decision that they'd have to give up on the free food and drink to head inside the stadium.

"With the number of t-shirt recommendations you've thrown out, you should be on commission, Stanley," Frank commented, once they'd made their way clear of the parking area.

Stan placed a hand on his expanding belly. "After the amount of various barbecued delights I've just consumed, I'm thinking of heading over and buying another shirt the next size up," he remarked.

Stella offered the area they'd come from one further admiring glance. "We need to arrange one of those tailgate parties at the TT races. Because that's one of the finest things to come out of

America since Jason Momoa," she insisted. "Or at least it *will* come out of America once I export the idea," she said.

Stan examined the small map printed on the back of their VIP passes, hoping to locate the appropriate entrance. "Right. If my orienteering skills are on point, then I think that's it over there," he offered.

"Yeah, I think the burly security guards with dark sunglasses standing in front of a velvet rope might also be a clue, Stanley," Frank suggested. "Hmm," he added. "Looks as if most of the people using that entrance have smartened up for the occasion. You don't think there's a dress code, do you?"

Stan returned his attention to the VIP pass in his hand. "Not that I can see, Frank. But we're in trouble if there is, as we've all returned our rented suits. And my original suit, along with my suitcase, is hopefully en route to the Isle of Man by now."

Frank, Stan, and Stella then presented themselves at the VIP entrance. "Yes, how do you do," Frank said to the man-mountain who was defending the door against intruders.

The doorman lifted his sunglasses up on his forehead, looking the three of them up and down, and then down and up. "Can I help you?" he asked, clearly unimpressed by what he was seeing if the tone of his voice was any measure.

"We're VIPs," Frank replied, positioning a strategic hand over the bit of barbecue sauce that had landed on his t-shirt at the tailgating party, resulting in an unsightly splodge. To the security guard, it must have looked like Frank was placing his hand over his heart, swearing to tell the truth. "That is, we're team sponsors," Frank added, along with a hint of a smile, as if he were having his passport photo taken.

"And we're on the TV," a grinning Stan declared, pointing to his likeness printed on the front of his shirt, hopeful that this might expedite their entry inside. "You might recognise me?"

The doorman shook his head in the negative. "No," he said simply.

Frank lurched forward, intending to show the doorman the VIP pass secured around his neck by a lanyard.

"Whoa! Stay behind the rope!" the guard firmly cautioned, taking up an intimidating defensive posture, as he appeared to interpret Frank's abrupt movement forward to be some kind of hostile threat upon his person. "Better think about what you're doing, buster. That kind of aggression will get you nowhere," the man warned.

The air burst out of Frank's balloon in an instant. After all, the fellow standing in front of him looking decidedly annoyed was nearly seven foot tall and almost as wide at the shoulders. "No, I wasn't... that is, I would never..." Frank pleaded. "No, I was just showing you my VIP pass, that's all," Frank insisted. "Certainly no aggression on my part, I can assure you."

The doorman took hold of the pass that Frank had removed from around his sweaty neck. "This is yours?" he asked sceptically, looking first at Frank's casual attire and then at the laminated pass.

"Absolutely," Frank advised brightly. But not *too* brightly, as he had no wish to antagonise the man further and there was no telling what might set the large fellow off.

"It's a fake," came the terse reply.

"A fake?" Frank asked, confused. "It can't be. You see, we're in the television programme that this race is promoting," he explained, glancing back to Stan as he said this in hopes that Stan might back him up on this.

Stan took a timid step forward. "Over there," he said meekly, indicating towards a nearby surface. "Just there, on the wall. You can see a poster advertising the show in question. If you look carefully, you can see our faces on it."

The gatekeeper did as Stan had suggested, appearing neither convinced nor impressed, however. That is, right directly before he burst into a laugh that was just as large as he was. "I'm just messing with you guys!" he revealed, slapping a hand against Stan's shoulders that nearly launched him back to their hotel.

"You are?" Frank asked, unsure what was going on.

"Of course. I know full well who the two of you are," the man said, unlatching the rope and stepping to one side to grant them access to the entrance. "Now get yourselves in there and have a fabulous day, you hear me? And while you're at it, tell Dave and Monty to kick some serious ass, okay?"

"We'll do that, no problem," Frank cordially replied. "And the whole bit about the fake pass?" he added, grinning like an idiot. "It was very funny."

Once inside, Stella finally had something to say. "Oi, you two are the biggest pair of kiss-asses," she told them. "Honestly, *the whole bit about the fake pass was so funny*," she added, doing her finest impression of Frank. "You should have just kicked him squarely in the bollocks, like I would, and walked straight past him. Bloody wazzocks."

"Sadly, we don't possess your unique gifts," Stan offered.

"Yes, and come to think of it, where were you when we needed you, Stella?" Frank entered in, slightly offended that she'd remained silent the entire time they could've most used her help.

"Why? It was entertaining enough to sit and watch you two sorry muppets squirm," Stella replied, chuckling away.

Fortunately, there were no additional wannabe comedians inside the venue, only a helpful greeter by the name of Paisley. "Hi, there, folks, how can I help you?" she asked, radiating a professional charm.

"Hi, yes," Stan replied, handing his pass over for inspection. "Hopefully we're in the correct area?"

"Indeed you are," Paisley happily reported. "I'd be glad to show you through," she offered. "We'll just need to provide you with some safety equipment so you can access the pitside garages."

"So we're not just in the padded seats with a complimentary programme?" Stan asked.

Paisley checked Stan's pass again, just to be sure. "No, these grant you the most favourable access possible," she insisted. "Right in front of the action. So close you can almost touch it."

"My favourite place to be," Stan advised. "We're ready when you are."

Paisley guided the three of them through the VIP catering section, just in case the copious amount of grilled meat they'd already consumed hadn't quite been enough for them (though of course Paisley had no way of knowing what the trio might have eaten earlier). Then, in a cloakroom near the circuit entrance, fireproof jumpsuits were issued along with a safety briefing, including a detailed talk about trackside etiquette.

And once the appropriate insurance waivers had been signed, Paisley handed the group over to one of her colleagues to direct them to their allocated team garage.

"This place is staggering," Stan remarked, looking up to the packed-out viewing galleries where they had enjoyed the action the day before. There were many fine seats to be had, for sure, though none with the same enviable trackside view they were going to boast today, of course. "Do you think we need to get some of these pitlane garages installed at our Jürburgring back home? Oh, and perhaps a VIP banqueting area?" he said, his gaze back down at eye level.

Frank appeared to like that prospect, particularly the suggestion of a VIP banqueting area. "Tell you what, Stanley," he said. "The moment we can regularly attract over forty thousand paying customers to our racing circuit, we can then upgrade from our rusting burger van. Agreed?"

"Agreed!"

"And can I get one of these jumpsuits once we're back home?" Stella asked, apparently quite taken with her bright orange outfit. "They're actually quite comfortable."

Frank nodded. "Of course you can, Stella. We'll get one each," he said, half-distracted and wondering if they'd already walked past their allocated garage, despite no words to that effect from their guide. "What number garage are we looking for, Stan?"

"Lucky number thirteen, Frank. Which, by my reckoning, is that one there," Stan advised, indicating to the unit up ahead.

"Number thirteen, Stan?" Frank asked with a worried frown, suddenly grabbing Stan by the arm. "Oh, I don't like that. I don't like that at all."

Stella rolled her eyes. "You don't believe in all that bad-luck superstition claptrap, do you?"

"I'm with Stella," Stan agreed, in full solidarity. "All of that walking under ladders and such? It's all rubbish. Just nonsense designed to keep the masses distracted and complacent," he advised, sounding almost like he knew what he was talking about. "All we need is a positive mental attitude, and everything will turn out just fine."

However, after eventually being led to lucky garage number thirteen, they were greeted, once inside, with the worrying vision of Dave, covered in sweat and screaming like a banshee, about to beat his allocated sidecar with the handle of a broom.

"Now, I'm not in any way mechanically minded," Frank felt the need to point out to his two accompanying associates. "But unless I'm very much mistaken, that doesn't look like a sign or portent that all is well in camp number thirteen. Not at all."

Chapter
TWENTY-ONE

Brad and Chip, along with a good number of local media representatives, were in attendance for the day's race, all charged with capturing the racing action for a curious nation. Yes, early indications suggested the show the brothers had made, *Isle of Man TT Aces*, was well received so far. Even so, the sport of sidecar racing was popular among only a select group of hard-core fans in the US, while remaining relatively unknown by the mainstream audience. Of course, with Clifford and his fellow TV executives now being firm fans of both the Isle of Man TT and the sidecar classes in particular, this was something they hoped to rectify. There was a real desire that the viewing public would embrace this type of racing and take it into their hearts.

For the sports channel reporters and such on hand, their goal was to capture every twist and turn of the action out on track. Brad and Chip, for their part, however, were more about documenting the human story as they had done for their programme. And with talk of a second series in the offing, today's exhibition race would provide an ideal opportunity to capture raw footage of some excellent behind-the-scenes action, the type which often proved to be an even better source of real drama, in their experience.

In fact, having arrived at the garage shortly after Frank, Stan, and Stella, the twins didn't have too terribly long to wait for their first drama of the day...

"And how are preparations coming along, gentlemen?" Chip asked, as his brother Brad pointed their camera into the compact but well-appointed pit garage. "Twenty minutes to go until race time, in case you didn't know," he added helpfully.

"Do you want me to stick that camera up your..." Dave shot back, the handle of a broom raised up in the air, poised for an assault on his machine's bodywork, it would very much appear. But upon seeing it was the twins, and knowing they had a job to do, Dave lowered his bike-bashing instrument and forced out a smile. "Oh, hello, treacles!" he said, trying his utmost to present a cheerful face for the camera.

Sadly, Dave's quaint colloquial form of address sailed straight over the Freestones' heads. Undaunted, the two brothers nevertheless pressed on. They stepped past the others, making their way in, with Brad then zooming in on the sidecar bike, examining it for any damage from Dave's previous, suspected attack. The paint appeared to be undamaged, however, with Dave's recent aggressive stance merely meant to show the bike who was boss, it would seem.

"So, guys. Talk us through the challenges," Chip offered, hoping to generate some back-and-forth between them.

At this point, Monty emerged from underneath the bike, covered in a mixture of sweat, grease, oil, and brake fluid. Indeed, there were more unwanted fluids on Monty's face than you may expect to find on the floor of an Amsterdam peep show. "Gremlins," Monty advised, sitting himself up, and then using the back of his forearm to wipe away some of the muck from his forehead.

"Gremlins, Monty?" Chip queried.

"Yep. Gremlins," Monty confirmed, looking directly towards the camera as he'd been taught in his media training. Well, one eye was, at least. "We've been working on this little lady since four o'clock this morning, and were just starting to get there," he said. "The suspension is tight, the engine was purring like a kitten, but then those horrid gremlins showed up uninvited to the party."

"There's an electrical issue," Dave wearily explained. "And while you might have all the ingredients for a lovely cake, if you run out of baking powder you might as well bugger off back to the hotel and spend the afternoon by the pool."

Chip had a rough idea of what Dave was saying and just hoped future viewers would as well. "So, the bike isn't firing up?" he ventured, using his limited mechanical know-how.

Dave nodded, tightening his sausage-like fingers around the broom handle he was still holding onto. "Well, she *was*," he said. "Then she *wasn't*... Then she *was*... Then she *wasn't*..."

"Erm, can't you just swap sidecars?" Stan suggested from off to the side, a bit bravely, if Dave's angry expression was anything to be worried by. "Aren't there any spares?"

Dave knew Stan was just trying to be helpful. "No, mate, there aren't any spares," he said. "And even if there were, we've spent the last two days perfecting the set-up on this bike. If we tried to head out on that circuit on another machine, one that we'd not fine-tuned for this specific course, then we'd probably end up in the wall by the first corner."

Monty pointed his spanner towards Brad and Chip. "Can you have a word with someone and see if we can perhaps have a one-hour delay?" he asked. "That way, we may have time to work out what's causing the problem."

Brad, still recording, looked over the top of the viewfinder. "I don't think they'll do it, Monty," he put forth. "You see, some of the networks are broadcasting live, and their advertisers would probably go apeshit if there was any kind of delay."

"Even though we're meant to be the stars of the show?" Dave asked. "I mean, there must be something. Can't you get on your phone and have a word?"

"I can ask the question for you, sure," Chip volunteered. "But like Brad just said, I wouldn't really get your hopes up."

"Monty, let's have another look at those battery terminals," Dave suggested. "See if it could be something simple. You know, Occam's razor, and all that, yeah?"

Frank, Stan, and Stella were likely starting to feel like spare parts. With no technical knowledge to speak of, there was little value they could add to the discussion. As such, spotting a handy electric kettle in the corner (not a common sight in the US, but placed there earlier by a thoughtful Brad and Chip to make their tea-drinking friends feel at home), Stan set to work making the team a brew, ably assisted by both Frank and Stella as there wasn't much else for them to do.

"It's a no-go," Chip reported a moment or two later, holding up his phone to indicate that he'd made the call. "The exhibition race starts on schedule, guys. Sorry, I tried. I really did."

Monty replaced the seat unit, satisfied that everything in regard to the battery was as it should be. "Bugger!" he shouted, loudly enough to be heard over the thunderous roar of the other sidecars leaving the pitlane garages on their way to the start line. "Bugger me sideways!" he added for extra effect, making clear his frustration.

Just then, as if Dave and Monty's day couldn't possibly get any worse, an all too familiar silhouette appeared in the doorway, masked by the harsh sunlight behind it and yet still instantly recognisable. "Are you not coming out to play?" Rodney Franks asked with a sneer, already fully aware of their technical issues. "If there's anything I can do to help you boys, you know you just need to ask."

"Thanks for the kind offer, Rodney," Dave promptly replied. "If you'd be gracious enough to lie down on the concrete floor and position your neck just beneath my race boot? Then that should fix our electrical problem, I reckon, and get us right out of this little pickle."

"What have I told you about the pillow talk, Dave?" Rodney responded, along with a playful flourish of his hand. "Honestly, what will people think?" he said. "Anyhooo... I'd best leave you boys to your tinkering, as we've got a race to win."

Rodney then turned to leave, but like all good performers there was always time for a cheeky encore, it would seem. "Oh!"

he said, spinning round, a solitary finger thrust skyward. "It's a shame you won't be taking home that fifty grand prize money. But rest assured I'll make sure it goes to a good home. Namely, me. I was thinking about using that bit of dosh as a nice down-payment on a new yacht for myself. What do you think?"

Rodney waited for a few seconds. However, no response was forthcoming. "No? Ah, well. I'll be sure to invite you all to the launch party," he said. "Toodle-pip!" he added, this time turning to leave for real.

Brad and Chip weren't likely to openly admit it at this particularly fraught time, but they knew that the sort of angry exchange they'd just witnessed was precisely what the viewing public wanted. So, like two children at Christmastime, perhaps, staying up late in the hope of observing Santa in the act, they'd positioned themselves in the corner, saying nothing, keeping themselves under the radar while the camera continued to roll.

"The smug, cravat-wearing, smarmy little bastard!" Dave spat out, snapping the broom handle he was carrying over his knee as soon as Rodney had left.

"Maybe this is all a sign," Frank offered, hoping their present troubles might be the catalyst required for the lads to possibly reconsider taking part in the race. "Maybe this exhibition isn't for you two. Maybe it's just not in the cards, yeah?"

"What's this? Are you on about your unlucky number thirteen bollocks again?" Stella asked.

But Stan was quick to jump to his mate's defence. "Maybe it *is* a sign, boys. And to be perfectly honest, I've never had a good feeling about this particular race either. So why don't we just pack up, have a few beers, and watch the action trackside, yes?" Stan held his optimistic gaze for several seconds. Then, lowering his head a bit, he added, "Some things in life just aren't worth killing yourself over. Do you know what I mean?"

"Yeah, a beer does actually sound like a pretty good idea right about now," Monty agreed, climbing to his feet and resisting the urge to give the nearby toolbox a kick with his hoof. "Dave...? What do you reckon?"

But Dave was in a distant place if his distracted expression was anything to go by. "Killing yourself over..." he mumbled to himself, cryptically echoing Stan's words. "Monty, what if it's a faulty kill switch?" he then asked, lurching towards the sidecar.

"We've tested the kill switch, Dave. And then tested it again."

The kill switch the boys spoke of was a nuclear button, so to speak, which when kept in its normal 'ON' position completed an electrical circuit enabling all of the bike's electrical systems to function. During racing, a cord is tethered between the rider and the machine. If, in the unfortunate occasion where a rider is thrown clear, the dead man's switch releases via the cord, safely shutting down the engine functions, including the petrol pump. It was a similar system to those utilised by jet ski operators. After all, if you fell off your jet ski out at sea, you'd want your machine to come to a graceful halt nearby, as otherwise it could be a long swim back to shore. While these safety systems were a great idea in principle, there were occasions, as with anything electrical, when things didn't quite go to plan. And via the process of elimination, having checked absolutely everything else they could think of on the bike and exhausting all other possibilities, this remained the only working hypothesis that Dave was presently left with.

"Yeah, but what if the actual switch is knackered, Monty?" Dave offered. "I mean, we checked all the wiring to the switch, but did we check the physical switch *itself*? We know from experience that heat and vibration does them in over time, yeah? And it's bloody hot outside. Really hot. And who knows how many miles this machine had on it before Clifford Tanner got hold of it, right?" Dave said. "Quick, grab the tool kit and we'll remove the rubber housing and try and override it!"

Monty looked at the wall-mounted clock. "But, Dave, the race starts in a few minutes, mate. And even if that were the solution, there's no chance we could even attempt it and still get to the starting line in time. I hate to say it, mate, but I think the bloody electrical gremlins have well and truly shafted us on this one occasion."

***

The eager crowd, numbering just under forty-three thousand according to the stadium announcer, were in fine spirits. It might have been the prospect of seeing the bikes soon to be out on the track or the result of one too many beers at either the tailgating parties outside or the refreshment vendors inside. But whatever the case, and despite the venue still only being half-full, there was a deafening cheer when the machines eventually made their way out from the pit lane.

It was only when all of the sidecars lined themselves up on the grid, however, that the absence of one of them became apparent to those watching on. As one of the two quickest outfits in the practice sessions, and its riders also the stars of the television documentary series, Dave and Monty were meant to be sharing the front row with Andy Thomas & Jack Napier. However, that honour was now for Team Rodney Franks alone to enjoy.

Because Dave and Monty were popular real-life characters in the show, their participation had been hugely anticipated. It didn't, therefore, take too long before disgruntled murmurings began to spread. As such, the stadium announcer soon took to his microphone to explain the technical reason for the pair's absence, much to the audible disappointment of the Dave & Monty fan club contingent (of which there appeared to be many members present).

With one ear on the announcement, Rodney Franks was in the middle of his final, motivating speech, kneeling beside his two riders at the front of the grid. "Did you hear that?" he asked with a giddy grin, momentarily halting his team pep talk. "Those two sorry oafs can't even keep their sidecar running!" he said, unable to contain his obvious delight.

But, to be fair to Andy and Jack, professional racers as they were, they were quite looking forward to an on-track tussle with

Dave and Monty, now that they were, machinery-wise, playing on an equal playing field. It would pose an interesting challenge, and one they didn't shy away from. Still, the thought that their main competition for the prize pot was now completely out of the equation was likely some consolation to them.

A booming claxon sounded, giving the onsite safety marshals their cue to clear the area of sponsors, crew, media, friends, and general hangers-on from the grid. And they certainly operated a tight ship, because in next to no time the only thing remaining out on track was nine sidecars gently revving their engines to keep their vital fluids circulating.

Then, receiving the required approval from the chief marshal, Clifford Tanner stepped out of the pit area armed with a green flag to get the race underway. And it was evident from his broad smile that this was a duty he was honoured to undertake.

With the flag raised, engines were now screaming, champing at the bit and desperate to be unleashed onto the oval circuit. Clifford, standing well clear of the magnificent beasts, gripped the shaft of the flag in both hands, darting his eyes over to the grid, and then dropped the flag like he was chopping wood.

Racing was underway in Las Vegas!

There was nothing quite like the sound of pure horsepower to send a shiver down your spine and raise the hairs on your arms, as Clifford had noted previously. And here it was intensified by a factor of nine.

At the Isle of Man TT, races were a time-trial where riders were released onto the circuit at ten-second intervals, meaning your main competition was against the clock. As a result, you didn't often get to enjoy the short, circuit style of racing when several machines were grouped together for any length of time. But here, in Las Vegas, all of the sidecars were hammering it around on their first lap with barely the length of a flea's hind leg to separate them. And the resulting sound was like Thor using his mighty hammer Mjölnir to bring godly lightning and thunder down from the heavens and onto the raging battlefield below.

With his team slightly extending their lead at the start of the second lap, you'd think that Rodney Franks would be rather enjoying the occasion. But curiously, your assessment would be wrong. Because down in the pit area, he was incandescent with rage. Flailing his arms at the race officials so wildly that he looked like some angry, multi-limbed Hindu god (albeit a very small one), Rodney was certainly not loving life right about now. And the reason for his ire... well, that would be the blue sidecar with the yellow splodge, with its engine now gloriously restored to life, presently being eased out of its garage and out towards the starting gate.

"What the blue bloody blazes is going on here? What do you lot think you're doing?" Rodney demanded, marching from the safety of his current position in the direction of the nearest person wearing a high-viz jacket.

"Sir, step back behind the pit lane marker! *Now*!" came the firm, immediate response.

Rodney did as instructed — reluctantly, as he had no choice — turning to find someone else he could vent his anger on. And he didn't have to search too far before finding another unfortunate steward who really was in the wrong place at the right time. "How are those two buffoons allowed to join the race when they didn't start with the others?" Rodney asked, stamping his foot down onto the asphalt to show just how serious he was. "I mean this is just ridiculous, and I demand that they're both dragged back to their garage this instant!"

The steward, a handsome, twenty-something lad with ginger facial hair and slightly untidy eyebrows, was initially at a loss for words. "Umm..." he offered, as his brain took a second to catch up with his mouth. "Well, I think the team have overcome their technical issues," he said. *"So they're permitted to join as soon as it's safe to do so,"* he noted, successfully regurgitating the portion of their steward's safety handbook that was relevant to this particular situation.

But Rodney still wasn't happy. In fact he was furious. "This is *absurd*, and I *insist* they're immediately disqualified!" he said.

The young man offered the sort of look you'd get when you weren't quite sure if your pals were playing some sort of practical joke on you or not. "Uhhh... right. You do know this is just a friendly exhibition race, don't you?" he responded. "With emphasis on the word *friendly*?" he said, deciding to walk away while he could keep his hands by his sides. After all, he was saving for a new PS5 gaming console and didn't want to lose his job over having to punch this guy in the face.

Unfortunately for Rodney, his complaints would need to end there as his path to possibly find somebody else to pester and annoy was now blocked by a defiant-looking Stella, flanked by Frank and Stan on either side.

"Ah, don't you just *love* the smell of burnt Castrol drifting on the breeze," Frank commented, nostrils flaring as he took in the acrid but alluring scent. "And it was *awfully* decent of the organisers to let the boys out on track, don't you think, Rodney?"

Brad and Chip, standing a safe distance away but still within earshot, grinned from ear to ear. "You're still recording, bro?" Chip asked. "Please tell me you are."

"You know it, guy. I'm getting all of this," Brad assured him. "Jesus, Mary, and Joseph, these guys are like a freakin' cameraman's wet dream come true," he joked. "Honestly, we're going to have enough film in the can for a third series if this keeps up!"

Chapter
TWENTY-TWO

Dave Quirk wasn't built for the heat. As he liked to jokingly remark, he could easily break into a sweat from simply bending over to tie his shoelaces. As such, with Dave wearing thick racing leathers as his legs were splayed over a vibrating, race-tuned weapon under the brutal Las Vegas sun... well, as you can imagine, he was feeling a tad uncomfortable.

From his stationary position in the pit lane, Dave teased the throttle, waiting for the signal from the marshal which would then set him and Monty loose onto the imposingly unfamiliar banked circuit. Of course he was desperate to get out there for some racing action, but also for the cooler breeze that would arrive when you're travelling at speeds in the region of one hundred and fifty miles per hour.

Even with his ears muffled by his helmet and the throbbing of his own engine, Dave could still hear the racing pack approaching, making the earth rumble like a freight train roaring up the tracks. Instinctively, Dave looked across his shoulder, receiving a positive thumbs-up from his buddy in the sidecar passenger seat to his left.

With the last of the pack finally through, and after receiving the required prompt, Dave immediately set about applying the throttle and releasing the clutch. First, second, and third gear came all too quickly as the machine snaked away under acceleration, with the bike's fuel tank currently full and the tyres still cold. In the blink of an eye, he was in top gear, all thoughts of heatstroke forgotten and the thrill of racing coursing through his veins.

The stampeding herd Dave was now chasing was, he reckoned, about half a lap ahead of him on the track. However, because of the technical issues he and Monty had encountered, the other bikes were already two, possibly three laps into the race before he and his pal Mr Montgomery had even got going. It was a significant disadvantage they would somehow need to recover during the hundred-lap race around the 1.5-mile circuit, especially when you considered that Napier and Thomas were two of the finest riders to have graced the sport, and some of the other current racers were probably no slouches either.

Teams were able to keep a tally of completed laps using the trackside electronic scoreboard. With this, the various riders could, for instance, calculate when they would need to stop to take on additional fuel, often an important strategic decision on which races were won and lost.

Dave made little progress over his first few initial laps, just being grateful he'd not been overtaken by the others considering he wasn't yet up to proper race pace. But with each passing mile, he felt like he was definitely clawing back some ground.

To mix things up a little, the race organisers had implemented a chicane section on the course, the riders being diverted off one of the straightaways and onto a special infield section of track with a set of twists and turns placed into it. This more complex portion of the circuit, it was hoped, would enhance the viewing spectacle and, as Dave remarked at the pre-race scrutineering meeting, would give the passengers something to do other than have a nice snooze as they travelled around a strictly oval track. As such, Monty needed to keep his wits about him, knowing just when to spring into action, shifting his position (and weight) to ensure the machine was as stable as it could possibly be when travelling through corners at high speed. Of course, if he came back up from the confines of the sidecar too early, his bulky frame would act like a ship's sail, costing them valuable speed, too late, and they'd likely struggle to safely and correctly navigate the tricky chicane.

But, as always, Dave needn't have worried, at least where his good mate was concerned, because, after years of experience at the TT races, Monty was always on point, poking his head up and shifting his position right on time and with the agility of an Olympic gymnast. Indeed, by their own admission, the pair of them would likely struggle to run a hundred metres in less than an hour, yet throw them both on a motorised missile and they were athletes in the truest sense of the word.

As they pressed on, Dave tried to relax and calm his breathing but it was proving difficult. In addition to piloting a relatively unfamiliar craft (aside from the fine replica paintwork) around a banked circuit for the first time in race conditions, he had the additional worry of their electrical issues. Because, while from a distance the tarmac appeared as smooth as a baby's bottom, up close and personal and travelling at warp speed, it turned out to be anything but. The vibrations running through the handlebars made Dave's fingers scream in agony; however, it was the kill switch workaround that was causing him the most anxiety, as he suspected the issue may have been caused by such vibrations in the first place. And he knew that if their workaround, professional as it was, failed, then not only would their race be over for them but they'd also be stranded in the middle of an active racing circuit with the nine other machines in danger of ploughing straight through them.

Despite Dave's concerns, he noted the pack was starting to spread out, with the first of the backmarkers in the group now within spitting distance of Dave's own machine (though with the other teams still being several laps to the good). There was also the first sighting of the black-and-silver outfit of Napier & Thomas. Spurred on by this good news and the steady progress he was making, Dave was starting to get a bit more comfortable with the banked track, rather enjoying it in fact. Although this was a completely different experience to blasting around the Isle of Man TT, of course, where one minute you'd be roaring through villages, the narrow streets lined with houses on either side little more than an arm's length away, and the next going flat out over the mountain section with only rolling hills and wandering sheep for company. Here, by contrast, it felt to Dave like they were racing on a wide motorway, albeit an oval-shaped one.

On his eleventh lap, Dave approached the chicane again, dropping down the gearbox, leaving his brakes alone until the last possible second and easing past another machine in the process.

"Shit!" he screamed when it became apparent the brake pads hadn't been briefed about Dave's racing style, fading like nobody's business. Whether the pads were an inferior product or if it was simply the outrageous track temperature, the result was that he didn't quite have the stopping power he was used to on his own machine. Ordinarily, something as significant as this would be a major disadvantage, although he took some comfort in knowing the rest of the field were riding in exactly the same conditions, and likely with similar brake pads as theirs. Fortunately, after a frighteningly unexpected trip through the grassy overrun, there didn't appear to be any damage other than a temporarily reddened face and perhaps some soiling of Dave's underpants that would hopefully come out in the wash.

***

Unlike the Isle of Man TT where no scheduled pitstops were required in the three-lap sidecar class, here, racing over a longer distance, the outfits could stop for fuel as and when required. However, like Dave and Monty, most of the teams didn't have their own dedicated pit crew with them. As such, the organisers provided qualified mechanics to act as their extended team. And as it was billed as an exhibition race, there was no intense pressure to conduct a pitstop at breakneck speed as you would at, say, a NASCAR race on this same track.

Or so one would think, at least. Others, however, might have something else in mind...

Rodney Franks casually rose up from his seat in the trackside hospitality tent, where VIPs, sponsors, media, and any of the assembled bigwigs could watch the action on big screens (if they couldn't be bothered stepping outside) with a glass of something cold to pass the time. Rodney smiled at the hostess. "The loo?" he asked. "Ah, sorry. The bathroom, I mean?" he said, having to rephrase, at which point he received the appropriate directions from the American.

But instead of heading to empty his bladder straight away, Rodney initiated a slight detour towards the pitlane marker that he'd been warned about by a marshal earlier. Just beyond the diagonally striped black-and-yellow hazard line, most of the mechanics were happily observing the race, waiting patiently for the first of the machines to require their attention. One of them, however, seemed more content to relax on an outdoor folding chair, head leaned back, topping up his tan.

"You, there," Rodney said, hoping to attract the sunbathing mechanic's attention, as the man appeared to perhaps be a suitable target for what Rodney had in mind. But Rodney was competing against the volume of forty thousand or so spectators in the stands and of course the action out on track. "Oi, you there!" Rodney shouted, receiving a cursory glance in his direction, at which point he extended and wiggled his index finger.

"Me?" the reclining mechanic asked, pointing to himself.

Rodney nodded, waving him over to his position behind the safety line.

"Yeah?" the mechanic asked on arrival. "What's going on?"

Rodney first looked over his shoulder, making sure none of the assembled media and their accompanying recording equipment were anywhere within range. "I'll keep this simple, as we don't have too much time," Rodney said, his voice now significantly lower. "What do you earn for a day baking out here in the sun waiting for something to happen?" he asked.

"I dunno," the fellow replied, caressing the hair on his chin. "I volunteered to be here. So nothing, I guess."

Rodney leaned in closer, conspiratorially. "How would you like to earn five hundred dollars for a couple of minutes' work?"

"Is the pope Catholic?" the mechanic asked.

"Erm... yes, I expect he is," Rodney replied, not really taking the man's meaning. As with many narcissistic sociopaths, Rodney sometimes had trouble discerning the subtleties of humour.

"No, I meant, does a bear shit in the woods?" the man asked. This, along with his raised eyebrow and crooked grin, appeared to finally convey his intended message.

"Ah, I see. A joke," Rodney said, forcing himself to return the mechanic's grin, in hopes of getting what he wanted.

"Wait. Five hundred?" the fellow said, appearing pleased by the amount itself but now slightly apprehensive about how that particular amount might be had. "What do I have to do for it?" he asked. "Because, I mean, no offence, five hundred is a lot of smackers. But if you're expecting, um... something *personal*. You know, like, personal services rendered, then, uh..."

It took a moment for Rodney to understand where the fellow was going with this. "Good god, man, no. No, nothing like that," he assured him.

"Oh, okay, that's good, then. Because when I saw your cravat and heard your English accent, I just assumed..." the man began, trailing off, as he didn't feel comfortable completing the thought out loud.

Rodney was on the verge of getting very angry, but he bit his tongue, still wishing to conduct some underhanded, shady business with the chap if at all possible. "Nothing like that," Rodney said again, and simply left it at that.

"Okay, what do you have in mind?" came the response.

"Well, when a certain sidecar comes in to refuel, I just need you to take your time, right? Obviously, I don't want anybody to get injured or anything like that. Just inconvenienced and delayed," Rodney put forth. "Do you take my meaning?"

"So you want me to suddenly forget where the fuel cap is? Something along those lines?" said the mechanic, appearing not at all put off by the idea if his widened grin was any measure.

Rodney, his earlier anger now brushed aside, found a sudden liking for this devious, oil-stained chap. Not quite as devious as himself, of course, because no one was. But close enough for the purposes of the job at hand.

"Perfect, my good man," Rodney answered.

"You know, a *thousand* bucks would certainly do awful things to my memory," the mechanic noted. "If you take my meaning," he added, mimicking Rodney's own language.

Perhaps this fellow *was* nearly as devious as himself, Rodney considered. He wasn't especially keen on forking over any more money than the five hundred dollars already proposed. Still, he had to admire this chap's chutzpah.

"Fine. A thousand it is, then," Rodney replied, taking another cautionary glance about to make sure nobody could overhear them. Then, after rummaging in his pocket, he produced a roll of notes. "Don't let me down," he insisted, handing over the agreed-upon amount. "So. Here's what I need you to do…"

***

Dave looked towards the electronic scoreboard, struggling to see through an insect-covered visor and taking a note to remove a tear-off the next time he slowed for the chicane. *"Lap thirty-six, David. You can do this,"* he said to himself.

Using a back-of-the-fag-packet type of rough calculation, he reckoned his forty-litre fuel tank would comfortably keep him going until the final quarter of the race. To be safe, he'd settled on heading into pit lane on or around lap seventy, subject to his earlier kill swich repair playing ball with that strategy. However, one of the frustrating side effects of racing on a heavily banked track, as opposed to the TT course back home, was the fact that the fuel in the tank frequently got heavily sloshed to one side, causing an occasional reduction in power (with the engine occasionally starved of fuel for a moment, and much preferring a more flat, level type of track to which it was ordinarily accustomed). Dave had first encountered this sensation during the practice sessions, observing that the situation worsened as the fuel level dropped, as that created even more room in the tank for the petrol to slosh around. However, once again, he consoled himself with the notion that the other machines must be experiencing precisely the same periodic drop in performance as he was.

By now, Dave reckoned he'd overtaken most of the field at least once, clawing back some of the deficit from his late start. That is, apart from the one team, unfortunately, whom he really needed to catch: Napier and Thomas. And he knew that keeping pace with their quality and experience on even a normal day was challenge enough. But throw in a three-lap handicap, and things were starting to feel like he was pushing water uphill with a fork. He was also losing even more confidence in the brakes, which seemed to have as much stopping power as using a spud gun on a charging bull elephant.

Soon enough, however, and giving him a much-needed motivational boost, was the sight of Andy Thomas and Jack Napier's leather-covered arses finally coming into view and getting a bit closer in the distance. "Oh, *hello*," Dave said to himself, gaining ground at a most pleasing rate. So pleasing, in fact, that Dave thought surely something must be up with the other team's bike. Whatever the case, Dave certainly wasn't going to complain. Taking advantage of the situation, he moved in close, tucking in behind them, towing a ride on their slipstream until the start of the next straight, coming up ahead, at which point he pulled out, slingshotting past them like they were standing still.

And it felt fan-bloody-tastic.

Dave resisted the overwhelming urge to flip them a raised middle finger from his new position in front of them, instead hunkering down behind his fairing as best he was able, hoping to dig away at their significant lead advantage.

All around the circuit, colossal video screens broadcast live footage for the enjoyment of the spectators. Dave, distracted as he was by more pressing matters at hand, had so far resisted the temptation to flick his eyes up and see what was going on. However, wondering if Napier and Thomas were experiencing some sort of technical difficulties given their recently reduced speed, this was now proving difficult. Trying to read a text message in your car when driving at normal speeds was, quite correctly, ill-advised. Similarly, trying to watch a large video monitor while travelling at one hundred and fifty-odd miles per hour was, quite frankly, ludicrous. Something that Dave found out to his peril when he nearly ended up overshooting the next bend, narrowly avoiding a race-ending visit through the gravel trap into a wall of used car tyres. But there was good news, he was pleased to observe — that being that, after having passed them, he was now gradually pulling away from Napier & Thomas, steadily increasing the distance between them.

Dave was counting down the laps. Despite the current gains he'd made, he couldn't wait to come in for a pitstop, just to give his throbbing limbs a rest and take in some much-needed liquid as his mouth was drier than a moth sandwich.

Thankfully, the electronic scoreboard soon showed that Dave and Monty had now completed seventy laps. He could only assume that Jack and Andy were tucked in somewhere behind, as the pair hadn't passed them since, and weren't visible anywhere ahead. Whatever the case, Dave wasn't chancing another look up to the jumbotron after his previous scare.

Approaching the final turn before the entrance to the pit lane, Dave manoeuvred to the inside of the track, dropping down the gearbox in preparation for their fuel stop.

Unbeknownst to Dave, Andy Thomas and Jack Napier, who had been gathered in mere inches behind them for the last while, mirrored their actions, slowing and following them in. It was a tried and tested tactic in any competitive racing: if you were already ahead of your nearest competitor on lap count, just tuck in behind, keep them in sight, and follow them home to victory. After all, they were already in the lead, so no need to put too much additional strain on their bike if there was no specific reason to.

Dave applied his sponge-like brakes, now slowing down to the strict 50-mph speed limit as he made his way through the pit lane, directed to one of three available fuel refilling stations just a bit further in. Once parked up in the designated area with the engine safely turned off, both Dave and Monty climbed out of their machine, immediately stretching out seventy laps of racing fatigue. Then, a marshal handed the pair of them a water bottle, each helpfully equipped with a long flexible plastic straw so they wouldn't need to remove their helmets.

"Oh, I've been dreaming about you!" Monty exclaimed, before taking a long and grateful drink of the chilled fluid.

Standing a few metres further up the pit lane, near the VIP hospitality area, Rodney Franks did his level best to discreetly attract the attention of one particular mechanic, the one with a thousand dollars in his pocket, to tell him that *now was the time* to put their plan into action. At first, when his gestures seemed to be ignored, Rodney was starting to believe he had been flimflammed. But when the mechanic then shot him a furtive glance, Rodney's confidence in his accomplice was restored.

However, as the biggest stars in the race were both in for fuel at the same time, most of the TV cameras were trained in on that particular area. As such, giving any sort of instruction was nigh on impossible for Rodney without being seen by a considerable audience. Fortunately, he'd already explained which outfit was to receive special attention, reviewing the plan well in advance. And yet the mechanic in question appeared dazed and confused in the heat of battle, with his recent furtive glance being not so much a *"Gotcha. I know just what to do,"* it would seem, but rather more of a *"Huh? What do you want from me?"*

Rodney pretended to scratch his nose while, in actuality, he was covertly pointing towards Dave and Monty's sidecar. *"That one,"* he said, mouthing the words. But by the time the instructions were received, the other pit crew members present had already sprung into action and were smartly attending to the petrol pumps, rendering Rodney's only plan of attack now redundant.

Rodney's compromised mechanic offered him a *what-the-hell-am-I-supposed-to-do-now* sort of shrug, receiving a furious glare in return. Then, he appeared to have a lightbulb moment if his goofy smile was anything to go by. Rather than scuppering things by slowly dispensing fuel as originally planned, he now took an oily rag from his back pocket and walked towards the two riders, who were also using their brief stop to change out their insect-splattered visors for fresh ones.

Conscious that fuel tanks would soon be topped up, now was the only chance for the rogue mechanic to carry out his nefarious Plan B before both machines left for the final stages of the race. "You're misting up there, buddy," he said, examining one of the newly fitted visors sticking straight out in its open position. "We can't have you going out there with steam on the inside of your visor," he advised helpfully, reaching up and giving the inside of the visor a quick going-over with his soiled rag. "Same with you," he said, taking a step to his left and attending to the other supposedly fogged-up visor. Of course it made little sense that the visors could've been affected like this, as being in the open position, the riders hadn't even breathed on them yet. But it was the best excuse the fellow could come up with on short notice, and it seemed to work, as the riders certainly had no cause to distrust him.

Seconds later, both visors were snapped down as the two teams were given notice that they were soon to be on their way.

"Hey, what the effing hell!" screamed a frustrated voice. "You used a filthy rag! How in god's name am I supposed to see out of this? Get me another visor, right now!"

Judging by the profanities continuing to be flung around the pit area, the mechanic's devious plan appeared to have worked an absolute treat. The only problem, as Rodney Franks was attempting to point out to him with his urgent, frantic gesticulations, was that the *wrong team's* helmets had been sullied.

"You absolute imbecile!" Rodney shouted towards his incompetent accomplice, as Dave and Monty successfully fired up their machine, accelerated down pit lane, and left Andy and Jack in desperation as they hurried to try and locate and attach new visors before they could resume their race.

Chapter
TWENTY-THREE

A rapturous round of applause from the lively crowd urged Dave and Monty on in the closing stages of the race. In fact, while enjoying seeing the refuelling situation unfold on the jumbotron, some seemed to believe it was pure spectacle, suggesting it was all orchestrated to simply amp up the drama, like something you would find in a televised wrestling match. Of course, they were more than happy to play along with this perceived artifice, booing certain particular participants with gusto and cheering others on with equal enthusiasm.

However, any suggestion of such pretence would find itself considerably wide of the mark, as the obvious fury displayed by Andy Thomas and Jack Napier was in no way rehearsed and a world away from make-believe. They were absolutely livid by the time it took for them to replace their visors and finally climb back aboard their sidecar. Not that it usually takes too long to change a couple of visors, necessarily. But as they'd only just swapped them out, there were no additional replacements immediately at hand, and it took the mechanics a good thirty seconds to locate another set and the same again to fit them. And if you're, say, enjoying the lovely view during the course of a leisurely Sunday drive in the car, for example, a minute will disappear as if it were nothing. However, when you're right in the middle of a fierce competition, and extremely keen on *getting back into that same competition*, thank you very much, a minute will feel like an absolute eternity, as sixty seconds could easily be the margin between victory and non-victory.

Frank, Stan, and Stella, who by now had long since vacated the pit garage to enjoy the action trackside, couldn't help but grin as Thomas and Napier powered away, both still shaking their heads in anger, but with nice, clean visors so they could at least see where they were going now.

"Have some of that!" Stella declared, raising a spirited reverse-victory-sign two-finger salute to send them on their way.

"That's not very sporting, Stella," Stan remarked, along with a chuckle, as he was nevertheless amused. "So, you're starting to enjoy your afternoon out at the races?" he ventured, noting the beaming smile on her face.

"I didn't understand why you two bellends spanked so much of your cash sponsoring Dave and Monty," Stella answered, not really breaking her attention away from the action. "But I think I'm finally starting to get it."

Stan was happy to overlook the casual and repeated bellend insult, just pleased that Stella was becoming a willing part of the team. "You know, I'm actually starting to think the boys can do this," he said, addressing both Frank and Stella now, who were standing on either side of him.

Frank nodded. "They're certainly hungry for it, by the looks of them."

Stella glared at Frank. "Oi, you're fat-shaming them now?"

"Eh, what? No, of course I'm not, Stella!" Frank answered, concerned for his own well-being for a moment, as an angered Stella was a dangerous Stella. "I'm just saying they're hungry for the *victory*. They want it more than Rodney's team, that's all," he assured her.

"I'm sure the chequered flag worth fifty thousand American dollars won't be slowing them down any," Stan suggested, scrutinising the electronic scoreboard. "Hey!" he added in an excitable manner, "If I'm reading that correctly, then Dave and Monty have recovered a good portion of the deficit on the field and are now only a lap behind the leaders."

Frank shook his head. "Nope, you're wrong," he said.

"Oh," a dejected Stan replied. "Maybe I didn't read it cor—"

"They've just crossed the start line again," Frank advised, pointing to the replica Big Blue Boiled Sweet flying past them at the beginning of another rotation. "So it's now only *half* a lap between them."

And Frank was correct. Because thanks to Dave and Monty's heroic efforts, along with the added involvement of an oily rag, any lead that Rodney Franks' team enjoyed was being steadily eaten into with each completed lap.

Up on the jumbotron, the footage displayed there onscreen had now switched from the trackside cameras to one of those installed onboard Dave and Monty's bike. And it made for compelling viewing. From this up-close and personal point of view, one could start to appreciate the rigours the riders endured as the machine's suspension waged a constant war against the banked tarmac track. And it was the sheer sense of speed that this perspective offered the spectators, helping them visualise in real-time just what the guys on track endured for their viewing pleasure. But what became apparent, also, was that the gap between Dave and the machine they were chasing didn't appear to be closing, and the available laps in which to accomplish that were now in the single digits.

Out on the track itself, Dave Quirk's arms were screaming at him to stop, the pain in his wrists rivalling the worst he'd ever felt. Was it that abscessed tooth he'd once had? The gout in his big toe that sometimes flared up from time to time? Or was it that kidney stone he couldn't pass, his very first one, with him certain at the time that he was dying? He tried to think of all the worst pains he'd ever experienced, and how they compared to this present one. Eventually, he had to force himself to stop, though, as dwelling on the pain was only exacerbating the painfulness of the very painful pain, and he needed to think about something else. He decided to focus instead on making progress in the race, and of applying himself to that end.

But no matter what Dave did, Napier and Thomas's talent was starting to show as they appeared — despite their recent setback vis-à-vis the visor imbroglio — to now gradually increase the distance between them. To Dave's dismay, the electronic scoreboard signalled the fact there were now only seven laps remaining, and hopes of a famous victory were starting to wane. If he was going to do anything, he knew it had to be soon. However, Dave was also aware that with similar engines at their collective disposal and therefore similar power, it was unlikely that he'd be able to pull back too much of the gap out on the open track. As such, Dave identified his best opportunity to do this as being through the unique chicane section of the course, where vital seconds could very easily be won or lost.

Unfortunately, the pair of riders standing in their way of victory were two of the finest to have ever graced the sport. So the chances of them making any sort of error were marginal, to say the least. But one thing Dave didn't do was give up, as he was no quitter, and while there was still hope for some sort of miracle then he would keep battling until the last.

And then, as it should happen, Dave's prayers might just have been answered, or at least dealt a good healthy kiss of life right there on the lips. Because usually, when you're jostling for the top spot in a race, the last thing you'd ordinarily hope to see is a bunched-up pack of backmarkers (those competitors vying for the lower positions on the leaderboard) up ahead, forming, in essence, a rolling roadblock. But that's exactly what Dave could now see. And if *he* could see it, then he knew that Andy and Jack could also see it as well.

As Dave predicted, the pack, moving at a slower pace, delayed Napier and Thomas, eroding their lead to no more than a few sidecar lengths before they were able to safely navigate themselves through the scrum. Dave followed the same route through, although there was a moment of panic when one of the backmarkers made an unpredicted manoeuvre, causing Dave to have to swerve at the last minute, sending him slightly offline and in danger of cancelling out his recent gains.

Once past the obstruction, and despite giving it absolutely everything he had and utilising all of the experience in his considerable locker, Dave simply couldn't get past the leaders, Napier and Thomas, instead having to settle on sitting in behind them and merely keeping them as close as he could.

Then, with merely two laps left to go, it was now or never if that big fat juicy cheque was going to be cashed in their bank accounts rather than Jack and Andy's. Keeping pace at two, maybe two and a half lengths behind, Dave knew the pair would soon have to slow for the chicane, as would he and Monty. Unable to out-accelerate them, Dave reckoned his only chance was to out-brake them, so to speak. Something he'd have only two remaining opportunities to attempt if there was going to be any chance. Get it right and victory was within their grasp. Get it wrong, however, and, at best, it was a trip into the gravel trap and probably the end of their race because of all the lost time it would cause. At worst, the other alternative was a trip into a vast wall of tyres that weren't quite as bouncy and forgiving as one might expect. Oh, and also *definitely* the end of their race.

Dave took a deep breath, doing everything he could do to override his natural instinct to apply the brakes beyond what his brain told him was the absolute last safe moment to do. With a sharp left turn into the special section of the course to navigate, Napier and Thomas must have had a similar thought, but physics dictated that you'd have to apply your anchors at some point; it was just a question of who had the largest set of cojones and was prepared to take the most risk.

"Wait for it... not yet... not yet... *Now*!" Dave said to himself, reaching for the brakes only at the very last possible second. However, there was next to nothing there, as his brakes were, as they say in the trade, completely bollocksed. As a result, tyres screeched from friction along the tarmac as they battled against the forces of inertia at too great a speed, and Dave's usually impeccable racing line was well and truly scuppered and completely twisted out of shape. Dave wrestled with the controls, throwing the sidecar into the first corner of the chicane with the grace of a boy racer out competing in his mum's old Ford Fiesta. He winced, knowing that with his excess speed, he wasn't heading towards the gravel trap at all, but rather directly towards Napier and Thomas's arse end.

The resulting impact momentarily snapped the handlebars out of Dave's already aching grip, but instead of spinning out of control, somehow, miraculously, Napier and Thomas's machine served to put Dave on the proper path. With the other bike acting as a barrier at exactly the right moment, Dave's machine had bounced right off of it, and once wrestling the handlebars into obeying him again, it had ultimately corrected Dave's trajectory (at significant sacrifice to Napier and Thomas's own progress). Startled, Dave enjoyed his new, improved course, steering into the next tight turn of the chicane with a gloriously unobstructed route ahead.

Dave didn't know if the other outfit was still active, there on the track behind them, or if they'd been nudged off route as a result of the impact, possibly off of the course and into the gravel trap. But Dave wasn't hanging around to find out!

Once clear of the chicane, Dave pinned the throttle, resisting the overwhelming urge to flick his eyes up to the jumbotron, his mind whirring faster than their sidecar's tyres. Were Napier and Thomas still in the race, mere inches behind them? Or had their efforts been scuppered, their machine now out of commission? Whatever the case might be, there was little point in agonising over it now, Dave reckoned, as all he could do at this point was keep his head down and focus on finishing his own race, making sure he didn't possibly slip up, ruining his and Monty's chances in the process.

Through his peripheral vision, Dave was just able to make out the energetic crowd waving flags, programmes, and extremities in the air. What he didn't know was if it was to cheer him and Monty on, or if it was to spur Napier and Thomas on for one last dash for victory. He certainly hoped the other two riders were still somewhere in the race, of course. Just not too terribly close behind would be nice, thank you very much.

Now on the final lap, it didn't take very long before Dave was approaching the chicane again for one last pass through it. Of critical import was that there was currently no sign of Thomas and Napier awaiting recovery, anticipating the pick-up crew to come and collect their disabled vehicle. This meant, of course, that they must still be out on track and circulating. But where, exactly, Dave simply didn't know.

"Come on!" Dave shouted to himself, this time taking a much steadier, more precise path through the chicane, quickly making his way through it.

Back on the main section of the course, there were only two more rounded corners on the oval track before the finish line now, but the fear that you were about to be overtaken and have your hopes dashed at the last second was all-consuming. As he came around the final turn, Dave finally caught sight of the race official poised with the chequered flag. "Please!" Dave yelled, squeezing every last ounce of horsepower out of their screaming engine, with no concern about how their useless brakes would eventually stop them.

Now on the final straight, Dave glanced beside him, first to his left and then to his right, but there was no sign of Napier and Thomas coming up alongside them and trying to overtake.

"Yes!" Dave screamed, as the replica Big Blue Boiled Sweet blasted through the chequered flag. The victory was theirs.

***

By the time Dave and Monty were well into the pit lane area and aiming towards their garage, their brakes were red-hot, smoking, and completely cooked after struggling to slow down considerably. And whether it was a result of that inadequate stopping power, his own sheer fatigue from the long, gruelling race, or simply a combination of both, Dave managed to completely overshoot their appointed garage, eventually coming to a rest, ironically, just outside Andy Thomas and Jack Napier's own allocated garage.

Dave immediately sat up, reaching over and throwing his arms around Monty, who had popped up from the safety of the sidecar like a hedgehog coming out of its hedgy nest to check and see if the weather that day was good. "We did it, mate!" Dave said, opening up his visor for some much-needed fresh air. "We only went and bloody did it!"

After giving Monty a series of very hearty pats on the back, such that Monty wouldn't need to be seeing his chiropractor any time that week, Dave then climbed off the bike, legs slightly unsteady and any aches and pains presently forgotten thanks to the adrenaline surging through his body. Thankfully, he could see Napier and Thomas emerge into the pit lane under their own steam a few seconds later. Dave had wanted to beat them, of course, but not at any cost. As a professional racer, you fought hard. But the most important thing, more than any victory, was that you all came home safely at the end of the day.

Conscious that his erratic manoeuvre in the chicane might have been interpreted as careless riding (or worse, even somehow intentional) rather than due to his rubbish brakes, Dave began making his way over to the adjacent, open garage, hoping to meet up with them there and explain the situation before their already fragile relationship was tested further.

Meanwhile, Andy and Jack approached, at speed, no doubt confused that there was a machine currently occupying the entrance to their pitlane garage. A helpful marshal raised an arm to quickly get their attention, and then motioned them towards the garage next door, shunting them over. Their machine then changed course, though this meant sending them directly into Dave's path, as Dave was nearing the mouth of this other garage as he prepared to enter it.

"Whoa!" Dave said, wondering if giving him a fright like this might be some form of payback on their part.

Dave attempted to take avoiding action, but unfortunately, so did Napier and Thomas's machine. As Dave quickly stepped to one side, Jack Napier abruptly switched course as well, intending to steer his bike clear of Dave but only ending up zeroing in on him once again. It was, of course, absolutely unintentional on their part to target Dave in this way. But to anyone watching on, it would have very much appeared to be precisely the opposite.

Napier & Thomas's sidecar was still travelling at a fairly good rate of speed as they came in, much faster than they would have liked, actually. And certainly much faster than *Dave* would have liked, as the front of their bike promptly made contact with his person, ploughing straight into him and flipping him into the air like a child's rag doll.

Thrown up and over the back of their bike, Dave landed in a heap, groaning and in obvious pain as Andy and Jack's sidecar eventually came to a rest.

"Medic!" yelled the nearest marshal, with an alarm sounding throughout the pit lane. "We need medical attention here!" the marshal shouted to whoever was listening, as he crouched down over Dave's crumpled form.

Very soon, a paramedic was at hand. "Can you hear me?" the man asked. "Are you conscious?"

"I think I am?" Dave half-joked. "Do me a favour and help me up, will you?" he asked, making an effort to sit himself up.

"No! You need to stay exactly where you are!" came the firm, immediate response.

"You're not going anywhere right now," the marshal added in, looking down at Dave's injured right leg, which was, sickeningly, currently pointing at an angle that nature never intended. "Stay right there, buddy. We'll get you to the nearest hospital as soon as we can, all right?"

"Is anything broken?" Dave asked weakly.

"Don't worry yourself about that. Just sit still and try and remain calm," the medic advised, not wishing to alarm his patient.

"If anything's broken, it's the fairing of that bike that hit you," the marshal offered, hoping to put Dave at ease, as much as was possible at least, with a little bit of humour. "You should see the mess you made of it," he joked, letting out a nervous, uncomfortable laugh.

"Nothing that a bit of T-Cut scratch remover won't sort out…" Dave said, right before resting his head on the warm tarmac, his eyes rolling back inside his upper eyelids.

Chapter
TWENTY-FOUR

When the Freestone brothers first pitched the idea of a docuseries about motorcycle sidecar racing, they both knew the associated risks and potential dangers of the sport (or any type of motorsport, in fact) were a grim reality for anyone involved. Each and every time one of those heroic racers put on their leathers and threw a leg over their machine, they were, all of them, acutely aware that if something were to go wrong the outcome could be, and often was, disastrous. And while the assorted riders, teams, and event organisers always worked tirelessly to identify and mitigate any conceivable risks, there was always a margin for error — be that mechanical error, human error, or even a result of Sod's Law (that is, if something *can* go wrong, it will).

It was the inherent nature of the sport and the risks related when it went wrong that made those who participated a special breed of competitor. They frequently did what the rest of the mere mortals who admired them so much could only dream of. They were warriors. They were the reason the sport was adored so much and by so many, both in the Isle of Man and beyond its fair shores.

Presently, it'd been one very long day since the horrific incident that soured what was supposed to be a moment of immense pride for Dave and Monty. After all, achieving victory on an unfamiliar bike, an unfamiliar circuit, and against a genuinely competitive field, was no mean feat. But instead of celebrating, Dave was lying in a sterile hospital bed surrounded by medical equipment, with tubes coming out of at least three different orifices (and possibly more concealed beneath the bedsheets). And if this wasn't bad enough, he was in a foreign country, thousands of miles away from home.

It was for that reason, then, that Frank, Stanley, Monty, and Stella needed absolutely no convincing that their scheduled return flight would be taking off without them on board. Indeed, as Stan was quick to remark, his suitcase would now probably arrive home long before he did. But if it meant having to buy another few outfits for him (and Stella buying several more pairs of knickers for herself), then that was a very small price to pay to ensure they were there for their mate when he needed them the most.

In the corridor just outside of Dave's hospital room, Brad and Chip hovered, with neither appearing especially keen on stepping inside. "You do it," Chip insisted.

"Me?" Brad replied. *"You're* the one holding the paperwork. *You* do it."

Frank, returning from the vending machine with a hospital tray full of coffee, smiled as he approached them from behind. "What sort of mischief are you two up to?"

Caught unawares, the twins turned to face Frank, with Chip nearly jumping out of his skin from the surprise.

"Holy shit, Frank, you scared me! Give a guy some warning next time, will you?" Chip said, taking what he was holding in front of him and tucking it behind his back as he was speaking.

Frank tilted his head, as if this would in some way improve his view of what Chip was now concealing. "I brought you both a coffee," he advised. "What was that in your hand? What are you hiding back there?" he asked, taking a step to his left in hopes of obtaining a peek.

"You may as well just show him," Brad said. "He's going to find out sooner or later anyway, so it's better if he hears it from us."

Frank's cheery expression hardened. "It's not about Dave, is it? Please tell me he's not taken a turn for the worse?"

"No, he's still comfortable," Chip answered. "Or he's heavily sedated, at least. So he definitely won't be feeling any pain right now," Chip assured Frank. "Anyway, no, it's actually about this," Chip said, finally revealing the wad of documents he'd been attempting to hide.

"Blimey, have you pair been writing your autobiographies?" Frank asked with a laugh, noting the size of the stack. But judging by the look on their faces, Frank suspected this wasn't going to be any type of good news, whatever it was. "Look, let me hand out the rest of these coffees before they go cold, and then we can chat through whatever it is that's on your mind, all right?"

"Okay, Frank, we'll wait here for you. Thanks," Brad said, taking hold of two of the coffees Frank was distributing.

The twins stayed out in the hallway, burning their lips on the scalding hot vending machine coffee that tasted suspiciously like brewed pencil shavings, as vending machine coffee often did for some strange reason. Eventually, Frank reappeared a short while later.

"So... what is it, boys?" Frank enquired.

Chip handed over the stack of paper. "It's this, Frank. This is the bill from the hospital so far. They forwarded it to the network, since NBC Boston was listed on the hospital intake form as someone things could be sent to, what with all you guys staying only temporarily in a hotel and everything."

Frank laughed, unsure if Chip was being serious, as the thickness of the pile suggested it was more likely to be a telephone directory than a simple bill for urgent healthcare services. Frank flipped through the first few pages, looking up to Chip and Brad and then back to the hefty invoice. By now, Dave had already had several operations: two to repair his badly broken right leg, and one for some injuries sustained from his heavy landing when he'd come down very hard on his shoulder and side. Of course, it could easily have been worse. A lot worse, in fact, as the doctors stressed that if Dave hadn't still been wearing his helmet at the time of the accident... well, Frank didn't want to dwell too much on that.

"They're charging for *everything*," Frank observed, running his finger down the first of the pages where every aspect of Dave's care, excellent as it was, was included on an itemised bill that continued on for a half dozen or more very expensive pages. Then, when he eventually reached the summary statement page at the end, it was Frank who was nearly in need of emergency treatment. "One hundred and twenty-four thousand dollars!" he exclaimed, incredulous. "Wow, thank heaven we've got the NHS back home, because *this*..." he said, using the stack of papers to fan himself down. "Well, I certainly wouldn't like to be the insurance company when they receive *this* little beauty," he joked. But when neither Brad nor Chip laughed, Frank started to suspect why the boys might be so concerned. "Wait. Dave *has* got insurance for when he's here," Frank pointed out, lest that crucial fact be overlooked. "Monty gave you a copy, yeah? I was there when he handed over the paperwork, wasn't I?"

Chip looked across at his brother, perhaps for moral support. "Well... the thing is, Frank, the insurance policy Dave and Monty signed up for was simply a travel insurance policy."

"Okay?" Frank said, uncertain as to what the issue was. "And that's a good thing, right?"

Brad shook his head. "Not in this particular case, Frank, no," he said gravely. "You see, competing in any kind of motorised racing is rarely covered under a standard insurance policy. You need to apply for specialist insurance, something both Dave and Monty *should* have been aware of."

Chip looked forlornly at his feet for a moment before glancing back up again. "Frank, the riders were all warned about this before they went out on even their first practice run," he said. "In fact, they each had to sign an agreement saying they understood this before they were allowed to do any kind of racing at all."

"I guess Dave and Monty just didn't quite realise this, somehow?" Brad suggested, along with a heavy sigh. "Or, I hate to say it, but maybe they just hadn't been paying too much attention to what they were being told..."

Frank began to walk in a circle, struggling to digest what he was being told. "Dave and Monty don't have the sort of money to pay this bill," he advised, telling the twins what they already likely knew. "Oh, Christ on a bike," Frank moaned, periodically slapping the collection of papers against his forehead as he paced in a loop across the floor, making himself look like some kind of strange, self-flagellating monk.

Chip offered a pained frown, like he had more to say but was perhaps reluctant to do so. But eventually, he must have felt he had no choice. "Frank," he said. "Frank, I don't want to be throwing gasoline on the fire. But just to be clear, that bill you're holding onto right now is only for services provided to date."

"But Dave's likely to be in here for *days*, possibly even *weeks*," Frank pointed out. Again, information the brothers were likely already aware of. "Oh, boys. This is an absolute nightmare."

***

Gradually, like waking from a deep sleep — which was precisely what was happening, actually — Dave's left eye slowly struggled open like a rusty gate. The bright, overhead light caused him to groan in pain as he forced the lid to its fully opened position. He tried doing the same with his right eye, but that one was even less cooperative and he now looked like he was simply winking. "Unnnh," he moaned, becoming aware of all the throbbing parts of his body that were now vying for his immediate attention.

In response to his troubled vocalisations, a head-shaped silhouette loomed over Dave, sheltering his one good eye against the piercing light. He stared, dazed, confused, and unable to focus in on exactly who it was that was looking down at him. He couldn't glean any details of the face, but he could eventually discern the imposing mass of tightly permed hair that framed it.

"He's awake," Stella said softly. Then, "He's awake! Dave's eyes are open! Well, at least one of them is!" she said, much more loudly now, so everyone could hear. Stella looked around the room, but in typical fashion, she found herself alone in there for the first time in many hours. So she quickly ran out into the corridor. "Oi! Frank, Stan, Monty, anyone!" she yelled, likely waking up most of the hospital ward in the process. "Dave's awake!"

She immediately returned to Dave's bedside, taking hold of his hand. "It's me, Stella," she said, her gruff voice shaking with emotion. "The others will be here soon," she told him, placing her head gently on his chest, looking up at his double chin. "You arsehole," she said affectionately. "We thought we'd gone and lost you, you great bloody pillock."

Dave had zero idea about where he was or what was going on. For all he knew, he'd just awoken from an extended nap (albeit a strangely pain-inducing nap) to find Stella getting nice and cosy on his chest for some strange reason. A startling sight, to be sure.

"Where... am... I?" Dave asked, struggling to form the words with unlubricated vocal cords.

Stella, with her face inches away from Dave's, smiled. "Don't speak, Dave," she said, very gently, the compassionate side of her nature apparently making a rare appearance. "Seriously, don't speak, Dave. Your breath is horrendous, mate," she felt the need to clarify.

Dave laughed, but then immediately regretted it, as he found the laughing hurt his ribs. Eventually, Dave's other eye opened, just in time to see Frank, Stan, and Monty come sprinting in.

"So we only step out for five short minutes, and *that's* when you finally decide to wake up?" Stan playfully admonished their patient.

"I wouldn't get too close," Stella cautioned, now watching the TV in the room, her nursing duties having been concluded. "At least not until he's brushed his teeth."

The others appreciated the warning, but they didn't care too much about some questionable personal hygiene.

"Come here, big guy," Monty said, arms outstretched like a hungry zombie anxious for brains. "Don't you scare me like that again," he said, with happy tears running down his cheeks. "Do you hear me, David Quirk?"

"I hear you, Monty Montgomery," Dave managed to reply, using his limited energy reserves to offer a smile. "Monty, did we win?"

Monty placed his hand against Dave's cheek. "We did, buddy. We showed them all what was what."

"Marvellous," Dave offered, a moment before he drifted back to sleep.

It was going to be a long and frustrating road to recovery, the doctors suggested. However, they remained hugely optimistic, confident that the shattered leg would heal nicely, as would his other injuries. And once they'd been able to speak properly with Dave, along with running all sorts of varied (and likely expensive) tests, they were satisfied he'd suffered no head trauma or injury to his brain — a real concern, as Dave, when he landed on his side, had smacked his head against the pavement as well. "No damage to his brain other than what was already there," Monty quipped at the time, pleased with his wit, yet receiving a disapproving glare from Stan for his trouble.

Still, it wasn't just the doctors who were owed an enormous debt of gratitude while they took care of Dave. In relation to the others, the hotel, despite being completely booked out, had still managed to find them all accommodation for the duration of their extended stay. And, in the circumstances, the airline was also completely flexible about their return journey home. For many, the prospect of a few extra days in Las Vegas, enjoying all the glitz and glamour that it had to offer, would prove largely appealing. However, for Frank, Stan, Stella, and Monty, they hadn't strayed too far beyond their hotel room and the route to Dave's hospital bed. Not that they'd especially wanted to anyway. Because having Dave now sitting up, talking, and cracking awful jokes, was quite possibly the biggest jackpot that anybody could ever possibly hope to score, as far as they were concerned, in this hedonistic gambling capital of the world.

And two other people having a slightly longer stay in Sin City than they'd originally intended, as it should happen, were Andy Thomas and Jack Napier, both facing serious jail time if it was proven that they'd mowed Dave over in a fit of rage. At issue was the fact that they had come in *much* too fast, making a beeline straight for Dave, and when Dave had attempted to step out of the way, they'd course-corrected and zeroed in on him *again*, ploughing right into him at full speed. It certainly looked very much intentional, despite Napier and Thomas's firm and repeated insistence to the contrary. And despite their pleas to be allowed to return home, the authorities would have none of it, not while the investigation was ongoing. This news didn't, however, prevent their team principal from heading straight to the airport at the first chance he could. Yes, Rodney Franks, eager to get out of Dodge as fast as humanly possible, buggered off, quick-smart, leaving his two hapless riders to face the music all on their own.

Of course, everybody was delighted to have Dave up and on the mend, but possibly none more than Andy and Jack. Ironically, Andy and Jack's salvation, and eventual permission to return home, came thanks to someone who at any other time might have quite enjoyed seeing them locked up and the key thrown away. Yes, Dave Quirk regaining consciousness not only saved them from answering a potential murder charge, but he was also able to substantiate their version of events: that being that their brakes failed because they were, well, useless (as Dave was able to attest from his own experience on his bike) resulting in them being unable to stop when Dave, trying to move out of their path, instead rushed directly into it. Thus making a collision inevitable. It was an unfortunate accident. But it was just that, an accident, as Dave was able to confirm.

And so, the morning soon arrived when Dave was due to be discharged. It was, of course, a time for celebration, because it meant they were all able to finally start the long return home. However, it was also tinged with a degree of anxiety, thanks to *several hundred thousand* choice reasons.

"Sod it, Monty. Just wheel me out when they're not looking, yeah?" Dave suggested, now sitting in his wheelchair, beside his hospital bed, in preparation to leave.

Monty nodded, considering the various options to make good their escape. "We might need some sort of distraction?" Monty proposed. "I once watched a film where the main character had to escape from a lunatic asylum, and—"

"You want a distraction?" Stella cut in, reaching for one of Dave's crutches. "Just say the word and I'll sort out the mother of all distractions for you. They'll think they've been hit by a bloody tornado."

"Do they have tornadoes in Nevada?" Dave wondered aloud.

"They will by the time I get through with them," Stella insisted.

Frank, who'd been assisting Stan in clearing out Dave's bedside cabinet, felt the need to interject. *"Ahem,"* he said. "And just how far do you think we're going to get before the hospital discovers that we've disappeared without making plans to settle the bill? Not very far, that's how far."

Stella returned the crutch, giving Dave a *just-you-say-the-word* type of look.

So far, there was still no real plan on how Dave was going to clear what was likely to be an astronomical medical bill. Knowing that they were scheduled to fly out later that day, a representative from NBC Boston was dropping by to arrange prompt payment of the $50,000 prize money, so there was that at least. And Monty, the amazing friend that he was, had already offered to throw his share of that cash into the Dave Quirk Emergency Medical Fund, to supplement Dave's contribution. But the fact that the administration staff had now been working out the final tally for well over an hour didn't really bode well.

By now, aware that Dave's overall financial situation wasn't exactly flourishing, Frank and Stan had already made a few phone calls back home to see what they could do in regard to possibly liquidating some assets to try and help plug up the remaining, enormous gap.

Stan removed his head from Dave's bedside cabinet. "Oi, you cheeky bugger," he admonished, holding up what he'd just discovered lying there on the top shelf. "I take it this is your mucky magazine?"

Dave blushed, which was a rare occurrence in itself. "I... er... that is... it was a gift..."

"Monty, for shame," Stan said, with an audible tut-tut, casting his eyes at the buxom blonde adorning the front cover.

Monty held out his hands, ready to protest his innocence. "Not guilty, your honour. But if you want me to examine it for clues...?" he joked.

"I bought it for him," Stella admitted. "Being stuck in here for days on end, I thought it would raise his spirits."

"I'll bet that wasn't the *only* thing raised," Stan remarked with a schoolmistress sort of look, delivering a bawdy line that wouldn't have appeared out of place in one of the *Carry On* series of films. "Although, as Dave was unconscious for much of his stay, I'm not sure how much skimming he would have managed anyway."

Just then, Brad gave a knock on the already open door. "Only us," he said. "We just wanted to come and say goodbye, and also maybe record a bit more, with you talking about the race before you go, assuming you're up for it."

"We've brought a visitor with us, too," Chip advised. "If that's okay?"

Dave nodded. "Sure, the more the merrier," he said.

With access thus granted and his presence duly announced, Clifford Tanner marched into the hospital room larger than life. "Dave, you gave us quite a scare!" he said, addressing the patient in the room, before offering a cordial smile to the rest of the room as well. As he cast his eyes about, he couldn't help but notice the item currently held in Stan's hands. "I hope I haven't caught you at an awkward time, Stan...?" he asked with a half-smile.

Stan took a moment to realise he was still clutching Dave's porno mag against his chest. "What? Oh! Oh, no. No, it's not mine, Clifford," Stan insisted, quickly throwing the magazine in question onto Dave's lap.

"I've been flat on my back, strung out on drugs," Dave pointed out. "What use would I possibly have for this?" he asked with a wry smile. "Honestly, Stan. There's no harm in exploring your own body, yeah? It's perfectly natural," he said with a wink.

"Nothing to be ashamed about, mate. Nothing at all," Monty chimed in, enjoying any opportunity to make Stan squirm.

Clifford appeared eager to move the conversation along. "Anyway, I can't stay for too long, guys," he said. "I just wanted to swing by and wish you *bon voyage*. I can honestly say, working on this project has been a total blast, and I can't wait to catch up with you folks at next year's TT races."

Frank took a step forward, offering his hand. "We'll be sure to make you very welcome, Clifford. A proper Manx welcome."

Clifford administered a hearty handshake. "I have no doubt," he said, smiling. "Oh, and while I remember. We've just had the viewing numbers for the second episode, which I can share if you have the time?"

"You appear happy," Monty noted. "So I'm assuming it's good news to share?"

"It is," Clifford was happy to confirm. "In fact, the figures are absolutely amazing!" he said, raising his hand for a quick high-five, which Monty reciprocated as best he could, given his wonky eye and resulting faulty aim. "So much so, that I've asked our two directors here to cobble together an additional episode to include all the hair-raising action from the recent race," Clifford added, glancing over to Brad and Chip.

"Culminating in the crash as the dramatic ending?" Dave asked, rapping his knuckles against his plaster cast. "Oh, and speaking of dramatic endings, Stan, would you want your magazine back?"

"Anyway, I gotta go," Clifford said, sparing Stan any further blushes. "But we'll be in touch soon to discuss the details for the second series," he added, clapping his hands together in anticipation. "Dave, good to see you're getting better. And, guys, thank you. It's been a genuine pleasure."

With plenty of existing footage for the recent exhibition race already available, Brad and Chip just needed to collect a series of sound bites to knit it all together. And having Frank, Stan, Dave, and Monty all in one place was too good an opportunity to miss before the group flew home. (Stella was there as well, of course, but she had stepped out of the room momentarily to go rustle up some grub for herself, as this watching-over-Dave situation was a hungry business.)

From day one, there was always the human element to their documentary work; that was front and centre in everything the twins set out to do. And now, following an incident that could have quite easily been a catastrophe — or at least, a far *greater* catastrophe than had already occurred — it was heartening to see how a group of friends all instantly came together when one of them was in need. It was this remarkable comradery that, as filmmakers, Chip and Brad hoped they could do justice to. In the relatively short time they had known the Isle of Man contingent, they'd grown to admire and deeply respect them all, and it was something the brothers were confident the viewing audience would do as well, taking them into their hearts just as they themselves had.

Having offered to drop the gang off at the airport and conscious of the clock ticking away, Brad and Chip started to wrap up the final portion of their interview, the subject of which was the patient himself.

"So," Chip said, just outside of the camera shot, "Dave, it's been a rollercoaster of a week for you. The highs of winning the race—"

"Which I don't remember," Dave cut in.

"Which you don't remember," Chip allowed. "And then, waking up in the hospital. Summarise the experience for me."

Dave immediately smiled as Brad, while operating the camera, slowly zoomed in, resulting in Dave's handsome face filling his viewfinder. After a few moments of quiet reflection, Dave started to speak.

"What you think is important," Dave began, looking directly at the camera. "That is, what you…" he said, before lowering his head for a moment. A tear welled up in Dave's eye before spilling over and running down his cheek. Dave laughed to himself. "You knew I was going to do that," he joked, pointing a friendly but accusatory finger towards Brad and Chip.

But they didn't speak, just waiting patiently until Dave could try and collect himself and continue.

"Right. What you think is important…" Dave went on, picking up on his original train of thought. "Really isn't," he said, waging a losing battle with his breaking voice. He cleared his throat, determined to finish conveying the thought he was attempting to get across. "You could have millions in the bank, loads of fancy cars, and houses all across the world. But that doesn't mean anything. Not really. No, *friendship* is what matters. Try waking up from surgery, after being unconscious for who knows how long, without friends, and I'll bet you that your fancy car won't fluff your pillow for you or fetch you some, uh… interesting reading material. And I can guarantee you all the money in the world won't crack the world's shittest joke and make you smile at the precise moment in your life when you need it the most."

Dave reached for one of the beige ankle socks provided to him by the hospital, the kind with the special rubber anti-slip soles, using it to soak up the emotion on his cheeks and about his eyes.

"Friendship and family are all that matters when you think about it. I mean, if you don't have that, then what's the point, really?" Dave concluded. "So, that's my summary, and what I'm taking away from this painful experience."

Brad slowly zoomed out, knowing that he'd just captured the perfect way to end their first series' addendum episode. "Thank you, Dave," he said, on a personal note, once his camera had been turned off. "And know that the two of us are proud to consider you a friend, buddy. Honoured and proud."

"Aww, hell, pass me that sock when you're finished, will you, Dave?" Chip said, dabbing at his face with the back of his hand. "You guys have got me going now, too!"

Packed up and ready to leave the hospital, there was just a short hop to the hotel to collect their luggage and then onward to the airport. But before that, there was just the question of the bill to work out, and for Dave to be formally released from the hospital's care. Of course, by now, both Frank and Stan had already offered assurances of assistance in regard to the bill, not wanting the worry about money hampering Dave's recovery.

However, Dave knew this financial situation was, to quite a large degree, his own doing. If only he'd taken the time to read through the paperwork about having the appropriate insurance policy, then he wouldn't be in this position. He'd have to come up with some sort of plan. What, exactly, he didn't have a clue. But on the basis that his assets weren't extensive, largely consisting of a modest amount of funds saved for his house deposit and a lime-green Honda Civic with an oversized exhaust pipe, then the prospect of declaring himself bankrupt was presently the frontrunner in a very small list of available options.

"Did Clifford happen to leave a cheque for us, by any chance?" Dave asked, as he was being rolled through the corridors to the hospital's administration office. "Because that would be pretty handy right about now."

Monty, pushing Dave's wheelchair from behind, shook his head. "Hmm, now you mention it, I don't think he did," he said.

"Even if they didn't, I suspect NBC Boston's credit is good around these parts, even all the way out here in Nevada?" Stan suggested, carrying Dave's few on-hand possessions, minus the now-binned magazine (which Monty, unbeknownst to Stan, had promptly plucked from out of the bin as soon as Stan wasn't looking, as after all, it was going to be a long flight home and a wee bit of choice reading material shouldn't have to go to waste).

There was a cold chill when you entered the administrative office in an American hospital. Gone was the warm sense of caring medical staff, replaced with formal folk wielding calculators, tapping away on spreadsheets with one eye on a profit-and-loss pie chart.

"Can I help you?" a studious-looking fellow with thin-rimmed glasses asked, peering up from behind the nearest desk.

"Er, yeah," Dave replied. "David Quirk, checking out," he advised, with a sense of impending doom about what was about to come off the printer.

"Um, okay," the bean counter in the nice suit replied. "So how can I help you, exactly?" he asked, as it wasn't often that people showed up at his desk on their way out the door, necessarily.

"We're here to discuss the bill," Stan said, stepping forward. "Specifically, we need to talk about a payment plan," he said, half-joking, though sincerely hoping this was in fact an available option. "Also, did somebody happen to leave a cheque for fifty thousand in here for collection, by chance? We'd been expecting to receive it earlier from someone, but, ehm…"

"Ah, you're the folks from that new TV series, aren't you? The one they've been promoting like crazy here in town?" the man behind the desk said, recognising them. "I like what I've seen of the show so far," he added, staring across at them without doing much else.

Frank looked at his watch, conscious that their return flight's check-in time was rapidly approaching. "That's us," he said. "Anyway, we just wondered about the bill, so we could, you know…"

"Ah, okay, let me check," came the helpful response, followed by some tapping of the keyboard. "Yeah, it's just what I thought, there's nothing outstanding left to pay here," he informed them. "You're all set."

Receiving this news, Dave was about ready to jump out of the wheelchair and somehow sprint towards the exit before the fellow changed his mind.

"Nothing outstanding left to pay...?" Frank repeated back to the man. "You're quite sure? Only the insurance situation that we—"

"A Mister Tanner — a Mister Clifford Tanner, to be precise — has already settled everything," the fellow cheerfully advised, double-checking the information on his computer screen, just to be sure. "You're all set," he said again.

"So we're free to go?" Dave asked, sounding like a prisoner with his parole papers being dangled in front of him.

"Sure, you're free to go," said the gentleman, a little confused. "Why? Did you think we were going to hold you here if you didn't immediately pay up or something?" the man asked with a laugh.

"Oh, uhm..." said Dave, a little too embarrassed to say out loud that he'd thought exactly that, essentially.

"Besides, I'm looking forward to seeing the rest of the show, so I'd never keep you prisoner here," the man joked.

Dave tapped a finger on his plaster cast. "Spoiler alert," he said. "It doesn't end on a high note!"

Once outside the hospital entrance and waiting for Brad and Chip to bring the transportation around, Dave breathed the biggest sigh of relief he'd ever breathed.

"Do you think the payment Mr Tanner handed over includes our prize money?" Monty boldly asked. "We won't see it now?"

"Yes, I think that's a given," Frank said. "And probably a small price to pay, considering."

Dave offered up an apologetic smile. "I'll make it up to you, Monty. I promise."

"*Pfft*," replied Monty. "It's only money, mate. Although, once you're up and running, if you wanted to buy me breakfast from Maccies for a while, I certainly wouldn't object."

"It's a deal," Dave readily agreed, offering out a hand to seal said deal. "And thanks, you two, for offering to help with the bill," he said to Frank and Stan. "Even though you didn't need to do it in the end, I want you to know the offer was most definitely appreciated."

"Our pleasure," Frank replied on the pair's behalf.

"Especially since we didn't actually need to do it in the end!" Stan chimed in.

"And Stella..." said Dave, shifting his attention once again. "Stella, thank you for fluffing up my pillows and reading me a story when you thought I was still sleeping."

"Those magazines will often have some very good articles in them," Stella answered.

"Yeah, so I've been told," Dave said, acting as if he'd never had the chance to look through that kind of ignominious publication before.

Stella leaned in close. "And if you ever tell anybody else about me reading stories to you in bed, you'll need surgery to fix your broken jaw, in addition to your existing injuries," she noted, with a firm-but-fair sort of smile.

"Taxi for Team Frank 'n' Stan?" Brad asked, winding the window down as he pulled up.

"You know," Stan said to Stella, apropos of nothing at all, really, "I think I could get used to travelling about without being burdened by luggage. It's rather liberating."

"I do talk sense at times, Stan," Stella said, as if that was ever in doubt. "And I hope they've fixed the poxy toilet in first class on that aeroplane of ours," she added, apparently having given the matter some previous thought. "Because I reckon I've got some unfinished business to attend to."

Chapter
TWENTY-FIVE

In characteristic fashion, by the time they'd returned home, it felt like they'd all been off the island for ages, when in reality they'd only been gone for a little over a week.

However, despite their relatively short absence, the welcoming committee at the Isle of Man's Ronaldsway Airport didn't disappoint. In addition to their family and friends, dozens of locals turned up to show their support to probably the most unlikely bunch of celebrities you'd ever be likely to meet.

Dave, in particular, was in the firing line for some serious affection, with concerned well-wishers landing more kisses on him than the pope's ring. He didn't mind so much, quite enjoying it in fact, especially when his beloved Becks landed a particularly sloppy one on him, much to her son Tyler's obvious disgust. (Tyler liked Dave just fine, of course. It was more a case of embarrassment on behalf of the adults, rather, as the two adults were insisting on acting shamelessly like adults.)

It was not long after this time that Dave began to contemplate the practicalities of his convalescence. Being in a plaster cast for the next few weeks wasn't ideal, for instance, when your rented house didn't have a downstairs bathroom, requiring a steep set of stairs to get to it instead. And while he wasn't going to be much use around the farm — "Nothing new there!" as a cheeky Monty, having a bit of fun, was quick to suggest — Dave still wanted to be on hand to lend his mate some moral support.

And to be honest with himself, he also didn't fancy the prospect of not seeing the farm animals for any length of time either. With all of this considered, it was decided that Dave would move into the TT Farm. At least until he was up on his feet once again. Until that should happen, as Becks was at pains to say, he was under strict instructions to relax, watch Netflix and such, and be thoroughly pampered. And he was absolutely *not* to exert himself under any circumstance! ...

"Right, Big Dave," young Dr Tyler said, cocking his head to show he was taking his responsibilities as seriously as the situation dictated now that Dave had settled in at his new, temporary lodgings. "Are you absolutely certain that you're comfortable?" Tyler asked, caring little chap that he was. "I can adjust your footrest if you need me to? You just say the word."

Dave looked down, checking the footrest was at the optimum angle for both his comfort and safety. "I believe I'm all good, buddy," he said, nodding in appreciation for the lad's concern. "Although..." Dave added, making out like there *was* a serious task that might just require Tyler's urgent attention. "You may want to check the pressure of the tyres?" Dave suggested. "It's always good practice to make sure you've got enough air in the wheels, yeah?"

"On it, Big Dave," Tyler responded, giving each of the tyres a good squeeze and a pinch. "I reckon we're good to go," he advised once his inspection was complete. "Permission to launch?"

Dave took a deep breath, acquiring a firm grip on the armrest. "I'm ready," he was pleased to report. "But this time, don't forget to factor in the slight gradient in the car park, okay?"

Outside in the glorious Manx sunshine, curious birds — blue tits, if their song was any indication — tweeted from the nearby trees, perhaps wondering what shenanigans were afoot down in the car park of the Isle of Man TT Farm. And they'd be right to be curious. With the parking area presently empty of cars, Tyler had carefully laid out, in a neat triangular formation, a collection of knee-high inflatable sheep. Originally purchased by Stan for the TT Farm's festive nativity scene, they were never used for the purpose intended, as the sheep's rather flirtatious appearance suggested they'd be more at home on a stag do than they would as part of a yuletide display. But now, they were getting a second lease of life thanks to Tyler and Dave's brilliant new game: Car Park Wheelchair Bowling.

Yes, Dave had achieved many lofty goals during his extensive racing career on three wheels, including victory at the Isle of Man TT. But now, sitting in a wheelchair with two big wheels and two teensy weensy ones, about to be launched into a flock of inflatable sheep... well, as Dave submitted to Tyler, this might just be the pinnacle.

Their first few attempts had been, putting it kindly, a learning exercise. On the first one, Tyler hadn't put enough shoulder power into his thrust, resulting in Dave coming up agonisingly short. On the second, Tyler hadn't accurately accounted for the slightly uneven surface of the carpark, resulting in Dave veering off towards the surrounding bracken bush. On the third and present attempt, confidence was high that the stars would align and all six of the vinyl yuletide rejects would thus surrender to Dave's indomitable will.

"We're going to get them all, this time," Tyler declared, lining Dave up for the current shot. "Do you think if we were able to buy a massive rubber elastic, we could launch you like a catapult, Dave?"

Dave had to admire the creative thinking on display. "Internet shopping was invented to solve problems such as that, my good man," he said. "How about we have a couple more attempts and we can go and do some research?"

Then, checking to make sure the coast was clear, Dave looked over his shoulder, spotting, actually, that the coast *wasn't* clear, with Becks advancing at speed. And she didn't look particularly happy, either. "Uh-oh," Dave said through the side of his mouth. "Dude, your mum is approaching from six o'clock. Make something up, and make it good."

Tyler looked down at his watch, even though he wasn't wearing one, confused, as he knew it was nowhere near six o'clock. "Are you sure you didn't hurt your head in that accident you had, Dave?" he asked, concerned about his patient.

However, Dave didn't have time to answer as Becks was soon upon them. "What on earth are you pair up to?" she asked, placing her hands menacingly on her hips, and then glancing over to the inflatable sheep. "Honestly, Tyler, I asked you to bring Dave out for some fresh air, and to…" she said, trailing off when she heard the sound of some loud snoring. "Don't you pretend to be asleep, David J Quirk! Because I saw you were wide awake when I was walking across the courtyard!" she scolded him, waging a battle against the smile that was forcing its way through. Then, turning her attention back to her son Tyler, "Right, mister. What's going on?" she asked.

Tyler chewed the inside of his cheek, looking out over the rolling Manx countryside for inspiration about how to hoodwink his lovely mum. "You asked me to take Dave out…" he said, telling his mum what she already knew. "And so we thought that it might be a good idea to– to, erm… to relax," he added.

"Yes? And?" Becks said, wondering where this was going.

"So I thought it might be a good idea for Dave to paint."

"To paint?" Becks asked.

"Yup. So I thought we'd paint some sheep," Tyler continued. "But there weren't any about to use as models, so we thought we'd just use these ones here."

Becks directed her son's attention to an adjacent field where, at a guess, roughly two hundred sheep could presently be viewed munching on the lush Manx grass. Which seemed to poke some serious holes in the credibility of his story. But more importantly, aside from which sheep might potentially be depicted, there was the suspicious lack of any painting-related materials at hand. "Right, so show me your artwork, then," Becks suggested. "Perhaps I'll buy a nice frame and we can hang it on the living room wall."

"Aaahhhhh," Dave said with a yawn, stretching out both arms above his head. "Blimey, is it morning already?" he asked, appearing discombobulated, and confused about his present location. "Tyler, what's going on?" he asked, along with a discreet smirk. "Why have you wheeled me all the way out here?"

"Do you pair think my head buttons up at the back?" Becks asked them. "I could see you launching Dave's wheelchair from the kitchen window. I just didn't know why, until now," she said, pointing her dishcloth towards the sheep. "Are you using Dave to play ten-pin bowls?"

"No!" Tyler immediately replied, protesting his innocence.

"Tyler...!"

"Honest, Mum. You can see we're only using six."

Becks shook her head in disbelief. "And *you*," she said, addressing Dave once again. "You've just had major surgery recently, and here I've caught you being launched, *willingly*, into a set of makeshift bowling pins."

"Oh, was that real? I thought it was simply a dream I was having," Dave remarked, eyelids heavy as he feigned sleepiness.

Becks stepped in close, placing a kiss on his unshaven cheek. "What are you like?" she said, unable to stifle a laugh. "Oi, you big crazy lummox," she said, giving him another kiss. "Anyway, the reason I came over here wasn't *just* to stop you from ending up in the hospital again. We're supposed to be at Monty's barbecue in twenty minutes. So let's go and get ready, you two, lickety-split!"

Tyler did as instructed, pushing Dave back towards the farmhouse. "Mum?" he said. "Mum, you don't happen to know where I can buy a really, really big rubber elastic, do you?"

Becks glanced down at her son. "What? Why are you asking me that?" she replied. "In fact, you know what? Nevermind. Because even if I *did* know where you could purchase one, I certainly wouldn't tell either of you two. I can guarantee that something would end up getting broken!"

***

"Alright, Lewis Hamilton," Dave said from the passenger seat of his Honda. "How about we try and get there in one piece?"

Becks grinned from ear to ear, giving the throttle a bit more attention. "I feel like a right girl racer driving your car, Dave. And I don't think I realised just how loud it was from the inside."

"Pardon?"

"I said that I... Ah. Very funny, Mr Quirk." Becks then flicked her eyes up to the rear-view mirror so she could get a look at the backseat. "So, sunshine. Just how many cheeseburgers do we intend on munching this afternoon?" she asked.

"Hmm. Three? Possibly four?" Tyler replied. "I was planning on taking it easy so that I've still got room for pudding."

"Smart lad," Dave said, voicing his approval. "I like your style!"

The garden party they were heading to was something Monty had kindly put together. Not only was it the ideal occasion to put his new Weber grill to good use, Monty had told Dave, but a nice opportunity for the extended gang to get together and enjoy a cold beer or three with some lovely food. Also, ever since they'd all returned from Las Vegas, Dave hadn't really seen as much of the others as he would have liked, aside from Becks and Tyler. Indeed, Dave was starting to get paranoid as Frank, Stan, and Monty always seemed to have some odd excuse about having to be someplace else when Dave wanted to make plans to do something. So much so, in fact, that Dave had felt the need to point out that whilst he wasn't exactly mobile, it wasn't like any of them needed to bed-bath him or change his underpants or anything like that. Just in case that was anything to do with their frequent absence.

Anyway, two things Dave Quirk especially enjoyed were cold beer and lovely food. And catching up with his best mates was an added advantage as far as he was concerned, so he couldn't wait to get the party started.

Shortly, Becks turned into Monty's street, sliding down her seat in embarrassment as she did so. "Dave, all the neighbours are looking at us," she observed.

"That's probably because of the loud exhaust," Tyler pointed out from the rear. "Or it could be to do with the funny green colour of the paint?" he considered. "Either way, you get used to all the peculiar looks after a while when you're zooming around in Dave's car."

"Eh, maybe it's because there's a big hunk of beefcake sitting in the front seat who also happens to be rather a major celebrity these days?" Dave weighed in.

"Nah, it's probably just the exhaust pipe, Big Dave," Tyler had to explain.

Becks pulled up outside Monty's house, pleased to turn the engine off and give her ears some respite. "Can I just remind you that you're already unsteady on your crutches this afternoon, Dave? So if you can factor that into how many beers you decide to consume, that'd be appreciated."

Dave opened his passenger-side door, carefully swinging his legs around and easing his feet out onto the ground. "Of course, my love. Anything for you."

Becks scurried around the car, eager to help Dave safely out and up into a standing position. "Here are your crutches," she fussed, making sure he was in one piece. Then, once Dave was entirely upright and properly situated, she took him by surprise by slipping her arms around his hulking frame. Not to help support his weight (because he didn't really need that at this point), but just because.

"What's this for?" he asked. "Not that I'm complaining, mind."

"I'm just glad to have you back in one piece," Becks advised, giving him a nice cuddle, although not one that could potentially knock him off his feet. "I do love you, Dave Quirk."

"I love you too, Becks. Oh, and also the little squirt blowing out his cheeks on my door glass," he said, offering Becks a kiss. "Oi, I'll need to get the Windolene out to remove your slobber!" he added a moment later, wagging a finger in Tyler's direction.

Dave hobbled up Monty's driveway, sniffing the air in firm anticipation of the aroma of food from the grill wafting his way.

But nothing. "How strange," he said, once he'd reached Monty's garden gate, peering over. "There's nobody here?"

Becks checked her phone to see if she'd missed any messages, a cancellation, perhaps. "How odd. We've not got the wrong day, have we?" she wondered, making her way to the front door and pressing the bell. "It must be the wrong day," she concluded, as the doorbell went unanswered. "Oh, how embarrassing. What am I going to do with the massive trifle I've brought along?"

"More embarrassing than driving Dave's car?" Tyler asked, helping his mum put things in perspective. "Oh, and about the trifle..." he said, looking down at the huge dessert dish he'd been entrusted with carrying. "I wouldn't worry too much about finding a home for it."

Dave started the short but difficult trudge back towards the car. "Ah, well, Tyler. I guess we'll just have to head back to the farm for another game of Wheelchair Bowling?"

"And maybe see if we can pick up a really big rubber elastic on the way home?" Tyler asked with hope-filled eyes. "Because if we had that, Dave, then I reckon we could take out the entire field of sheep if I made sure my angles were correct. Whaddya think?"

"Only one way to find out, champ!"

Once they'd reached the car, Tyler opened the door, placing the trifle he was carrying inside, and then taking hold of Dave's crutches while Dave situated himself so he could climb back in.

"Oi! Where do you think you're going?" a familiar voice called out, louder than the paint job on Dave's car.

"Jesus, Monty!" Dave said, startled. "Where *are* you?" he asked, looking around and about, as he'd heard Monty's voice clear as day but couldn't tell where it had come from. Dave then glanced back over to the garden gate they'd just left behind, as that seemed a logical enough place to look, but Monty wasn't there.

"If you're going to soak me with a hose or anything like that, you'll be taking me to the hospital for a new plaster cast once we've had a couple of burgers and a beer!" Dave warned, still looking this way and that.

"There he is," Tyler said, pointing over as he spotted Monty across the way.

Dave turned at the rate of speed of a heavily laden oil tanker. "Where?" he asked, with the sun now in his eyes.

"Standing by the front of that house," Tyler said, pointing a little pointier with his finger this time.

Dave eventually located his chum across the road, standing on the neighbour's porch and leaning against the front of the house near the door. "Are you stealing old Mavis's post again, Monty, or did you kick your ball into her garden?"

Monty waved a hand, encouraging them over. "Nothing like that, Dave," he assured him. "Come over here! I need to show you something!"

"You don't think he'd actually soak us with a hosepipe? What with you being injured and all?" Becks asked, taking up a position behind both Dave and Tyler so that they'd take the brunt of any practical joke first.

Dave proceeded across the road with caution. "Could you not have come over to *me*, Monty?" he joked, clearly struggling. "And why is there no smell of barbecue?"

With Becks's assistance, Dave was eventually able to shuffle over and make his way through Mavis's lovely white picket garden gate, offering it an admiring glance as he often did when visiting Monty's neighbourhood.

By the time he made it halfway up the garden path, moisture was starting to form on Dave's clammy forehead. "I do think you may need to come to me, Monty," Dave said. "Either that or a piggyback wouldn't go amiss."

Just then, however, the red-gloss front door opened, revealing a grinning Frank and Stan standing just inside. Stella appeared briefly as well, just behind them, but then just as quickly disappeared.

"Right, you lot are starting to freak me out," Dave noted. "And what have you done with poor old Mavis?" he asked. Ordinarily, Dave would never consider the others as being capable of murder or other nefarious deeds. But with Mavis currently nowhere to be seen, and Frank, Stan, and Monty bizarrely making themselves at home on her property, he was beginning to have his doubts.

Dave looked to Becks for any possible answers, but her befuddled expression suggested she didn't have the faintest idea what was going on either.

Frank and Stan lingered in the doorway, with it appearing very much like they were, quite suspiciously, attempting to conceal something behind their persons. Mavis's dead body, Dave could only assume at this point.

"We've got something for you, Dave," Frank teased.

"Do I... do I really want to know what it is?" Dave asked, filled with dread.

"Well, it's actually for all *three* of you," Stan gently corrected Frank, in reference to Dave, Becks, and Tyler.

With that, Frank and Stan separated, taking a small step away from each other and finally revealing what they'd been obscuring from view. With a great deal of relief, Dave could now see that it was not a corpse.

"This is for you," Frank said, and with Stan's assistance, they presented the estate agent's 'For Sale' sign that had previously been plunged into Mavis's front lawn.

By now Dave had some inkling about what was going on. But he didn't dare to believe the suggestions his brain was offering.

However, it was now Monty's turn to step to one side. And when he did, he revealed a polished wooden plaque affixed to the outside wall, just beside the door, with the words *Casa Big Blue Boiled Sweet* engraved in fancy italic lettering. "Frank and Stan asked me to come up with the house name," Monty explained. "You can change it if you like. But I just thought—"

"I absolutely adore the name, Monty," Dave said, now daring to believe what, a few short moments before, he'd only dared to believe. "Someone's going to have to go back to that hospital and fetch my crying sock because here come the boohoos again."

"Right, what's going on, exactly?" Becks asked, stepping beside Dave and taking some of Dave's weight, as he appeared nearly ready to keel over. "Firstly, what sock?" she said. "And, secondly, who bought a house?"

Frank and Stan climbed down the porch steps to join them on the garden path. "I'm not sure I remember about the sock thing," Frank said. "But the house situation I can answer."

Frank then went on to explain how both he and Stan had purchased the house on Dave's behalf, knowing that Dave had been finding it impossible to scrape together a deposit large enough to be able to purchase the home of his dreams (having to settle for something much less dream-worthy and rather more nightmarish instead).

The amount of the deposit Dave would have put down was Frank and Stan's gift to Dave — times *three*, in honour of Dave, Becks, and Tyler. They were also allowing Dave to pay back the remaining amount directly, with Stan and Frank now acting as personal mortgage lenders rather than the much less flexible bank (who wouldn't lend Dave enough to buy a Wendy house). This meant an added savings of hundreds of pounds a month in interest, as the boys were providing the loan for Dave interest-free. This way, what was once unattainable was now easily and blessedly affordable. Besides, as Frank went on to say, there had been the distinct possibility of him and Stan shelling out a considerable amount of dosh on some boring old medical bill that wouldn't have brought joy to *any* of their lives, while this, on the other hand, was a *much* better use of that money.

And the house being discussed, as was very obvious to Dave by this time, was the one formerly owned by Monty's neighbour Mavis. Ever since Dave first had designs on buying his own special place for the three of them, it'd always been Mavis's house he imagined in his mind's eye when he drifted off to sleep at night, as it was a gorgeous little home and would have been absolutely perfect for his needs. So when Monty initially told him it was for sale, he was elated. With that elation quickly turning to intense frustration, however, with the realisation he would never be able to afford it in a million years. This was devastating not only because the house was everything he'd dreamed about for his expanding family, but also because of the extra advantage of having his best mate living right across the road from him.

"I... I don't know what to say," Dave said, not really knowing what to say.

"Wait, this place is going to be our new home?" Tyler asked. "Seriously?"

"It certainly looks that way, buddy," Dave told him. "I reckon we could even get our own herd of sheep for the garden," Dave added, confusing the others who weren't in the know about the beauty and brilliance that was Car Park Wheelchair Bowling (minus the car park in this instance, of course).

"Come on inside," Frank suggested. "And if we've all been a bit absent of late," he offered apologetically, "well, let's just say that Mavis's colour scheme was a bit—"

"A bit shite!" Stan offered, rendering his critical assessment. "Honestly, so we've had the paint brushes out to make it perfect for your arrival in Casa Big Blue Boiled Sweet."

Dave looked first at Becks and then at Tyler. "After you," he said to them both. "And you know, Becks, I'd carry you across the threshold if it weren't for these crutches and this bleedin' plaster cast."

"May I?" Monty asked, ready to scoop Becks up in his arms and assume that particular duty.

Dave smiled. "Be my guest, Monty."

"Oh, by the way, Dave, your mum, along with all of the other invited guests, are in the back garden waiting to surprise you," Monty said, laden with Becks in his arms. "I'm only telling you in advance because I didn't want you getting a fright and falling over, as you'd be quite heavy to pick up again. I also took the liberty of buying you your very own Weber grill. It's sat back there right now as well. So in answer to your earlier question, the reason you can't smell the food cooking is that you'll need to light the grill for yourself the first time you use it, yeah? Otherwise, it's like a newborn duckling thinking the first person they see is their mother. And I didn't want your new Weber grill thinking I was its mother, Dave, you know what I mean?"

"Strangely, I think I know exactly what you mean, Monty," Dave answered.

With Tyler's help, Dave negotiated the few steps up to the house. Once inside, Dave came to a complete halt, taking a whiff of the fresh paint now filling his nostrils. "Hang on, everybody wait! Don't go any further!" he said.

"Do you need to have a seat?" Stan asked, looking around for one. "Wait there and I'll go and fetch you a chair."

"No, no, I don't need a seat," Dave replied, slowly running his eyes over Tyler, Becks, Monty, Frank, and finally back to Stan. "No, I wanted to just tell you lot that you're all the best thing that's ever happened to me," he said, welling up once again. "So, if it's at all possible... I'd just like a group hug, yeah?"

"We can do that," Stan readily agreed, what with him being a regular and enthusiastic hugger.

"Oi, where's Stella?" Dave asked, wishing to include her. "I thought I saw her in here...?"

"She's guarding the meat," Frank explained. "She won't let anyone else touch it."

"Ah. To make sure no one puts anything on the grill until I get here?" Dave asked, impressed by Stella's thoughtfulness.

"Don't be daft!" Stella called out from the kitchen. "It's to make sure I get all the biggest pieces! I'm putting my name on them!"

Dave laughed, but he insisted on Stella joining them for the group cuddle, to which she reluctantly complied (reluctantly, that is, because she hated to take her eyes off the meat).

Soon smothered under a sea of arms, Dave enjoyed every last second of it. "I love you bunch," he said. "You're all completely and utterly bonkers. But I wouldn't change you for the world. Thank you for being you."

"Good. Now we've got that claptrap out of the way, can we finally get the food started?" Stella complained, removing herself from the scrum. "Honestly, my poor stomach thinks my bloody throat's been cut!" she added, offering the very faintest of smiles as she did so.

The End

Unless you want more? You're the boss. Get in touch or leave me feedback on Amazon and your wish can be my command! In the meantime, be sure to check out my other books detailed on my website below.

www.authorjcwilliams.com
authorjcwilliams@gmail.com

Printed in Dunstable, United Kingdom